The Wicked Garden

LENORA HENSON

ISBN: 978-0615785370
ISBN-13: 0615785379

DEDICATION

For Sophia.

ACKNOWLEDGMENTS

Special thanks to my constant cheerleaders Joanna Devoe, Brooke McNutt, Gabby McNutt and Joleen Minarik. You kept me on my path with your tireless enthusiasm and support. Thank you to my extraordinary editor and research champion, Jessica Jernigan. It's been an incredible journey. Thank you to cover model RaeChelle Leiken. Thank you to Jennifer Adele, Robert Scrimpsher, and Emalie Babb for sharing your knowledge. Thank you to Mom and Dad, for fostering my creativity. Thank you to Sophia Henson for your patience and being the coolest kid I know. Thank you to Jim Murphy for everything.

PROLOGUE

Scotland, Early 1600s

An unholy stench—sulfurous, metallic, sweet, and fatty—swirled in the late June breeze. The wind blew indifferently; the element of air was unmoved by the day's terrible events. The element of fire, however.... The blaze seemed to be relishing its work, consuming its victims like ravens falling on a fresh carcass. The pyre's hunger for human flesh seemed desperate, eternal.

Hidden on a hill nearby, a girl sobbed quietly. The smell made her stomach turn, and being with child, she could not stop vomiting. Wiping tears, bile, and greasy black ash from her face, she decided to take action. She knew it was too late to save her twin. Her sister had been strangled to death like the others before the fire was set. She could not save her, but she could join her in the flames. It was where she felt she belonged after what she had caused. It would be her redemption. They would find her soon enough anyway.

The decision was made, but just as she moved toward the fire, she felt herself being pulled back. She struggled wildly as powerful arms held her tight. A scream rose in her throat, only to be silenced by the familiar, weathered hand of her grandmother. The girl had little strength left to fight as she was dragged from the gruesome scene. The gentle summer breeze sent burnt hair and charred flesh trailing after her. She would never see her sister again. She would never be redeemed. She would never be forgiven, and never seemed a very long time.

Part One

Carbondale, 1940s

Epona stood on Pringle Street, eyeing a two-story Victorian in a quiet neighborhood, well away from the bustle of the university. It was a lovely house, well-built and carefully maintained. Her head was canted gently to one side as she considered it from across the road.

This was the place. She had seen it in a vision.

It was dark, and a light rain drizzled. This was something of a distraction. Earth was her element. Water pulled at her too strongly. It wanted all of her, just as it had wanted her mother, and her mother's mother.... So many women in Epona's family had ended their lives in water.

And this was why she stood in the dark rain before a stranger's house on Pringle Street. It wasn't just to save her own life, but also to protect the ones to come. She had to break the curse, and there was something inside the house on Pringle Street that she needed if she was going to do that.

Epona sensed that she had company—otherworldly, if she had to guess. She could see that there was a thickly wooded area out back. The presence from the forest was by her side with a movement as instantaneous as thought.

Fairy.

"You've arrived." The voice in Epona's ear was soft and seductive.

"Indeed," she replied. She knew that she had to be careful with this one. Epona ventured a quick sideways glance. The creature standing beside her was delicately made, and not nearly as tall as Epona—few women were—but she had a powerfully beguiling presence. Epona knew her kind. In fact, she now realized with a start, she knew *her*.

"Penelope received his seed last night, with the energy of the new moon," the fairy said.

"Yes, Claire. I know. I saw it in a vision. That's why I'm here." Epona stood very still.

"Aye. Your gifts are still strong. *You're* strong. You've reached, what—fifty-some years now? You were never meant to make it past forty."

Epona took a deep breath of cool, misty air. "I have no choice but to live. I have a responsibility to help fix what has been broken. To heal the past."

"You think you're stronger than the past?" Claire's tone was incredulous, almost condescending.

Epona turned and looked directly at the fairy. Claire's long black hair shined like a raven's wing and her skin was impossibly smooth. "I don't know if I'm stronger than the past, but I'm damn sure going to strengthen the future."

A small grin grew on Claire's face. "Whit's fur ye'll no go by ye."

Epona nodded. "Whit's fur ye'll no go by ye."

The pair stood in silence for a moment.

"He might come back, you know, to reclaim that which you seek," Claire said.

"But I need those journals." Epona looked inside herself, she looked toward the future. She saw a man climbing the stairs that led to the front door of the house on Pringle Street. He had a head of wild curls and aquamarine eyes.

"I have to get inside that house, Claire. Now, before it's too late."

The fairy gave an appraising look. "You're the strongest woman your family has ever seen. Do what you came to do."

Epona closed her eyes, centered herself, and chanted a string of words beneath her breath. When she opened her eyes, she was inside the house on Pringle Street. The first thing she saw was a new sofa, beige with pale roses, an echo of the riot of flowers that grew all around the house. The whole room was suffused with the same bright coziness. This home radiated warmth and peace. Epona gave herself a moment to take in some of the healing energy. The magic she had just worked was strong stuff. It would probably leave her weak for days—weeks even. After she had regained a little strength, she scanned the room, looking for the object of her mission.

There it was: a worn leather messenger bag. Epona pulled out one of many journals and tried to flip through it, but she couldn't seem to open the covers. Charmed, probably. Well, she hadn't time to worry about that now. She put the journal back in the bag, stilled herself, and uttered the spell that would send her back outside.

Nothing happened.

She had no choice but to try the front door, even

if that meant making unwanted noise. The doorknob wouldn't turn.

"Damn it," she whispered. She tried every opening spell she knew. None of them worked. She tried not to panic.

Suddenly, Claire was next to her. "Leave the bag."

"Why?"

"Because it won't allow you to take it. It's not meant for you. Take the journals and leave the bag. The bag is for the messenger."

Epona had no idea who "the messenger" was, but she knew she had no choice but to trust Claire. She pulled out the stack of journals, dropped the satchel, closed her eyes, and recited the words that would carry her silently from the house.

She felt the chill breeze and the cool drizzle that meant she was back outside, but, when she opened her eyes, she still saw the front room of the house on Pringle Street. The scene had changed—the lovely floral sofa was now a sagging wreck—but the atmosphere was the same. There was love, laughter, joy, and, above all, that healing energy. Epona saw a young man with wild curls and aquamarine eyes, and she saw a bohemian beauty with hair almost as red as her own.

She saw an amethyst necklace.

She saw a tiny woman with a sleek, brown bob sitting on the threadbare sofa.

She saw scenes of abuse, pain, and horror.

She saw betrayal.

Whit's fur ye'll no go by ye.

CHAPTER ONE

Irvine, 2010s

He only beat her when he felt it was necessary. That's what he told her anyway. When he felt it was necessary, she would most likely receive a blow to the back of the head. When he felt it was *more* than necessary, he would hit her in the stomach. And when he felt it was *very* necessary he would beat her senseless. But only when necessary.

The recipient of this punishment was Gretchel Shea.

Gretchel lived on an ordinary street, in an ordinary subdivision, but this woman was far from ordinary. She was, first and most obviously, beautiful, with hair the color of red velvet cake and white skin brushed with pale pink freckles. She was tall and lithe and gracefully made. These, however, were just the outward signs of her difference, which were visible to anyone. Were you to look into her gray eyes, you might catch a glimpse of her true nature. You might find yourself thinking, *Here is your life, child, please come and live it.* Looking even deeper, you might think, *This woman is the rise of creation, she is the question, she is possibility, she is creativity, and she is sex on a stick.* You might discover that you could not look away.

But Gretchel would never let that happen. She had become very good at hiding her difference. She had become very good at hiding herself.

Sitting on an ordinary beige sofa, she was the very image of tranquility. The ability to appear calm, to be still and quiet, was a skill Gretchel had worked hard to master. She was not the still, quiet type. Aphrodites never are. But Gretchel had decided long ago it was safer to keep her true nature hidden. At first, it was painful. Eventually, she grew indifferent. And, in any case, she felt she deserved the pain and the numbness that followed.

Once upon a time, Gretchel believed that she had been a very bad girl, and now she was paying the price. At the moment, she was paying that price by sitting very still, watching a video montage of famous putts. Famous putts? Yes. The Golf Channel is one of the severest punishments devised by the gods for women who renounce their own divinity. That's what Gretchel had decided, at least. As she gazed blankly at the screen, she imagined that she was Amethystos, a maiden pursued by wild, drunken Dionysus. A maiden whose prayer for protection was answered when Artemis turned her to stone. She was safe, but dead—inside and out. Gretchel understood Artemis's cruel logic. She had arrived at much the same conclusion herself, which is why she was sitting there, watching Tiger Woods sink a putt for birdie.

Lately, Gretchel had become aware that she could not stay still forever. She could feel a flicker of the light she had tried to smother, like a knife-blade of flame that would not go out. Her true self—the spirit she had buried—was surging back toward the surface. She was afraid of what would happen when her stony façade cracked, but she could not suppress a jolt of excitement. *Oh*, she thought, *it's about damn time.*

Her hip jerked. This involuntary motion made her heart race. It sent a ripple of energy around the room. Gretchel turned to see if her husband had noticed. He hadn't… yet.

It would be dangerous to come back to life, perhaps even deadly in a paradoxical sense, but she was ready to take the chance. *As if I have a choice*, she thought as she felt the flame burn brighter within.

Her nose twitched, and her sense of smell awoke. Inhaling deeply, she smelled her old friend. Alcohol. The painkiller smelled like salvation, as she remembered how it quieted her torturous self-hatred, but it also smelled of damnation, of powerlessness and shame. Either way the smell seemed to be fuel for the awakening fire.

Gretchel peered down at her husband's glass. The thin, caramel-colored liquid sparkled under the lamp, and the ice cubes clanked about in a beautiful dance of promised oblivion. Her hand was only inches away. She felt two forces within her. The first force was the addiction, and it was undeniably powerful. The other force was her will, which was making itself known to the addiction like a wolf baring its incisors to protect its young from harm.

She could hear the instinctual growl inside her soul, and knew she mustn't take a sip, but a distant tug laughed wickedly in her mind. The laughter was familiar and malevolent. Something was not right. Or perhaps it was absolutely right. She had long ago lost the power to discern.

She took her eyes off the glass, just as Phil Mickelson chipped his way onto the green. A grin erupted on her face, shattering her perfectly practiced half-smile. Phil was pure of heart. She could feel it.

She turned away from the TV, and gazed out a window into the cold, dark night. A salt truck crunched by the house, making its way around the subdivision. It was an ordinary December evening in Illinois. Ordinary.

But it shouldn't have been ordinary. It was the Winter Solstice, and Gretchel should have gone back home to Snyder Farms. Troy had forbidden her joining the Bloome family for its celebrations, and he certainly didn't want their children involved.

Gretchel sighed gently as she looked beyond the window glass, through a white haze of precipitation, wondering if it was snow or sleet, hoping that her daughter's travels were safe.

Her sense of restlessness grew.

She shifted on the sofa, stretching her long legs, smoothing the wrinkles from her gray yoga pants. Her husband shot her a look, and she froze.

"Are you watching?" he growled. The lovely smell of Scotch whiskey washed over her again, her nose twitched, and she felt the stirrings of another internal battle.

Troy clenched his jaw until Gretchel could see a vein pop out in his forehead. She obediently shifted her eyes back to golf.

She wasn't a bad golfer. She could powder it off the tee like a female John Daly, but her short game wasn't so good; it never had been, and she honestly didn't care if it ever improved. Troy cared though, which was why Gretchel was spending Winter Solstice with Tiger and Phil.

She brazenly snuck a peek outside the window again, just as a blustery gust caught the pocket of a ratty white trash bag and sent it sailing. She watched as it loop-de-looped through the air.

A hand popped her on the side of the head. "Goddamn it, Gretchel! Pay attention!" Troy hissed.

Troy Shea. What the world saw of the man was the epitome of public achievement: school board member, avid volunteer, country club regular, Sunset Automotive's most successful salesman, and everyone's favorite guy to run into. He was a looker too, complementing his trophy wife with a fierce handsomeness. His big, dark eyes and perfect smile made women weak, and his fit physique left their men jealous. Troy's image was of the utmost importance, and so, for seventeen years, Gretchel had kept their family's secrets safe.

Timidly, she rubbed her head, and turned back to the TV. But her heart was racing, and an odd sensation was working its way through her body. Suddenly, her mind was filled with a dozen voices arguing and screaming. She felt strife and utter despair. A volcano of passion erupted within her being. She felt as though she were being pulled in all four directions, and she heard a voice that was not a voice, but a vibration echoing in the very depth of her soul. Startled and frightened, she sat straight up on the sofa.

"Whit's fur ye'll no go by ye!" she shouted.

Troy turned to her, stunned by the outburst. It had been a few years since he'd had to enforce the heavy punishment. He shook his head in disappointment, and then grabbed his wife by the arm, and pushed her up the stairs of their sprawling two-story home.

Troy flung open the double doors of a walk-in closet and threw Gretchel to the floor.

"Assume the position," he commanded. She was breathing heavily, but she didn't dare let out a cry for mercy. She did as she was commanded as her husband pulled a fraternity paddle from the wall.

She endured blow after blow. Her bottom and thighs were bright pink by the time he wore himself out. He finally replaced the paddle, and knelt down to her face. "You know I don't want to hear that witchy bullshit in my house. Ever."

"I didn't—," she began, but a sharp blow from his open hand shut her up.

"I never thought I'd have to do this again," he said, shaking his head in disappointment. Then he shut the door, and locked it from the outside.

Gretchel could tolerate a lot of things, but being locked up was not one of them. Quiet tears began to pour out of her haunting eyes. "Whit's fur ye'll no go by ye," she mouthed, but no sound came out. Gretchel knew what was about to happen. She tried, and failed, to stop herself. With shaking hands, she unclasped an amethyst pendant from around her neck. Vibrating with raw fear and wild energy, she was no longer a woman made of marble. She was unprotected, and alive. Magic filled the air, and the precious stone was ready for its new owner.

CHAPTER TWO

Irvine, 2010s

In Gretchel's dream, a siren wailed. She was shocked awake by a variety of panic she'd almost forgotten about. The siren was a familiar fixture in her dream world, but, for seventeen years, she had been immune to it. Ever since Eli had put the amethyst necklace around her neck, she had been safe—well, not safe, exactly, but protected from some of the more fearsome terrors that lurked in her mind. Now that she had given the amulet away, all that darkness was crawling back to the surface.

Her heart racing, Gretchel jumped out of bed and scurried to the window. Everything looked normal, but something had changed. Her intuition had been dormant for years—deadened by drink for a time, and, later, suppressed by the amethyst's power—but she trusted the feeling in her gut and looked outside again. Her attention was drawn to the white trash bag snagged in the branches just outside the window. It had been there since the Solstice. It thrashed in the wind, but it was nothing. She dismissed it as she continued to scan the neighborhood. By the natural light of the full moon and manufactured glow of the street lamps, she could make out a gray wolf padding down the road. She gasped, and the wolf turned toward her and howled.

Gretchel closed the drapes, and she tried to close her ears to the mournful wail from outside. *Wake up!* she told herself. *There are no wolves roaming this gated community.* She rubbed at her sleepy eyes, and tried to adjust herself to reality, but the dream that had awakened her still clung like fog.

Right before the siren had sounded, she had come face to face with the night mare, the black horse that had first invaded her sleep when she was a teenager. She had been in a field of poppies when she saw it galloping toward her. She couldn't get away. She reached out for help to no avail. The horse reared in front of her, and then lowered its head to fix her with its huge black eyes—and then she heard the siren. It was a horrible dream. *The damn necklace*, she thought, *I shouldn't have given it away. I'm going to go crazy again.*

She glanced at the clock. 4:32 am. There was no use going back to bed when the alarm would soon be blaring for her morning run. She was brushing her teeth when a dreadful feeling washed through her. Something devastating was going to happen, she could feel it. Something that would change her life. She was ready for something to propel her out of the godforsaken inertia of the last seventeen years, but she wasn't entirely sure if she was prepared for a new type of hell.

She went to her walk-in closet. Above a full-length mirror hung the fraternity paddle. It was there as a visual reminder to sustain her fear and submission. It had worked that way for a long time, but it wasn't working this morning, just like it hadn't worked on the Solstice.

Gretchel moved aside some sweaters, and pulled out a box that housed items she once used for ritual. Concealing it from Troy was a necessity, lest she face a beating. Troy wasn't much of a Christian, but he was pretty sure that his carefully cultivated image did not include a pagan wife. It had been a long time since she'd even opened the box. It was easier for her to just go through the motions of being Troy's gorgeous, adoring spouse, and she had been doing whatever was easier for quite awhile.

Gretchel closed her eyes as she lifted the lid. A musty smell—the scent of things long hidden—floated toward her. The first thing she saw when she opened her eyes was an old rag doll. She pulled it out of the box, held it tight to her chest, and began to shake.

Oh, wise ones, please forgive me, she prayed. *Please be patient. I've lost myself, and I know I need to change, but I don't know how. It felt right to pass on the amethyst. It was time to take it off. But I'm afraid without it—afraid of myself. Please protect me.*

Gretchel slipped a hand inside her robe and touched the scars on the right side of her torso. The skin felt tender and ached as if the wounds were fresh. On the edge of an abyss, Gretchel tried to retreat into the illusion of normalcy she'd wrapped around herself for so many years. *It's all in my head*, she thought. *The necklace was just a piece of jewelry. The wolf was just the fragment of a dream.*

She heard a lone howl, and her skin prickled. It was a sign. Change was surely happening, whether she was ready for it or not.

∞

Later that morning, Gretchel stood in a daze at her kitchen sink. It was New Year's Eve, and her wedding anniversary. She couldn't believe it had been seventeen years. It was worse than a prison sentence. *'Til death do us part? If only.* Gretchel couldn't believe that she'd *ever* be free of Troy.

The toaster popped, startling her.

"Salon day?" Troy asked, grabbing his plate of bacon and eggs.

Gretchel nodded. She was showered and dressed after her subzero run. A silk scarf covered her hair. It was navy blue and white, and had been a gift from Troy. It matched the fitted navy cardigan she wore over a crisp white shirt, and navy slacks from the Troy-approved winter casual collection.

She glanced at her husband, who sat at the island in the kitchen eating and reading the sports section of the St. Louis *Post-Dispatch.* It was Friday, and he was going to work as usual. If he did nothing else for her, he was a good provider. Sometimes, she tried to convince herself that was why she was still with him.

She lived in a beautiful home. She always drove a brand new car. She had everything that money could buy a stay-at-home mom in a small, sleepy town. Focusing on how blessed she was, had always made life easier to handle—until now.

As a teenager, when her family came close to losing everything, this kind of lifestyle seemed very safe, but now it didn't seem to be enough. *No,* she disagreed internally; *it's not that it's not enough. It's more than enough. It's just not* me. *This is all a lie.*

It may have appeared to the outside world as if she had achieved the American dream, but behind the veil of country-club living was the truth: She was married to a man she hated; her sixteen-year-old daughter was a pistol and constantly antagonizing her husband, and her fourteen-year-old son was becoming an ungrateful monster like his father. Gretchel herself was nothing more than the adhesive that kept the family together, and the glue was losing its hold.

Once upon a time, she had been an art student with an affinity for the natural world. Growing up, Gretchel had turned to art to get through the very toughest times, and her garden had always been a refuge. Troy wasn't interested in art, and he wasn't about to let her replace their perfectly manicured lawn with a mess of herbs and wildflowers. So, she had a house full of white walls and a philodendron above the kitchen cabinets, dying from lack of attention.

The last time she had done any painting, Gretchel had been beaten and locked in the basement for two days. It hadn't been the act of painting that had gotten her into trouble so much as the subject of her work.

Catching herself remembering those aquamarine eyes, Gretchel gave herself a shake and wiped toast crumbs into the sink. She wondered where the nostalgia was coming from. *It's the damn necklace*, she decided.

She picked up the last piece of bacon and began to nibble, when Troy came from behind and snatched it from her hand. "Aren't you on a diet?" he asked, shoving the bacon in his own mouth. "I'll be home around six, so make sure you're ready, and tell the faggot to do something different with your hair. You're due for a change."

Yes, I am, she thought.

She'd forgotten they were going out for dinner and drinks to celebrate their anniversary. With friends. They weren't *her* friends, of course. Well, one of them was—or, at least, he had been. But that was a long time ago. Gretchel didn't have any friends now.

She had just finished cleaning up the kitchen when her son walked in with a grumpy groan.

"French toast," he growled, pulling up a stool and laying his head on the island.

An unusual wave of anger rushed over Gretchel, turning her face crimson. "I'm not a short order cook," she snapped. She grabbed a box of cereal and slammed it down inches from her son's head.

The boy was stunned. It had been a long time since his mother raised her voice to anyone. He watched her curiously as she grabbed the ringing phone from its cradle.

"Hello," she said.

"Hi, Gretchel. It's Ben."

"Hey, Ben. Zach's right here."

"No!" Ben's voice cracked. "I need to talk to you."

"All right. What's on your mind?" Gretchel noticed Zach's eyes grow wide as he poured milk into his bowl.

"I really don't want to have to be the one to tell you this, but…."

"What's wrong, Ben?"

After a brief pause, the boy's words came out in a rush. "Troy is screwing around with my mom."

Panic and anxiety washed through Gretchel like a

tsunami. "Excuse me?"

"Troy and my mom are, you know, bonking." Ben had regained some composure.

"What?"

Ben spoke slowly and loudly. "My *mom* and your *husband* are doing the nasty. Having sex. Am I being clear, Gretchel?"

Gretchel leaned against the island as she felt herself losing strength. "No," was all she could mutter.

"Yes. Last night I overheard my mom talking about divorce."

"*No!*" Gretchel wailed.

"Look, I know my mom's a bitch, but I don't want my family torn apart. Make him leave her alone, Gretchel. I've got to go, she's coming."

Gretchel wiped at the tears running down her face, and looked at them on her hand with a certain fondness, as if they were long lost friends come back to comfort her.

Zach glared at his mother. "He told you about Dad and Michelle didn't he?" Gretchel was speechless. "He just couldn't leave it alone," Zach said, throwing his cereal bowl in the sink and storming out of the house. Gretchel heard the front door slam.

She had known that Troy was sleeping with somebody. He'd put her in the hospital three years before, and hadn't touched her since—well, not unless he was hitting her. She knew he'd taken a mistress after that, and she'd been grateful to whoever that mistress was, but why Michelle Brown? *Of all the women in Irvine, why Michelle?* she thought.

It was bad enough that Troy worked for Michelle's father. It was bad enough that Gretchel was forced into being friends with a woman who despised her. And it was bad enough they had to be neighbors. But this was the last straw. This reeked of karmic payback, and she wondered if her punishment would never end.

Gretchel looked out the kitchen window, and tried to find some glimmer of sunlight, but her world was covered by a cloudy midwinter sky. She had known that she was ready for a change, but this wasn't what she'd had in mind. Not at all.

CHAPTER THREE

Irvine, 2010s

Teddy Wintrop paced across the thick beige carpet in Gretchel's bedroom. He was irate, but as Gretchel's best friend, he knew it was his job to keep calm and gently guide her out of the chaos Troy had created.

Teddy had nearly fallen over in shock when Gretchel had called him crying. He could hardly remember the last time she had cried—or shown any emotion at all, for that matter. He had been trying for years to coax her back to life, just as he had done before, back when they were teenagers.

The disappearance of the Gretchel Teddy knew had been a gradual process. During the first seven years of her marriage to Troy, she still had a spark. Teddy thought that maybe he was the only one who could see it, but he wasn't. He was just one of the few who cherished it unconditionally, and he had to watch helplessly as Gretchel's husband thrashed it out of her. After a particularly brutal episode three years ago—one that required a hospital stay—every emotion Gretchel seemed to express was forced and fake. Her spirit had slipped away.

Teddy glanced at her huddled on the bed, like a beaten puppy. He shook his head, and continued to pace. Gretchel had been acting strange lately—strange even for her—and Teddy had been checking in with her every day. He knew that Troy was beating her again. He begged her to file charges, even though he knew she wouldn't.

Teddy also knew that Gretchel wasn't wearing the amethyst pendant she had worn constantly for almost two decades. He had spent a lot of time with Gretchel's family over the years, and, although he struggled to maintain his skepticism, he knew that he had seen magic manifest. Grudgingly, he had become a believer.

That was why he was so concerned about the fact that Gretchel had given away the amethyst. From the moment Eli put it around Gretchel's neck, she had abstained from alcohol. If asked, Teddy probably wouldn't say that the stone actually had healing energies, but he had to acknowledge the power it had over Gretchel. Within hours of Gretchel giving the pendant away, her world had turned upside down.

As hard as it was to see her hurting so much, this display of genuine feeling gave Teddy hope. The Gretchel sobbing on the bed was like a wild animal being taunted—disoriented, hypersensitive, ready for a fight.

Teddy was ready for a fight, too. He had felt nothing but contempt for Troy from the moment he'd first encountered him, and he hated what he'd done to Gretchel over the past seventeen years. It was just like Troy to sleep with the one person Gretchel truly loathed. Teddy was sorry to see his best friend undone by this betrayal, but he was more than willing turn it into a catalyst for change. Of course, his slight form and complete disinterest in manly combat meant that he wasn't about to confront Troy physically. Teddy's instinct for intrigue and his love for Gretchel were his strongest weapons.

Teddy turned away from Gretchel and gazed out the window, thinking. He noticed a ratty, wind-torn trash bag hanging from a tree in the front yard. He watched it flutter as he said, "Leave him, Gretchel. Leave today."

When he looked back toward the bed, Teddy saw his friend looking up at him with red-rimmed eyes.

"Leave?" she asked incredulously.

"Just pack up and leave. Go to the cottage. I'll go with you. I'll hire a bodyguard. I'll *be* the bodyguard if necessary. Just go!"

"I can't just leave!" she cried.

She had tried to leave before. The first time was early in her marriage. That attempt ended with her brother Marcus in jail for assaulting Troy. She had tried again after Troy had beaten her and locked her in the basement for a few days, but she succumbed to his apologies before she even made it out the front door. Teddy had been sure she'd finally leave after Troy put her in the hospital, but that was the attack that changed her—made her completely numb and almost invisible. Now, it seemed like the real Gretchel—the fierce, wild girl he had known—was back. Maybe this Gretchel could find the strength to get away.

Teddy tried to be reassuring. "It may not be as bad as it seems."

"Well, this is how it seems to me, Mr. Glass-Half-Fucking-Full," Gretchel spat, "When Michelle's dad died six months ago, he left Sunset Automotive to her. If Troy divorces me, he'll be free to marry her. That manipulative bastard is probably sleeping with her so that she'll let him take over the company. Michelle hates me. I'm sure she'd be delighted to take away my financial security while she takes away my husband and breaks up my family. I'm sure they're already trying to figure out how to make it look like *I* was the one who broke up two marriages."

Teddy gave Gretchel a chance to catch her breath, and then rebutted, "Point taken, but you have the upper hand in your power struggle with Michelle. You've had the upper hand for years."

"No, Teddy. We both called a reluctant truce. And besides Troy still has the video tape. What if he shows her? And if he hasn't, he will. Did you think about that?" Gretchel's voice rose and her eyes flashed.

"No, I didn't think about that."

"What if she's already told him everything about my past? What if she's told him about Beltane? She's going to destroy my family. Oh—my kids!" Gretchel began to sob.

Teddy walked to the king size bed, and climbed up beside her. "This was a marriage of delusion from the beginning, Baby Girl. You *chose* to put yourself in this situation. I know it. You know it."

"Yes, Teddy. You're right, Teddy. We both know that. But it doesn't matter what we know!" Gretchel snapped.

"It *does* matter," Teddy retaliated, "because you have to take responsibility for your role in this mess. You don't deserve to be treated this way, and you have to quit acting as though you do."

She stared out in to space, ignoring him. "They're

going to destroy me."

"So your reputation suffers. This won't be the first time, will it? So you lose everything again. So what? You're still alive, and don't you *dare* tell me you don't deserve to be," he threatened as he saw her preparing to protest. "Your kids will forgive you. You can start over, Gretchel. Isn't that what you want?" He laid his hands on her shaking fingers. "You're a survivor, Gretchel. You've done it before and you can do it again."

"I don't *want* to do it again. I want to start over, but not like this. I want to be prepared. I want to be in control," she said ripping up a tissue.

"Well, this is way out of your control. You took off that necklace for a reason. Now let go and get out."

"Where do I even start?"

"Monday morning I'll come over after Troy leaves for work. We'll go through the finances, we'll figure out exactly where everything stands. We'll scour the house again for the tape. Maybe we'll find it, maybe we won't. Either way we're going to get you through this, but you have to stay focused. You cannot let internal distractions get in your way."

"*Internal distractions*? Is that what we're calling the voices now?"

He shrugged. "For lack of a better phrase."

"Thank you."

"You can thank me when you're safely out of this marriage," he said. Teddy put his arm around her thin shoulders and gave her a squeeze. She gave him a peculiar glance.

"What in the hell are you grinning about?" she asked.

"It's just so good to have you back, Baby Girl." Teddy planted a kiss on her forehead, and eased into the padded headboard as she slumped against his chest.

∞

Teddy steamed as he drove to work. Gretchel's marriage to Troy had been a trial for her and her kids, but it had taken a toll on him, too. Cautious where Gretchel was impetuous, a steady voice when Gretchel was utterly unhinged, Teddy had helped his friend through experiences that still made him shudder when he pondered them.

Teddy had appointed himself the role of Gretchel's protector a long time ago. His first glimpse of her was a phantasm seared on his brain: A redheaded Amazon clutching her middle, mesmerized by the sight of a burnt up truck. Teddy knew who she was—Gretchel was not someone you would mistake for anybody else—but his first glimpse of her was almost like a ghost sighting. She was ethereal, barely clinging to this world.

Teddy and his recently divorced mother had just moved to Irvine and were renting one of the houses on the property owned by Gretchel's family. Once people knew where he was living, they were eager to pass along rumors about hauntings in the patch known as the Wicked Garden, and macabre stories of the Witches of Snyder Farms. Teddy wasn't afraid, though. He was just curious, and his paradoxical personality—equal parts extrovert and underdog—quickly made him a favorite of Miss Poni, matriarch of the family.

It was through the old woman that Teddy finally

met Gretchel. Miss Poni led him into a room in an ancient cottage nestled close to the shore of a massive misty lake. She announced, "Gretchel, this is Teddy," and the flame-haired beauty sitting at a window turned to face them.

Teddy knew that Gretchel hadn't spoken in months—not since the last suicide attempt. He was well-equipped, though, to fill up the empty air with mindless chatter. He repeated celebrity gossip from magazines. He described his crushes. He showed Gretchel dance moves he'd been working on. Her eyes followed him, but it was only when he pulled a brush out of his knapsack and stroked her long hair, softly, over and over again, that she smiled and spoke.

"You're my angel, Theodore Wintrop. They've sent you to look after me, haven't they?"

Teddy wasn't sure if *they* had or not, but he already felt like her caretaker.

After that afternoon, Teddy loved Gretchel like a sister, and she loved him back. She trusted him with all of her secrets—even the ones he could barely stomach. In her clearer moments, she sought his advice, and even took it—until she met Troy. Teddy would never forget that night.

He was attending community college in Irvine. Gretchel was a freshman at Southern Illinois University at Carbondale. Teddy knew that she had settled down a bit since starting school, but he also knew that she was always one drink away from the self-destruct button. Teddy also knew that her party persona had less to do with revelry and more to do with quieting the voices in her head, and he had a bad feeling that Halloween in Carbondale wasn't the best environment for keeping Gretchel out of trouble.

The town had a reputation for wild Halloween

celebrations. Gretchel's family had begged her to come home for the weekend. Gretchel was sensitive to the fissures between this world and the Otherworld under normal circumstances. Samhain was no time for her to get lost in a chaos of cheap beer, frat boys, and girls in sexy vampire costumes.

But Gretchel refused to go home. Teddy assured her family that he'd watch over her. Of course, he had no idea of what that night would bring.

Teddy was hardly a stranger to serious partying, but he had never seen anything like a Carbondale Halloween. The masses of partygoers were buzzed up and out of control, and Gretchel was no exception. Teddy was pretty sure that they hit every bar on The Strip—some of them more than once. By early morning, the crowd felt dangerously restless, and Teddy was begging Gretchel to let him take her back to her dorm before any real trouble began.

It was not to be. When she was drinking, Gretchel was attracted to mayhem like a pirate to rum. After the bars closed, she led Teddy into the streets, toward the wild heart of the crowd. Teddy held onto Gretchel's hand, and let her drag him through the madness. She was dressed as a redheaded Alice in Wonderland. Teddy was dressed as himself.

The scene was rowdy, like a Kindergarten classroom without a teacher—if the Kindergartners were college students full of adrenaline, hormones, and alcohol. Some of the revelers were dressed in costume, but most wore flannel shirts and torn jeans. Bands trying to bring grunge to the Midwest finished their sets, and, after bartenders announced last call, hordes of students poured out into the already-crowded streets.

Teddy and Gretchel were in the heart of the mob. When they heard yelps and cheers coming from a few yards away, Gretchel couldn't tolerate not knowing the source of the excitement. "Put me on your shoulders. I want to see what's going on," she told Teddy.

"Gretchel, you're six feet tall! You'll break my back!" Teddy exclaimed.

"Hop on," a taller, more sturdily built kid told her.

"No, Gretchel. We have to go," Teddy said, trying to pull her away.

She gave him a sad look, and Teddy stomped his foot.

"Fine. Hop on the linebacker and take your look, but only if you promise to get us out of here before this turns into a full-blown riot."

Gretchel climbed aboard the obliging set of shoulders. Her goofy, inebriated grin dissolved.

"What do you see?" Teddy inquired, wringing his hands, as if he were the nervous White Rabbit to Gretchel's Alice.

"It looks like a car's been flipped over about a block down the street. Something's on fire. There are guys hanging from a tree, and there's a huge fight," Gretchel shouted.

Teddy started to panic. "We should go, Gretchel. Now!"

It was too late. A gorgeous redhead floating above the crowd was hard to miss, and the men surrounding Gretchel had definitely taken notice. They began chanting, urging her to show a little more skin. Instead of flipping up her shirt like so many of the young women around her, Gretchel flipped the boys a double bird. This only made the chanting more insistent, angry instead of playful.

"Gretchel, stop antagonizing them," Teddy chided, "You're going to get us killed."

Suddenly an ambulance siren went off in the distance, and Gretchel screamed.

"You've got to get down!" Teddy called. He watched as she held her hands to her head, and wobbled on her perch. Teddy was terrified. He knew that the ambulance sirens had triggered a flashback—a bad one. Teddy got on tiptoe, and looked for a way out of the seething crowd.

He felt someone tap him on the shoulder, and a voice with a Scottish burr said, "You'd best keep your eye on that one." Teddy turned and saw a beautiful young woman with raven hair and tulle fairy wings.

He followed her pointing finger across the street, and saw a young man watching Gretchel quietly and intently. This dark-haired man-boy exuded an eerie calmness in the middle of pandemonium, but Teddy didn't feel reassured. He felt as if he were looking at the devil himself. Teddy turned back to the girl in the fairy costume, but she was gone.

Gretchel was screaming, ducking her head, trying to protect herself from invisible assailants. The crowd of men thought she was just being coy with them, and chanted even louder. They grabbed at her legs, trying to pull her to the ground.

"Hold still! I'm about to drop you!" the guy holding her yelled.

Gretchel couldn't hear him. She was somewhere

else, and it wasn't a happy place.

Teddy laid a steadying hand on her leg and said, "Gretchel, it's okay. Just get down. I'll help you."

"They won't be quiet," she cried. Teddy knew she wasn't hearing the sirens anymore. She wasn't talking about the deafening sound of the riot. Gretchel was hearing voices in her head. "Make them stop," she pleaded.

She squeezed her eyes closed, and grimaced as if she were in pain. It was rare for her to hear the voices when she was intoxicated. Something was terribly wrong. She kept bending down like she was ducking from something, and holding her head with her hands.

"Dude, please let her down. I have to get her out of here," Teddy begged the man holding her.

The crowd was still chanting for her to show herself, the sirens blared, and then Teddy watched—like he was seeing it in slow motion—as the quiet guy across the street looked directly at Gretchel and launched an empty beer bottle. It struck her in the forehead, knocking her backward into the mob. The crowd roared, cheering the fall of the bitchy redhead who wouldn't show her tits.

As she lay on the ground, blood gushing from her head, a few kind people gathered around to help her. Teddy ripped off his jacket and pressed it against the wound, trying to stop the bleeding.

After a couple of minutes that seemed like hours, Teddy and the others were able to get Gretchel on her feet. Teddy was trying to guide her out of the chaos when a voice beside them said, "Come on. Let's get you out of this mess. I'll take you to my place." Gretchel stopped as someone grabbed her arm.

Teddy turned around and a chill ran down his

spine. "She needs to go to the hospital," Teddy asserted, slapping at the hand fastened on Gretchel's arm.

"Back off, faggot."

Teddy gasped. He was terrified. He knew that this guy was pure evil, and he knew that he was no match for him.

"No one talks to my friend like that, asshole," Gretchel growled as she shoved her captor in the chest.

He just laughed. "Chill out, Red. You're coming with me. I'll get you cleaned up," he said, beginning to maneuver through the crowd.

"I'm not leaving Teddy."

"I've got a warm bed and more booze."

Gretchel hesitated, and that was all the opportunity the guy needed. He tightened his hold and started pushing Gretchel through the legion of students before Teddy could tell Gretchel what this man had done to her—before he could even protest. He tried to chase after them, but he was carried off in the riot. He felt the pepper spray before he saw any cops, and he hit the ground writhing.

Teddy never found Gretchel that night. He struggled for hours through streets crowded with people, just trying to get back to her dorm. She wasn't there, of course, so he slept a few hours in the bushes. Later that morning, he was pacing and waiting when a red convertible pulled up. Gretchel stumbled out, looking like Alice had missed Wonderland and taken a tour of Hell instead. Teddy glared at Troy behind the wheel, but he just grinned and roared off.

Gretchel's head was haphazardly bandaged, and

Teddy was silently praying that she didn't have a concussion. He was worried, relieved, and furious.

"You had sex with him," he accused.

"He saved me," she said.

"Saved you? Saved you? He was the one that threw the beer bottle, Gretchel. He looked right at you and aimed."

She stared at him for a moment, as if she understood the implications, but was more than willing to ignore the truth. "Well, he made up for it. He took me to breakfast at Mary Lou's, and gave me a hundred bucks for a new outfit."

"So, you're a hooker now?" Teddy fumed.

"Don't you ever call me that!" Gretchel's eyes blazed, and Teddy steeled himself for a slap. He had crossed a line, and he knew it. He was able to stammer out an apology while Gretchel was deciding whether or not to hit him.

"What about the voices you heard last night? They were trying to warn you right before he threw the bottle, weren't they? You were ducking and holding your head. They knew something was going to happen. You *knew* something was going to happen."

"What voices?"

"You started hearing the voices when the ambulance siren went off."

"I don't remember a siren, Teddy, and I didn't hear any voices," she said, but he knew she was lying through her pretty white teeth. "I barely remember getting hit with the bottle. Just let it go. So I got another wound that will turn into another scar, and a nice guy helped me out. I slept with him. Big deal. Can this fight be over?" she asked.

But the fight wasn't over. Not by a long shot. He had fought with her the rest of the weekend, and for a good part of the next seventeen years.

CHAPTER FOUR

Irvine, 2010s

Gretchel left the salon with her long hair trimmed and styled differently enough to please her husband. Her phone rang just as she got into her car. It was her mother. After a brief conversation, Gretchel set out for Snyder Farms. The infamous property on the outskirts of Irvine was comprised of three houses, a lake, and two thousand acres of fertile farmland. It was where she was raised, the place she still thought of as home.

"Mama, I'm here," Gretchel announced as she walked through the kitchen door of the old farmhouse on the hill.

She was welcomed by Suzy-Q, a beautiful white Saluki. There had been a dog of this breed on the property for nearly a hundred years. They were a family tradition and Southern Illinois University's mascot. Gretchel got down on her knees to give the hound a tight squeeze. Suzy-Q licked her face and nuzzled her shoulder, almost knocking her over. Gretchel glanced up at her mother.

"She's never this happy to see me. In fact, she

usually ignores me."

Ella Bloome eyed her daughter strangely. "Suzy-Q's very sensitive to change. Baby Girl, something's afoot, and I think you should take heed, just like the rest of us."

"Mama, what's wrong?"

"Holly had a vision last night."

Gretchel dismissed her niece's precognitive gift. "Her visions don't always come to pass, Mama."

The sound of a bone-shaking, crackling cough came from the living room. Ella scowled, distracted. "Miss Poni's cold isn't passing. I'm off to get some fresh ginger and fennel. She's refusing to see a doctor, but if it persists another day, I may need you, Marcus, and Cindy to help me force her."

"I can't force her, Mama. She never forced me when I was sick," Gretchel sighed and let Suzy-Q nuzzle her again.

Ella knelt down to her daughter and the hound. "Holly saw a funeral in her vision."

Gretchel felt the color drain from her face as a chill ran down her spine. "No," she whispered. Then more loudly, "No. Holly's visions are wrong as often as they're right, and Miss Poni would know if she was dying."

"Miss Poni doesn't tell all of what she sees." Ella shook her head, and wiped away a tear from the corner of her eye. She rose and pulled on a heavy winter coat. "I won't take too long; just a few errands."

"Take your time."

Her mother stopped, and took a closer look at Gretchel. "Baby Girl, are you okay? Have you been crying?"

"No. No. I'm just sick of this weather. You know

how I get in the winter," she mumbled.

"I can't see how it's different from the other seasons. You haven't turned with the wheel in years." Ella gave her daughter an appraising look. "You should see a doctor, too. You're skin and bones."

"I'm fine, Mama. Just go," she said as she shooed her mother out the door.

Ella eyed Gretchel suspiciously, and then she motioned toward the living room. "The over-the-counter cold medicine I've gotten Miss Poni to take is making her all kinds of loopy. Be patient, Gretchel. I won't be long." And with that she was out the door.

Gretchel peeked around the corner, and saw her ninety-seven-year-old grandmother sitting in a cushioned rocking chair, an old book across her lap. She wasn't moving. Gretchel panicked.

"Grand Mama, are you okay?" she asked. She felt her grandmother's pulse and shook her gently.

"Aurora? Is that you, honey?" the old woman asked.

Gretchel stared at her in disbelief. She hadn't heard that name spoken in decades. She put her hands to her mouth. She pushed back a sob and an overwhelming urge to lose consciousness. Her eyes fluttered, her head swam, but she slowly brought herself back to reality. The crone was staring at her, waiting for an answer.

"Grand Mama, it's me, Gretchel. Mama went to do her running, so I'm going sit with you for a while. Would you like a cup of tea or something to eat?"

Miss Poni stared blankly. The old woman was confused, and Gretchel didn't think she had the courage to deal with it. Not today.

A familiar light came back into Miss Poni's eyes. "No, Baby Girl. I'm just fine, but it sure is nice of you to come sit with me. I've had a terrible cold. I'll be sound in a few days, and you won't have to worry 'bout coming 'round so much. Your mama shouldn't have to be watching me like a hawk, either," she said as she pushed her ancient cane against the floor to start the chair rocking. Gretchel stared awkwardly at her grandmother. She was being abnormally sweet. It must have been the medicine.

"Mama's fine. I'm sure you took good care of your mama when she got older. It's just something daughters do," Gretchel said.

She took a seat on the sofa, and her sense of panic subsided. She thought about how glad she was that she wasn't taking care of her own mother, who was seventy-two and still a force to be reckoned with.

She was also grateful to her older brother, who had taken control of the family farm when he was just twenty-three. Marcus had graduated from SIU, and was preparing to start a masters program in agricultural sciences when he left it all to run Snyder Farms.

He had worked hard to save his family's livelihood, and within a few years he pulled the farm out of the red, only to be slammed back down during the flood of '93. He rose to that challenge, too, and, now, the farm was not just surviving but thriving under his management. The third house on the property was the one that he had built a few years after he got married. Marcus was committed to the farm in a way that Gretchel never had been and never could be, and, for that, she was thankful.

"The women in my family died young," Miss Poni said, almost to herself. Then the old woman lifted her head and raised her voice. "I've never told you this, but my mama, she died young. She was very sick, Baby Girl. The spirits made her sick, and I don't just mean the Scotch. She drowned in a pool of guilt and shame long before she ended her life in the cottage lake. You know that lake's haunted, and now you know who was calling you when you tried to do yourself in all those years ago."

Gretchel was barely listening. She was busy dreading the evening ahead.

"How much do you know about our ancestors, child?" Miss Poni asked.

Gretchel snapped back to the present. "Just bits and pieces, Grand Mama. I know that the cottage has been in our family for a long time, and that you were born and raised there. I know it was built for your mama, Miss Mary Catherine Miller. I know a neighbor willed Snyder Farms to you. Of course, I've heard plenty of stories about the ghosts in the Wicked Garden, and you know I've seen them." *And don't you dare bring up the ones I put there Grand Mama*, Gretchel thought.

"You don't know a goddamn thing about those ghosts," Miss Poni rasped, a sneer contorting her face. Gretchel was used to her grandmother's cantankerousness, but this took her aback.

"I would welcome the chance to be educated, Grand Mama," Gretchel replied with all the poise she could muster. "But you don't know what I know. You have no idea."

The ancient woman wasn't fazed by her granddaughter's sass, only surprised; she just shook her head. "Yes, well, it would be good to get the truth out. There are stories we need to tell. Yours is one of them,

Baby Girl. It's time. I can feel the north wind blowing changes our way."

It'll be a cold day in hell before I tell my *story*, Gretchel thought. And then she thought about Holly's vision. She knew she should hear what Miss Poni had to say before it was too late, but she wasn't ready to think about life without her Grand Mama. She pushed the thought of the woman's passing to the back of her mind.

"I think it's time for your stories on TV, isn't it?"

"Gretchel, I want you to do something for me."

"What do you need, Grand Mama. Do you want another blanket?"

"No, no, no. I want you to go down to the cottage after your mama gets back and fetch me the painting of the poppies. I need something pretty to look at."

Gretchel couldn't stop the tears from reaching her eyes. "Can Mama do that for you? I'm kind of on a tight schedule."

"In a rush to get back to your prison cell, are you now? Does the warden know you've come to fraternize with the Witches of Snyder Farms? Should I expect torches and pitchforks within the hour? Do I need to load the shotgun so I can take care of that abusive son of a bitch once and for all?"

"Enough!" Gretchel yelled.

Miss Poni eyed the girl with interest. She hadn't fought back in many years. The old woman noticed what was missing from her granddaughter's neck, and nodded to herself. "I'd really like to see that painting, Baby Girl. I *need* to see it. Something's stirring in this cold winter wind, and I want those pretty poppies to keep the shadows at bay."

"Okay. I'll get you the painting. Just please watch

your stories, Grand Mama," Gretchel replied. She walked into the kitchen, and burst into tears.

∞

"Can you come back for dinner tonight—bring the kids, maybe? I know it's your anniversary, but it's not as though you care," her mother asked as she put groceries away.

Gretchel let the jab roll. "We're going out with the Browns." Gretchel felt her mother's loneliness in the pit of her stomach. "Mama, why don't you have Thomas over for dinner? I haven't heard you talk about him for a while now."

"I'm just fine with the way things are. Now you run along, and make sure you tell Troy how much I despise him."

"I can't leave just yet. Grand Mama wants me to run down to the cottage to get the poppy painting."

Ella stopped unpacking her bags, and turned to her daughter. She began to cry. "The poppies. She's going to leave us soon," she muttered. "I can get the painting, Baby Girl, you don't need to trouble yourself."

"It's not a big deal, Mama. I'll be back in a few minutes," she said.

"It's a blue moon. Do be careful."

Gretchel drove toward the cottage. It was less than a mile away. As soon as it came into view, she felt a bittersweet ache spread across her chest. The cottage at Snyder Farms was her real home. She had lived there twice in her life: once as a teenager and once as a young married mother. Both times she was barely getting by, financially and mentally. The house was technically hers, but only on the condition that Troy never set foot on the property again. Miss Poni had made it clear that she would cut Gretchel out of her will if she had good reason to believe that Troy had been there.

Troy had pushed the matriarch too far. When he sent Marcus to jail, Miss Poni had been angry. When she saw the bruises on Gretchel's body that had provoked Marcus to violence, she had been outraged. Her initial response had been to terrorize Troy with the old family shotgun and promise to bury him in the Wicked Garden. The threat of disinheritance had been a welcome de-escalation.

Gretchel shook the horrid memory from her head, only to be struck with yet another. As she pulled into the gravel driveway, her eyes were pulled toward a burnt-out pickup truck sitting phantomlike in the snow, surrounded by dead vegetation. The Wicked Garden had claimed the vehicle many years before. Gretchel touched her waist, and had to fight to catch her breath.

She pulled her attention away from the desolation and toward the cottage. Kinder memories fell softly in her mind. The cottage was a breathtaking piece of architecture in the middle of nowhere—even in the dead of winter. With its crooked chimney, sloping roof, and arched doorway, the cottage looked like something right out of a fairy tale. For the first time in her life, Gretchel wondered if maybe this fairy tale didn't have a happy ending. A shiver ran through her as she put the key into the lock.

She flipped on the lights. No one had lived there since she and Troy had moved out. She didn't like to remember that time.

The interior was beautiful, exactly the home Gretchel had always dreamed of. Miss Poni had had it completely renovated three years before. For a little while, Gretchel assumed that her grand mama was softening in her old age, willing to lift her ban on Troy. But she soon learned that Miss Poni was just trying to lure her granddaughter away from her husband.

It was cold inside the cottage. She pulled her coat tight, and looked toward the pictures on the mantelpiece. On one side she saw her great great grand mama and her great grand mama. On the other side were Miss Poni and Ella. She wondered when her picture would be added to the display. Was she even worthy of being added? She had shamed the family. They tried to deny it, acting like nothing had happened for the sake of her sanity.

In the middle of the pictures sat an old bottle of Scotch. Whiskey had been a mainstay in the house, but this bottle had been untouched for decades. Without thinking, Gretchel reached for the amethyst that was no longer there. She would have to find strength from within, her first real test.

She took a deep breath and moved her gaze from the bottle to the antique Remington shotgun that hung above the photos. It was said to have belonged to her great-grandmother, and there were stories aplenty of the times it had been fired.

Above the shotgun was a huge mounted buck that Gretchel had prayed to as a teenager. It was her Horned God. She had shot the buck herself, bow hunting, when she was only twelve. There was a time when the beast had offered her guidance, when she was still able to hear the knowing inner voice, before she felt nothing.

She glanced at the bookcases built around the fireplace. The shelves held many of Miss Poni's books—some of them impossibly old—as well as volumes on art, gardening, magic, herbs, and mythology. There were a few novels—classics, mostly—and collections of poetry, too.

And then there were her own books—the books Troy had forced her to leave behind. She walked closer and let her eyes linger on her favorite authors: Jack Kerouac, Tom Robbins, Carlos Castaneda, Kurt Vonnegut, Lewis Carroll, and, of course, her very favorite: Graham Duncan.

Duncan had come out with seven new books since she'd married Troy. Seven books that she hadn't read. There was a time when his books were her only friends in the world, when she had been sure she had a telepathic connection with the author while reading his words.

The precious first-edition signed copy of *Hermes In Heat*, given to her as a gift, was missing from the bookshelf. It had been missing since Ame was a baby. Troy had probably burnt it in the cottage fireplace, along with *The Spiral Dance,* her *Bhagavad Gita,* and the *Tao Te Ching.*

Gretchel was brushing her fingers against the spines of her books when she heard a snapping sound. Her eyes turned back to the photos on the mantelpiece, to her ancestors, but they were all still. It was the house settling. She was just being jumpy. She touched each silver frame, one by one.

"I gave the amethyst away. I had to. So what am I supposed to do now?" she asked, and then the tears began again. She dropped into the overstuffed storybook chair, where Miss Poni had read to her as a child, and wept.

When she had calmed a bit, she turned to look at the painting her grandmother had sent her for. Its field of orange flowers was vibrant against the pale green of the wall. Gretchel hated this painting. She cursed the thing, and the voice that commanded her to paint it.

She heard another creaking sound, this time from the direction of the master bedroom. Alarmed, she got up and crept into the room, but there was nothing there—nothing but the painting of a phoenix hanging above the bed. This was more of her work. Gretchel felt a tightness in her throat as tears gathered in her eyes. She walked to the dresser and let her fingers circle the rim of an ancient silver loving cup. She remembered the last lips to touch it, and she began sobbing again.

Gretchel sank onto the bed, curled into a fetal position, and surrendered to the pain. It seemed like today she was making up for more than a decade without tears. It was exhausting. She needed to sleep. She just needed to rest for a while. She closed her eyes, and cried herself into slumber.

Wake, ye weak bloody bampot, a voice shouted.

She be a bit of a crabbit, an er heid's mince, said another.

Aye, but she's got to wake up before the pain in the bahooky arrives!

Gretchel opened her eyes inside a dream. It was dark, but she could see stars in the sky above and a huge full moon glowing bright. Her movements felt strangely fluid. It took her a moment to realize that she was immersed in water. It was warm and comforting. She felt a strong, healing presence surrounding her. She moved her hands and let the water wash over her naked shoulders. Then she saw them.

Several women were circling her, all of them redheads. She was in the middle of a grove, soaking in a huge cauldron. She could see the flames of a bonfire glowing madly nearby. There were sparkles of fairy wings flickering about in the moonlight.

It's a braw bricht moonlit nicht, and for Hogmanay no less.

"I don't understand," Gretchel said.

I tol ye, her heid's mince. She asks for help, and doesn't listen.

Keep the heid, an older woman said, then she addressed Gretchel. *She says it's a good, bright moonlit night for New Year's Eve. Blue moon it is. There's magic in the air. New beginnings. Wind blow'n in yer favor, lass. Been blowing that way since the Solstice.*

Aye! the women agreed in unison.

Gretchel was slightly unnerved by her lack of nervousness, and watched apprehensively as the ghostly figures seemed to float around her. They kept an eye on her, too, as she simmered in the huge pot. But their gazes weren't frightening. In fact, they were as warm and gentle as the element in which she soaked.

Her tensed muscles relaxed as she allowed herself to be held by the water, watched over by kindly eyes. As the tribe of red-haired women circled her, Gretchel felt tiny bits of herself merging back into place, like pieces of a puzzle connecting, or the skin closing over a scar. *Yes, that's it,* she thought. The more they danced, the more whole she felt. They were healing her. She knew, without knowing, that this was a ritual as old as time, and she allowed herself to surrender to it. For the first time in almost twenty years, her heart was open.

But the moment didn't last.

Ah, piss. The bloody devil's bride's a comin', one of the women called.

Startled, Gretchel was jolted out of restorative bliss and back into panic mode. The women were panicked, too, running from the clearing and disappearing into the mist that surrounded it. Turning her head this way and that, trying to identify the source of their terror, Gretchel saw her greatest fear approaching. She hadn't seen this apparition in seventeen years, but now she was back: the Woman in Wool.

Slowly and steadily, the entity walked toward the cauldron in the grove. Her bland blue wool dress was filthy and tattered. Her bare feet were covered in dirt and blood. Her hands were claws, ravaged by time and hard work. Her hair was a tangled red nest. But her face.... Gretchel might have thought she was the most beautiful woman she'd ever seen if that beauty wasn't marred by the purest evil.

Gretchel splashed at the water, frantic. She looked again for the women who had been with her moments ago, but she knew that they were gone. She looked for the flutter of fairy wings and saw none. She was alone, naked and defenseless, with her worst nightmare. She finally managed to pull herself out of the cauldron and set off running across the grove and into the forest. Gretchel was a fast runner, but that didn't matter in a dream. She turned back, and saw that the Woman in Wool was catching up with her without ever hastening her terrifyingly deliberate pace.

"Leave me alone," Gretchel shouted. She felt like she was running in place. She couldn't make her legs move fast enough.

Suddenly a wolf howled and the Woman in Wool dropped to the ground. Gretchel felt a slight tinge of relief, until she felt the first flames licking against her legs, her belly, her breasts. She was burning. There was fire all around her. She heard the ambulance cry and jerked awake.

After a moment of confusion, Gretchel realized where she had awakened. Being trapped in the nightmare would have been preferable.

For the first time since the accident, she felt the full impact of what had happened. There was nothing—no medication, no alcohol, no madness, and no charmed amethyst—to protect her from the pain. It felt like a vacuum had sucked her heart right out of her chest, and then blew it back in with unimaginable force.

She couldn't breathe. She pounded on the dashboard, frenzied, until finally she took in a stinging breath of bitter cold air. She wrapped her hands around her waist as tightly as she could. Her abdomen cramped with remembered loss. Her arm ached from a long-healed break, and the ghostly pain from her side nearly sent her into a psychotic episode.

Looking around the old pickup truck's charred interior, she remembered everything. *Everything*. She closed her eyes and let the memories wash through her fully and completely.

And then the truck vibrated as she let out a banshee wail that could have awakened the dead—and maybe had.

She kicked at the door. It wouldn't budge.

"Help me!" she screamed.

She tried pulling up the lock on the passenger side. She couldn't grip it, and her bare hands were seared from the cold.

"Gretchel!" She heard in the distance.

She finally realized what she had to do. She began climbing out the window.

"Gretchel!" She heard again.

She hesitated, and looked back in the cab, just as she had done twenty-five years before, but this time there was no one there to reach out to. Then she pushed herself out of the truck window almost the exact same way she had done before to save her own life.

"What in the hell are you doing?" bellowed her mother.

Gretchel looked around as she stumbled away from the truck, shaking wildly.

"How did I get here?" she cried. She pulled herself up and looked around again, noticing that the sky was dark. She smelled smoke—burnt flesh. She felt her waist again.

She heard shuffling behind her, in the Wicked Garden. She turned around to see her daughter's black horse staring her down from the fenced pasture. The horse never came this close to the Wicked Garden. Epona neighed and bucked as if she'd been spooked.

"Gretchel, it's almost 5:30. Mama reminded me you were coming here. Have you been in the Wicked Garden this whole time?" her mother asked as she helped her up from the ground.

"I have to leave. We're going out for dinner. Look

at me. I'm a mess."

"What were you doing in the truck?" Ella cried.

"Mama, I have to go!"

Backing out of the drive, Gretchel saw the shotgun laying in the backseat of her car. She gasped at the sight. She had no idea how it got there, and she didn't have time to take it back to the cottage. She sped down the country road hoping she could get a shower before Troy got home. Then the voices started. She hadn't heard them while she was awake since... since...

Noo, jist haud on!

She's aff er heid.

Yer bum's oot the windae, Mama, let er go about it then.

Will ye look at the bloody huge chebs on the chootker!

Aye. Huge fer a Skinny Malinky longlegs.

On and on they went, uninvited guests that wouldn't go away and wouldn't shut up.

Gretchel was pulling into her own driveway before she remembered that she hadn't taken her grandmother the painting she'd been sent to fetch. But, then, she suspected that Miss Poni had another motive entirely in sending her to the cottage.

CHAPTER FIVE

Irvine, 2010s

It was nearly six o' clock when Gretchel got home. She put her car in the garage and thanked all the gods and goddesses she could think of for the service door. The last thing she needed was for the neighbors, particularly Michelle, to see her carrying a shotgun into the house. Once she was inside, though, she had no idea what to do with the thing. Nowhere felt safe from Troy, and she certainly didn't want her kids to find it. Then it occurred to her that Ame had been staying with Holly and had no plans to come home anytime soon. Gretchel slid the shotgun under her daughter's bed, trusting that she'd have a chance to take it back to the cottage before Ame's winter break was over.

After cleaning herself up a bit, Gretchel retreated to her walk-in closet—sacred space and occasional prison—and collapsed to the floor. The voices had faded, only to be replaced with anxiety and fear. She had to keep it together. Troy had already picked out the clothes he wanted her to wear. She was surprised that he hadn't chosen shoes, too. She fingered a gray wedge and tried not to think about her afternoon at the farm. She had to focus on surviving the evening ahead. One calamity at a time, she reasoned.

She replaced the gray wedge, picked up a black heel, examined it, and then threw it across the small room. She was a barefoot kind of gal, a woman who could run over rocks without the slightest cringe of pain. She closed her eyes and tried to recall the feeling of grass between her toes.

"Strange place for a nap. Or are you in trouble again?"

Gretchel jumped at the voice of her teenage daughter.

"Ame, you scared me! What are you doing here?

Ame looked at her strangely before saying, "Uh… I live here?"

"I thought you were staying with Holly until it was time to go back to school."

"I came back to get some clean clothes. Is that a problem?" Ame didn't wait for an answer before she sat down next to her mother. "Have you been crying? Why didn't he lock the door?"

"I'm not crying. Please be quiet," Gretchel begged.

"What's wrong? Did he beat you again?" Ame asked, suddenly furious.

Gretchel shook her head. Her daughter carried enough burdens without having to deal with rumors of the affair.

"You found out about Michelle, didn't you?" she asked. Gretchel looked up, stunned. It wasn't the first time Ame had been able to read her mind.

"How did you know?" Gretchel asked.

"Zach told me when I got back from Champaign last week. That's why I've been staying with Holly. I was afraid I'd lose it and accidentally knock Dad down the stairs, proceeding to stomp on his face until his skull cracked open, allowing blood and what I think might be a brain to ooze onto our lovely wool carpet. But it would be an accident, of course, just like it has been when I've explained my black and blues all my life," Ame said. Gretchel looked down in shame. "Mom, why are we still here?" Ame's voice rose and cracked, making her sound more like a little girl than an angry teen.

"I just don't have everything figured out yet," Gretchel whispered.

"We need to get out for real this time," Ame said. Gretchel looked deeply into her daughter's eyes. They were wise eyes, and gray like her own.

"Teddy and I are going to come up with a plan. The best thing you can do right now is to just carry on. Keep saving your money. We may need it," she said, trying to smile.

"Like I'd take a penny from Dad anyway," Ame said. "I can't believe he's banging Michelle Brown, of all people. The neediest soldier wouldn't ride that nag into battle."

Gretchel tried, and failed, to stifle a bark of laughter. "Where on earth did you hear that expression?"

Ame grinned, "Miss Poni, of course."

"Well, stop it. You're just making things worse."

Ame's grin faded as she looked at the fraternity paddle, and then back to her mother. "I don't think things *could* get any worse."

She left the closet, slamming the door. Gretchel turned back to her shoes. Her blood was boiling now. Troy hadn't destroyed her family; she had. Teddy was right. She knew that whatever circumstance she was in was a result of a choice that she had made, but she wanted to be mad at Troy. She wanted to blame him. If only for a few minutes, she needed to blame him.

She pulled out her ritual box, held the old rag doll and began to pray.

Troy suddenly pounded on the closet door, and she jumped. "I told you to be ready at six," he shouted.

She instinctively glanced above her full-length mirror to the paddle.

∞

Troy was putting his coat on in the living room, when Gretchel carefully walked down the stairs in an ungodly pair of black stiletto boots. They were dripping with confidence, and she at least needed to appear as though she had some. Troy looked her over longer than normal.

She steeled herself as she walked past Zach and Ben, who were playing a video game in the living room. She headed straight for the kitchen. She didn't want to look into the eyes of the child who had broken the news. It would be too much. Just seeing the two boys together was almost more than she could handle in her current state.

"Where's Ame?" Troy demanded.

"She's getting ready to go out," Zach answered.

Troy looked to the boys. "Hey, Ben," he said. "I left my briefcase in the car. Would you run out and grab it for me?"

Ben looked at Zach, and then toward Gretchel in the kitchen. The boy had grown up around this family. He was familiar with the code. He grabbed Troy's car keys, and quickly moved toward the back door.

Troy walked to the steps. "Giant, get your ass down here."

Ame came bouncing down the stairs. Troy was six foot tall, and Ame towered three inches above him, which Troy found absolutely infuriating,

"What's up, Shorty?" Ame asked her father.

Troy's face flamed, but he decided to let that one pass. "Another bottle of Scotch is missing. Don't think for a second I don't know what you're up to, Giant. No booze tonight. If I smell it on you when you get home, you're grounded indefinitely. You can kiss your job goodbye, the car, everything. I'll make sure you're kicked off the volleyball team, too. Do we have an understanding?" he barked.

Gretchel watched the showdown from the kitchen. She prayed for Ame to just keep her mouth shut.

"I don't drink little man, so quit accusing me of things I don't do."

"You're a liar. I know that's why you were staying at Holly's. You two little witches have been getting hammered on my booze again," he spat.

"I can't wait to get out of this house and away from you," Ame muttered.

"No booze or I'll take your college money and buy a fucking boat," he threatened.

"If I don't get a scholarship, I'll pay for college myself," Ame rebutted.

Troy laughed. "Right, and you'll end up a whore like your mother."

Gretchel slapped a hand over her mouth, and tried like mad to stop the tears from falling freely down her face.

"I think I'd rather be a whore than take a dime from you. Somehow it seems more respectable," Ame said.

Troy smacked her across the face, and then shoved her hard. "Don't underestimate me, you colossal waste of sperm," he threatened.

Ame shoved him back, and he nearly fell into the wall. She raised her fist, and Gretchel screamed from the kitchen. "Stop it!"

Troy, Ame, and Zach all looked her way, shocked into stillness. Gretchel had not screamed in many, many years. Ame dropped her fist, and Troy straightened himself.

"Zach, if she comes home drunk, you tell me."

Zach looked at Ame apologetically, as she rubbed the red mark on her face. Then he turned to his father and gave a barely perceptible nod.

"You'll always be a little coward," Ame hissed at her brother. As she ran back up the stairs, she stopped midway and looked back at Troy. "Your moment's coming little man. You're not long for this world."

∞

She knows. That was all Troy could think when he got in the car, and saw Gretchel's face. She looked like she'd been crying, and he couldn't remember the last time she'd shed a tear.

He tipped his head and looked at her sweetly.

"What?" she asked sharply. She found it unnerving how he changed moods so quickly. It was too easy for him to put on whatever face suited his needs or his audience.

"What would it take to make you happy? Whatever you want," he said.

She looked down at the Tiffany watch he had given her on their last wedding anniversary. He'd given her nothing for her most recent birthday, and nothing was exactly what she wanted from him. She turned her head away, and looked out the passenger side window. She glanced at the garage door, and then at the huge house. It was too big for them—too big for *her*, with too many white walls that left her feeling cold and empty. Tears began welling up in her eyes.

The voices were stirring. She could hear their mumbling, but within the background noise of her psyche, she also heard–or was it *felt*?—a clear whisper, *The tree.* A sob caught in her throat as she glanced up at the sky. The full moon was illuminating the white trash bag that was still caught in the oak tree's branches. Then Gretchel's eye was drawn by a shadow, moving. She felt butterflies in her stomach, but tried to dismiss them, *Just a raccoon, probably.*

She turned to her husband. "You should get that trash bag out of the tree."

Troy leaned over her, and looked through the window. "I don't know if I have a ladder tall enough. Can't maintenance do it?" he asked.

"Would it kill you? You asked me what would make me happy. *That* would make me happy. It's been there for over a week." Her mouth filled with the taste of venom.

He sat back shocked by her outburst. “It’s really in your best interest not to talk to me that way,” he threatened. He tried to intimidate her with his stare, but instead her eyes were scaring *him*. They were the wild gray eyes of the witch he once knew.

She glared at him bitterly. “Would it kill you, Troy?”

He took a deep breath, mulling over the consequences if he didn’t comply. If she knew about the affair, she appeared to be deciding whether or not to make it an issue. He needed her to keep her mouth shut and let it go, because he was very close to sealing a deal that would make him a very rich man. He shook his head.

“Thank you,” she said, and turned away.

He glanced back at her as he pulled out of the driveway. She was still so smoking hot it made him sick, but he would never, ever tell her. Maybe she would let him touch her tonight, just for old time’s sake; it was their anniversary, after all. Surely she’d healed by now; his guilt surely had. Michelle was nothing compared to Gretchel. Maybe Gretchel was just jealous. Maybe they needed to be intimate. Maybe she’d do him like she used to, when a keg and a couple hundred dollars was all he needed to get her to do the crazy stuff.

She’d been out of her damn mind in college, with the psychotic babbling and screaming in the night. Troy was convinced he was the one that cured her shortly after the hippy left town.

He rubbed the inside of Gretchel’s skinny leg, and she jerked. “Don’t pull away from me sweetheart. I own you.”

She turned on him with a look of pure contempt.

"You're not good enough to own me," she spat. *No! What have I done?* Gretchel wished for a moment that she could take back her words, but she willed herself not to show Troy how scared she was.

Troy's eyebrows turned up. The crazy had returned. He bit his tongue, pulled his hand back and had to force himself not to hit her. His patience was wearing thin. He didn't need to save the best ammunition for the divorce. He had his own ace in the hole, but apparently Michelle had so much dirt on Gretchel they could bury her twice and still have leftovers for that garden she always wanted.

"Gretchel, do I need to pull out the VCR?"

All the rage left her face, leaving it a rumpled mess of despair. Only he could debase her in such a way.

"You wouldn't," she whispered.

"Try me."

CHAPTER SIX

Irvine, 2010s

The country club was right around the corner—it was just like Troy to drive instead of walk—but, by the time they reached the parking lot, Gretchel could swear steam was shooting out her ears. Her outrage sounded like surf crashing inside her head. The voices mumbled above its steady throb.

The windaelicker's bluffin'

Aye, he's jus lookin' for a nasty shag, love.

Troy parked behind the building, and tried to make it to the other side of the car to open the door for Gretchel just in case anyone was watching, pretenses being of utmost importance. Gretchel was still fuming. She swung the door open, just grazing his testicles.

"Knock it off," he growled nervously, and then shot an anxious wave to some acquaintances that were walking past. "Evening. How's that new SUV suiting you in this weather, Jim?" Gretchel could not have been less interested in the response.

They rounded the corner, and Gretchel noticed a

figure sitting on the stone bench just outside the country club door. She fell to her knees.

"What the hell is wrong with you?" Troy hissed as he grabbed her elbow. Gretchel was shaking uncontrollably. Troy looked in the direction of her fixed gaze, and then turned to survey the pristine, snow-covered grass surrounding them. "What the fuck are you looking at? Get up, you crazy bitch." Troy's low, angry voice was barely audible above the noises inside Gretchel's head.

He dug his fingers into her arm, reaching through coat and clothes to crush the flesh beneath. Troy pulled Gretchel from the ground. "Careful now. It's slick," he told a couple walking toward them.

Gretchel kept staring at the bench, shaking, and clutching at her throat, while the Woman in Wool eyed her eagerly.

As Troy opened the door to the country club, Gretchel pushed passed him and ran for the bathroom.

"What's wrong with Gretchel?" Cody Brown—Troy's best friend and Michelle's husband—asked.

Troy rolled his eyes, and motioned for the bartender to get him his usual Scotch. "On her period."

Cody knew that couldn't be true. Gretchel hadn't had a cycle in three years.

∞

"No. Oh, no." Staring into the ladies' room mirror, Gretchel panicked as discreetly as she could. She felt like she was going to vomit. She opened a stall door and knelt down, waiting for something to come rushing out. Nothing came. She turned herself around and sat on the floor, her back against the toilet.

She reached into her purse and fished around for her cell. She started talking as soon as she heard the click on the other end. “Teddy, she’s back!”

“Where did you see her?”

“Outside the country club.”

Teddy was quiet for a moment. “I’m coming to get you,” he said.

“No. You can’t,” she cried.

Teddy sighed. “Gretchel, you’re dealing with a pretty major trauma, and you’re still adjusting to life without the amethyst. You’re in a state of shock. If you insist upon enduring this evening, my advice is: Breathe mindfully, eat something, and think pleasant thoughts.”

“Why is she here? Why do they keep punishing me?” she cried.

“Gretchel, enough! If you’re going to spend the evening with Troy and Michelle, you need to pull yourself together. I’ll come to your place first thing tomorrow morning.”

“Yes. Please. I’m freaking."

You should be, he thought.

∞

Gretchel sat down at the table. Michelle grabbed the chair across from her. Gretchel avoided eye contact by pretending to take an interest in her husband, who was bantering with several couples at the bar.

She thought about how easy it had been for Troy to make friends when he had moved here to her hometown. He fit right in to the country club set. She did, too—at least on the outside. Everything she despised about the town, she had become a part of.

When they moved to Irvine from Carbondale, she had assumed that Troy, being from a posh suburb of Chicago, would hate it, but it was quite the opposite. He had become a big fish in a little pond. He quickly found a job at Sunset Automotive. Michelle's father owned the dealership, and while Gretchel hated the fact that he was working there, they were broke, about to have a baby, and needed the money.

As the world's greatest liar and a practiced charmer, Troy was able to surround himself with an adoring clique in no time. They all treated him like a god. Even Cody—who Gretchel knew to be so much smarter than the rest of them—had fallen for Troy's nauseating charisma.

She sat quietly, sipping a glass of water and trying to push back the resentment. She was afraid if Michelle said the wrong thing she would reach across the table and stab her with a butter knife.

"You look tense. Why don't you order a Scotch," Michelle smiled. She flipped back her naturally blonde, spiral-curled hair. Gretchel twitched. She detested this woman. Loathed her. It was so much easier to ignore her when she had the comforting weight of her talisman against her throat. Now the intense feelings of abhorrence were bubbling up to the surface.

"I'm fine," Gretchel said flatly.

"Oh come on, Gretch. Lighten up a little. One drink won't hurt you," Michelle chuckled, and sipped at a glass of wine.

Gretchel raised her hand to her neck by instinct,

clutching at the amethyst that wasn't there.

"You know, don't you?" Michelle asked. "I can tell. It's about time you figured it out. Looks like the ball's in your court yet again… Gretch."

Gretchel clawed at her own legs to keep herself from committing murder. She took a deep breath, and stared the woman down. "It's not over yet… *Chelle*," she whispered.

"It wouldn't be any fun if it were," Michelle smiled, and then turned to welcome her husband and Troy back to their table.

"Next shotgun season I'm hunting at the cottage, are you in?" Troy asked Cody. Gretchel's eyes grew wide at the realization of what he'd said. He wasn't just going to destroy her; he was going to try to take away the one and only home she had left in the world.

Cody furrowed his brow. "I thought you weren't welcome at Snyder Farms."

"The old hag's out of her mind. I've heard she never leaves her rocking chair these days," Troy said.

Cody glanced at Gretchel. He noticed her trembling lips and the tears quivering at the corner of her eyes. "I don't think it's a good idea. It's in the will, Troy. If you hunt there, Gretchel loses the cottage. Miss Poni was dead serious," Cody said.

"To hell with her and the broomstick she flew in on," Troy growled.

Cody shook his head. "I'm not going down there."

"Why, you afraid of ghosts?" Troy snickered.

Cody and Michelle both looked at Gretchel, who was trying to hide behind the menu. Cody had a sad, sympathetic look in his eye. Michelle giggled.

"Well, I'm not afraid of ghosts… or witches," Troy said and grabbed Gretchel's hand under the table, bending back her fingers until she nearly screamed.

As soon as he let go, she grabbed her purse and coat and stomped out of the club. She had reached her limit.

It was bitterly cold outside, but it felt like heaven. Gretchel was burning up from the inside. She turned to see if Troy had followed her, but the only person she saw was the Woman in Wool sitting underneath an oak tree.

"Leave me alone!" Gretchel screamed.

"Baby Girl, I'm taking you home?"

She zipped around to see Cody. She turned back to the tree. There was no one there.

"This isn't happening," she whispered to herself.

"You don't look good. Is something going on?" Cody put his hands on her shoulders. They were warm and comforting. "Are you hearing things again?"

"Just leave me alone," she whimpered, but she didn't push him away. He embraced her, and she buried her head in his chest.

"Look, Troy's pissed, and he told me to take you home," he paused. "Are you aware of what's going on, Gretchel?"

She started looking around for the Woman in Wool. It was all in her head, she tried to convince herself. Then she tried to focus on what Cody had said.

"Yes, I know. Just take me home. I've got to get out of here. I'm sick. I've got a migraine, the flu, whatever you want to tell them. I've just got to get out of here."

Cody led her to his huge truck, but she hesitated at the door. The sense of *déjà vu* was almost overwhelming.

Before she could stop herself, she screamed as loudly as she could.

∞

By the time she got home, Gretchel felt a little less crazy. She'd jumped out of the truck in the middle of Cody's tirade against their cheating spouses. Inside, the boys were still in the living room playing video games. She informed them she was sick, and going to bed.

"She's not sick. She's just pissed at my dad," Zach said.

Gretchel froze at the top stair landing, listening.

"Well maybe your dad shouldn't be messing around with my mom. He's a jerk." Ben retorted.

"Yeah, well your mom's a bitch. They deserve each other."

"I bet Troy's trying to get control of the dealership. Why else would he cheat on your mom? She's hot. Every guy in town wants her."

"My mom's an insane train wreck," Zach spat.

"Still hot, bro."

"C'mon, man. You're talking about my *mom*," Zach mumbled. Then he looked around for his mom, and pulled the missing bottle of Scotch from between the couch cushions.

Gretchel sighed, shook her head, and continued her way up the stairs. She couldn't cope with her son's drinking. Not right now. Resisting the urge to join him was taking all the strength she had. She continued to the master bath, struggling to make sense of everything that had happened in the last few days. After years of maintaining a perfect veneer of anesthetized normalcy, Gretchel felt her life spinning out of her control.

She ran a hot bath. This ablution and her habit of rising early to greet the goddess of dawn were the only rituals she had left. Had Troy known what these practices meant to her, he would have found them incompatible with their upwardly-mobile, gated-community lifestyle, but he just thought that his wife enjoyed a long, steamy soak and an early-morning run.

As she eased herself into the water, Gretchel was reminded of the dream that had come to her in the cottage. She returned to the scene before the Woman in Wool had arrived. She willed herself to feel that sense of safety again. Yes, her life was spinning out of her control, but maybe she could trust that fate had something in mind for her besides an endless cycle of silent pain and carefully sustained numbness. Gretchel let the warm water hold her, and allowed herself to indulge in a memory that she'd been afraid to revisit for ages. Once, long ago, she had heard the voice of fate incarnate. She had heeded that voice, and it had led her to the boy with the aquamarine eyes.

∞

Carbondale, 1990s

The end of her freshman year of college was quickly approaching. She had barely passed all her classes, what with the hangovers, her job, and Troy. He had announced he was going home to Chicago for the summer. They had been dating–if one could call it that—since Halloween. She was going to be glad to be rid of him and his horrible friends. But she couldn't go home herself. Not yet.

She didn't know how she would be able to afford to stay in Carbondale for the summer, but she was determined to find a way. Otherwise she would be back in Irvine working on the farm. She didn't mind the work; she just wasn't ready to go back. Even though she desperately missed the countryside and the cottage, Carbondale had been a fresh start for her.

She told herself it was also the perfect opportunity to break away from Troy. Teddy had been right. He was a predator, and nobody would ever believe how evil he could really be.

Her plan had three steps: Find a cheap place to live, work hard all summer, and disappear from Troy's life forever. It was a big campus, and even when she returned to the dorms in the fall, she would find a way to steer clear of him.

But it was May already, and she was running out of time to complete the first part of her plan. She was at Mary Lou's, reading *The Daily Egyptian*, when the ad caught her eye. "ROOM OPENING: Free rent and utilities. Minimal household tasks required." followed by a phone number. Gretchel couldn't believe it; it just seemed too good to be true. She ran to a pay phone as fast as she could.

A man answered, and she remembered how the voice had made her feel blissfully loved—safe, even. She didn't know that hers was the nineteenth call. She didn't know that the nineteenth call was the one the man on the other end of the line had been waiting for, or that he'd gotten the message to wait for the nineteenth caller in a dream.

"I'm calling about the room in the house on

Pringle."

"It's open immediately. Tell me, honey love, do you have a green thumb?"

Gretchel was perplexed. "Yes, I was raised on a farm."

"Stupendous. You'll have three roommates," he said, and then took her name and contact information. "Do you have any questions?"

She had quite a few, in fact. "Do I have to prove I'm in school? Do I pay any rent at all? And do I meet you or something? I mean I don't even know your name."

"I know you're in school, I can tell. No rent, no utilities, and intuition tells me we will meet someday when the time is right. Timing is everything, honey love."

"And your name?" Gretchel asked.

"You can call me Peter—or Pan, if you have a sense of adventure. Are you the Wendy type?"

"I'm more of an Alice," Gretchel said.

What planet was she on? Things like free rent, and anonymous landlords that called themselves Peter Pan just didn't fall out of the sky.

"Why are you doing this? I mean, it seems too good to be true."

The man laughed. "No need for the paranoia, honey love. I recommend you trust the blessings that come your way. You wanted this, did you not?"

"Well, yeah, but what's the catch?" Gretchel inquired.

"There is no catch. I like to give," he said.

"What do you want from me besides the upkeep of the house?" she asked.

"The question is what do *you* want besides the

upkeep of the house? Your world is malleable, my dear. Chew on that for awhile. What is it that you really want?" Peter asked, and then hung up before she could even begin to answer that huge, never-ending question.

What did she want then? She wanted forgiveness, she wanted justice, and she wanted closure. That was the main reason she had gone to SIU for school. She had avoided her real intentions all year, but that day, after that phone call she knew she had to find Devon—an old family friend—and make things right. She needed to see him, to talk to him. She needed to face a part of her past that had been nothing short of beautiful and pure, but had turned disastrous.

If she saw him then she could move on, at least a little. She could focus on what she really wanted, which was to learn, to experience, to connect with the earth on levels she never had, and then take all that and release it back out into the universe. Above all, she was craving connection, intimacy, and someone who understood how to ride the waves. Someone who would understand her quirks, someone who was capable of having an intellectual conversation, someone who understood that sex could be not just a hit and run accident, but also a nice long drive in the country. And she didn't just want someone; she wanted the boy with the aquamarine eyes—the eyes she had searched every face for after the eve of her fourteenth birthday, the night that changed her life forever.

Gretchel closed her own eyes and let her mind drift back to that night. Her throat began to close with unshed tears as she replayed the conversation she'd had before she left the house that night. Clairvoyance was a gift that appeared in every generation of her family, at least as long as anyone could remember, and the boy with the aquamarine eyes had appeared in a vision that was clearly intended for Gretchel. There had been more to that vision, but Gretchel was young enough—and foolish enough—to only hear the parts she wanted to hear.

If she could only go back, she would heed the warning contained in that vision, she would stay home. Everything would be different. *Everything.*

But she hadn't listened, and she couldn't go back. The Wicked Garden had always been cursed, but Gretchel was responsible for a few of the restless spirits doomed to walk through its weeds forever. And forever was exactly how long she would carry that blame. A ripple of guilt washed through her.

Gretchel sank down deep in the tub, letting the water reach her chin. She came back to the present—which wasn't much of an improvement. Waking up in the truck had spooked her—badly. This wasn't how she wanted to start her new year. "But what do I want? What do I really want?" she asked herself aloud. *I still want the boy with the aquamarine eyes. I always will.* Then her thoughts shifted back to Troy, and all she could think about was burying him in the Wicked Garden. His was a soul she would gladly consign to that unholy, unhappy place.

∞

Irvine, 2010s

"Goddess, guide me."

Gretchel was in the back yard, her arms stretched toward the blue moon.

She had married Troy because she felt that she

deserved him. She felt that she needed to be punished. She let him take away her power, and then she had sacrificed her children to her own guilt and shame. No more.

Gretchel held Troy in her mind, and then, chanting words she had learned from Miss Poni, she banished him.

Where you come from, I care not
Where you go, best you be gone
Leave me now and let it be
The bond is cut, so by this done.

She let her words sink into the snow at her feet. She let them rise up to the stars. Then she turned back toward the house and went inside to face whatever future she may have wrought.

CHAPTER SEVEN

Irvine, 2010s

It was just past one in the morning. Gretchel looked out the window when she heard a car roll into the driveway. She was surprised to see that it was Ame's. Gretchel's hand clutched the curtain as her mind flashed to the shotgun still hidden under her daughter's bed. Then she saw another set of headlights. It was Troy. Gretchel ran down the stairs and into the kitchen. She pulled Ame away from the refrigerator.

"Stop it," Ame protested.

Gretchel looked into her daughter's bloodshot eyes. Ame was either drunk or stoned. Given that Ame had gone straight for the guacamole and chips as soon as she got home, Gretchel was pretty sure it was the latter.

"You're out past curfew. Your father just got home. Go to your room and get into bed, *now*!" Gretchel hissed as she dragged her daughter up the stairs. Gretchel had just shut the door of Ame's bedroom behind her as Troy reached to open it.

"Drunk again, Giant?" Troy was talking to Ame,

but Gretchel could tell that he was the one who had had a few too many. Again.

"No. She's not drunk. You are, and don't you dare lay a finger on my daughter."

Troy turned toward his wife, seemingly surprised to hear her voice, and knocked her onto Ame's bed with a fierce backhand. "That's for contradicting me. I'll pay you back for embarrassing me tonight later."

Then he looked to Ame. "You were out past curfew." He rubbed his chin, savoring her punishment. "Say goodbye to your horse tomorrow."

"You can't do that!" Ame screeched.

"The hell I can't," Troy yelled. "Everything you have belongs to me. Tomorrow, I look for a buyer." He paused. "On second thought, I think I'll just shoot her in the head."

Gretchel lay on the bed, holding her jaw. Troy rarely hit her in the face. Facial injuries showed. Gretchel sat up, and looked into Ame's eyes. They were blazing. With an impossible shock of recognition, Gretchel knew that they looked just like her own when she was at her wildest. She wasn't surprised when Ame launched herself at Troy, jumping on his back, trying to choke him with her arm.

"Ame, *no*!" Gretchel tried to intervene, but an elbow caught her in the head. Zach rushed into the room. He, too, tried to restrain his sister.

Troy finally swung Ame around and off him. She landed on the floor with an impact that shook the house. He jumped on top of her and pummeled her repeatedly in the stomach. Gretchel felt a surge of energy rip through her center. She reared back and kicked Troy in the face. He pushed himself against the wall, touched the blood that gushed from his lip, and stood up.

"That was a big mistake, Gretch," he said.

"Not in front of Ben," she whispered. Troy looked to the doorway. If he was concerned about having a witness, he didn't show it. He got up, slowly walked to his wife, punched her hard in the gut, and pushed her back onto the bed. His cold gaze took in both boys. "Go. Now. Get out of this house."

"You're going to kill them! They didn't do anything wrong!" Zach cried, tears of sheer terror streaming down his face.

Troy gave his son a look that communicated a familiar threat. Zach stood frozen, and then pushed his wide-eyed friend out the door. Troy locked it and turned back to his wife and daughter. Clumsy from drink, he dropped to the floor and climbed atop Ame, who was still trying to catch her breath. He straddled her, pinned her arms above her head with one hand, and began unbuttoning her jeans with the other.

"Well, it appears that, for once, you're speechless, Ame. I think it's time that I shut you up for good, you worthless bitch." Ame couldn't speak for sobbing. Troy glared down at her. "You're a no good witch like your mother. You don't deserve any better than this." Then he spit in her face.

"Mama," Ame whispered hoarsely.

Troy felt cold metal against his temple.

"Get off her," he heard his wife say in a low, guttural voice.

Troy's gaze turned slightly to meet the barrel of the antique shotgun. Then he looked into his wife's eyes.

She had always been wild, and there had been a time when he had delighted in exploiting her special combination of abandon and self-loathing. He had certainly seen Gretchel crazy. But now he was seeing something else. Something that terrified him.

Gretchel pointed the shotgun at his face. "Get. Off," she repeated. Her breathing was heavy, but she held the gun steady.

"Gretch, this isn't what it looks like," Troy desperately pleaded.

"Get off," she said again, "And get out." She drew the shotgun up, pulling it tight against her chest.

"I take it all back. I'll never hit her again. I swear."

"Get out of this room," she screamed, "And get out of this house!" The metal met Troy's forehead.

He climbed off Ame and backed out of the room. Gretchel slammed the door in his face.

∞

Gretchel lowered the shotgun, gently. The calm sense of purpose that had descended on her when Troy attacked their daughter started to dissipate. She was shaking as she helped Ame climb into bed.

"The gun.... why was it in my room?" Ame asked. Gretchel started to sob. Unable to speak, she just shook her head. "Mom if you don't do something to change this for us, I'll never forgive you. You have to fight. If not for yourself, do it for Zach and me."

What remained of Gretchel's heart cracked, and then disintegrated into a fine powder of guilt and remorse.

Gretchel swallowed, pushing down the rising bile.

"I will make it right. I will do everything in my power to make it right," she said. Power. She had power. She could feel it inside, like a ball of light expanding and pulsating.

"Lock the door behind me, Ame. Do not open it for anybody but me."

The voices started as soon as she began walking down the steps.

'Bout time the amulet come off.

Aye, we be trying to reach ye since the bloody blue-eyed chap left ya cryin'.

Ye been hiding behind that purple gem. Served ye well 'nuff, but ye can't hear a bloody thing.

Even gie ye a skelpit lug!

Aye.

The devil's bride 'ill have you finish 'im off, but dinnae! Dinnae! Tis not your place to take his life. Ye got to break the cycle, love. Nature'll do 'em in. Let the elements do the deed this time. Whit's fur ye'll no go by ye.

Finish what ye've started, tart. Do it fer yer bairns. Most of the voices in Gretchel's head were anonymous, attached to nothing and no one she had ever seen, but not this one. This was the Woman in Wool.

If Troy was still in the house, she *would* blow his head off. She listened for movement. Everything was quiet. He was, perhaps, just smart enough to stay out of her way.

Gretchel was digging through the fire safe, looking for the documents she and her kids would need to start a new life. The shotgun was at her feet.

Before Gretchel even realized that Troy was behind her, he grabbed her wrist and twisted her arm behind her back.

He's oot his face!

Keep the heid! Keep the heid!

Kill him! the Woman in Wool screeched.

"Nobody else is going to love you like me, Gretch. Nobody else is going to be able to look at your disgusting body, your burns and your scars. I'm the best you're ever going to get, so let's just go to bed and pretend nothing ever happened." His voice was hot in her ear, and she could smell the Scotch on his breath. He would never change. Had she ever really believed that he would change?

Gretchel shifted her hips to the left, and used all the strength she had to drive her free right fist backward into Troy's testicles. His grasp on her arm weakened, Gretchel flung his arm away and reached for the shotgun.

Troy, curled up on the floor, raised his hands in defeat. "Gretch, I'm sorry," he gasped. "I can't lose you. I'd do anything for you. You know I would. You can't leave me. I'll break it off with Michelle, I'll find another job, we can move, whatever you—"

She leveled the gun to his chest. "I want the tape, Troy."

"It's gone!"

"Bullshit. Where is it?"

"I swear to you, it's gone."

"You're lying. Where's the tape, Troy?"

"I destroyed it. I did it for you! I love you. I've always loved you. We can fix this. Just put down the gun."

Gretchel drew back the hammer.

Kill him! The Woman in Wool screamed again. *Kill him!*

Gretchel stared at her husband over the barrel of

the shotgun. "All right, Troy. I believe you."

He sagged with relief.

"But there's still something I want from you, Troy. Can you do something for me, Troy?"

"Anything, Gretchel. Anything!"

"I want you to get that goddamn trash bag out of the goddamn tree. That's what I want from you, Troy."

Gretchel left her husband cringing at the bottom of the stairs.

She knocked on Ame's door, and waited for her daughter to let her in. She tucked the covers around her daughter, and, after giving Ame a kiss on the forehead, Gretchel settled herself into the rocking chair facing the door, the shotgun across her knees.

It was several hours before Gretchel let herself fall asleep, but, when she did, she slipped into a dream almost immediately. She was in a clearing. She was cradled in warm water. Women danced around her, chanting in low voices. She felt the gun in her hands, and shot the first man she saw.

CHAPTER EIGHT

Irvine, 2010s

Gretchel woke to the sound of a shotgun being fired.

When she opened her eyes, she saw her daughter's room. She saw her daughter, asleep in her bed. The gunshot had been in her dreams. Gretchel shuddered, remembering the events of the night before.

Ame stirred and turned to Gretchel.

"Happy New Year's, Mom. You were screaming in your sleep. Nightmare?"

"Yeah, I guess it was a nightmare. How are you?"

"I feel a little sore. Did I get my ass kicked last night?" Gretchel couldn't suppress a wry smile. Only Ame could be this diabolically sarcastic. "Really, Mom, I think that this *could* be a good year for us, but only if we make a move. Holly had a premonition. She saw a funeral. We need to get out of here before dad kills one of us—or you kill him."

"Your grand mama told me about Holly's vision. She thinks that it's Miss Poni who's about to die. But, look,

Ame, Holly's visions are never clear. There's no need to panic."

"No need to panic? You were here last night, weren't you?"

Gretchel heard the tears in her daughter's voice. She rose from the rocking chair and put her arms around her girl.

As she held Ame, Gretchel looked out the window. There was movement in the front yard. She saw Troy climbing a ladder, while Zach and Ben held it steady at the bottom.

Ame followed her mother's gaze. "Look at him. He's trying to get that stupid trash bag out of the tree," she said with a mirthless laugh.

"I asked him to get it down," Gretchel said, wondering why she had been so fixated on that stupid bag. Last night, she could have asked Troy for anything. Why hadn't she made a wiser choice? Why hadn't she *ever* made a wiser choice?

"What an idiot," Ame chuckled. "He can't reach it. He's going to crawl across that branch. I've got to get a picture with my phone."

Gretchel laughed too. Troy *did* look like an idiot trying to crawl across a very thin branch, very high up in a very tall tree, to reach a plastic bag.

"Look," Ame said. "I think the branch is cracking."

Gretchel watched flittering sparkles of sun dance around the bag and the branch. In the blink of an eye, the branch snapped, and Troy fell to the snowy ground below.

Part Two

Scotland, 1970s

Summer Solstice, just before dawn in the lowlands of Scotland. The boundary between light and dark was obscured, but one thing was clear: Diana Stewart's acid trip was starting to get interesting. She watched, rapt, as the sky stretched its arms and yawned a dirty white cloud into the black morning. She watched as the cloud disappeared. She watched the sky go back to sleep. Diana had watched this happen over and over again for an intense half hour.

Then she felt a shift in her awareness. She sensed movement all around her. She felt something tug at her long brown hair. The tug turned into a yank, and Diana felt herself being assaulted by a flurry of tiny hands. She flailed, swatted, and swore as minuscule fingers twisted her hair into knots. Almost by accident, she caught one of her tormentors snared in its own handiwork. She plucked it from the tangled mess of her hair and held it in front of her face.

It was a diminutive thing, faintly luminescent, with shimmering wings. A fairy. *This*, Diana thought to herself, *is what happens when a folklorist drops acid on midsummer morn. Although I would have thought that a tripping folklorist might come up with something a little more authentic than wee Victorian vermin.* She gave the fairy one more glance before she flicked the nasty creature away from her with a sneer of disgust.

"All right, you filthy little things. You asked for it." She grabbed another and flipped the diaphanous nuisance toward the forest.

Confronted with this fearsome counterattack, the fairies disengaged from Diana's head, regrouped, and flew in formation toward the forest. Diana watched them go until just one remained.

This lone fairy flitted and darted just outside of Diana's reach. "I'm Claire," she piped. "Follow me."

As Diana looked at Claire, she felt a shift in her awareness again. Where, just seconds before, a tiny winged being had been hovering, now there was a young woman dressed in a gown that would have been in vogue during the Regency. Diana found it hard to focus on this dress—it seemed to be simultaneously there and not quite there. Sometimes it looked as if it had just been delivered from the dressmaker's shop; sometimes it looked like a frail construction of cobwebs and dead leaves. But there was nothing ambiguous about Claire's face. It was captivating, and her hair—which fell about her pale shoulders—was a deep, sumptuous black. Diana's irritation with the earlier assault was replaced by a growing sense of uneasiness. *This*, she thought, *is a proper fairy. Best watch my step, even if she is just a hallucination.*

"Follow me," Claire repeated, holding out her hand.

Diana remained wary. "Why would I want to do that?"

Claire didn't reply. She just shrugged gracefully, and then turned to join her troop.

Diana looked around her parents' lush estate. It

had been in her family for centuries, as had the wealth that accompanied it. Diana had been raised in the States, but she spent her summers at Castle Belshire, and she knew the forest that surrounded it like the back of her hand. Still, she was apprehensive as she looked toward its threshold.

The landscape seemed still. Diana's mind was not. As the midsummer sun crested the horizon, she made her choice.

Diana had just finished her final year of college, where she had studied religion and mythology along with psychology. She was a privileged young woman. She had no need to work, and yet she was drawn to the field of psychology—just like her parents, her grandfather, and her great grandfather had been. Her father and mother, Charles and Miranda Stewart, had become pioneers in the field of transpersonal psychology. They had made amazing progress with psychedelic psychotherapy until the use of LSD had been outlawed.

The ban hadn't stopped Diana. The acid she was on was from her mother's lab. She knew she was being irresponsible. Taking a trip in an uncontrolled environment was not wise, nor was it approved of by her parents. But she had felt so compelled to take the hit. As soon as she awoke in the wee hours of the Summer Solstice, she immediately slipped it onto her tongue.

Diana had come to Scotland with her lover. She was taking a break before plunging into graduate school. He… Well, it was best for him to be out of the States for a little while. Diana had hoped that they could both take it easy for a couple months, but relaxation just wasn't one of

Diana's greatest strengths. She was driven like her parents. She couldn't relax when she tried.

Just the day before, she had been perusing the castle library in search of a novel to help her unwind—something in the way of Emily Brontë or Jane Austen, perhaps. Instead a large, dusty book sitting alone on a mahogany table caught her attention. Ever the scholar, Diana opened the book where it had been marked. It was a volume of Scottish folklore, and the chapter to which she turned was called "The Solstice Twins." One twin, it seemed, had been tried and executed for the crime of witchcraft. The other drowned thirteen years later.

Diana was intrigued by this fragment of history—in fact, she was captivated, compelled. It wasn't just the uncanny synchronicity of discovering the Solstice Twins the day before midsummer, although that was part of it. She also sensed that something had gone horribly wrong all those centuries ago. Innocence had been punished. Justice had been perverted—she felt an instinctual need to uncover the truth and an irrational pull to undo a karmic perversion. Diana was hardly the type to act on instinct—this was one of the many differences between her and her lover—but the pull she felt toward the Solstice Twins was irresistible, and their story was swirling in the back of Diana's drugged-up mind as she followed a fairy named Claire out of the early-morning glow of the Summer Solstice and into the thick, wet dark of the forest.

Diana kept walking until she came to a small clearing surrounded by trees. She hesitated. She didn't like this spot. Never had. As a young girl she had been chased through the forest by a fierce creature with brindled fur and barred teeth. When she told her parents that it was a wolf, they assured her that Scotland's last wolf had died centuries before. But Diana knew that the beast she'd encountered was no mere dog. The animal's pursuit had ended here, in this very clearing. Diana had fallen, breaking her leg, and, suddenly, the wolf was nowhere to be seen. Now, Diana paused among the trees, trembling. After a taking a few moments to banish this bad memory, she took a reluctant step into the gloomy clearing.

Diana could see fairies flitting through the dark, dense leaves above. Other than that, she seemed to be alone. Claire had either rejoined her flying friends or she had disappeared. Diana was about to get extremely frustrated with herself for trusting a fairy when she heard the sounds of movement—the rustle of dry leaves, the snap of a twig—nearby. The hair on her arms stood on end as she backed into a gigantic oak.

The old woman had come out of nowhere. Diana clutched her chest and sucked in a frightened breath. She could hear the thumping of her heart in her ears. Then she remembered, *I'm tripping. And I know an archetype when I see one. Crone. Wise woman. Symbol of intuitive wisdom.*

"I've been waiting a long time for you, child."

"Just who the hell are you calling a child?" Diana pulled herself up to her full height—all four feet, eleven inches. Her hand was on her hip, and a scowl on her face. She was willing to see what this trip might have to teach her, but she wasn't about to let a hallucination condescend to her. "I'll have you know that this *child* just defended a groundbreaking thesis on…"

"Quiet!" the crone squawked.

Diana bit her tongue, and really looked at the

woman before her. Her hair was long and gray, her face wrinkled and worn, her eyes white and ghostly. She gripped a weathered cane with one hand, and held something concealed in the other.

"I'm sorry," Diana said. "You frightened me." Diana gave the crone another long look. "Do I know you?"

"Aye, girl," the old woman grumbled, "At least you should. Have you no gratitude for the one who gives you what you seek?"

What I seek, Diana thought, *What* do *I seek?* She eyed the hag suspiciously, and decided to let the LSD—and her thesis-fatigued brain—do their thing. "Forgive me. I'm very pleased to meet you, and I'm sorry if I kept you waiting."

Diana probed her mind. She *did* know the crone. She had seen this woman many times in her dreams. In her dreams, Diana knew that there were questions she needed to ask her, people only the crone could help her find, but she never knew what questions to ask, could never identify the people she needed to find. Now, with the crone from her dreams standing right before her, Diana still found herself utterly mystified.

The old woman came closer. "You must take the amulet. The time is approaching."

The crone opened her clenched hand and reached toward Diana, who took what the old woman offered. It was a necklace. A surge of energy crossed between them. Diana could see a silvery light spread through her fingers and sink into her palm. She felt it journey up her arm and dissipate into her body.

Diana shuddered, and then looked at the amulet.

"It's beautiful," she whispered. She let her thumb roll over the center gem. It was a deep purple amethyst surrounded by tiny diamonds. "Shall I put it on?"

"It's not for you. Your son will know to whom it belongs."

Diana was trying to be polite to this archetype, but she couldn't stop the incredulous snigger that slipped out of her throat. She had just graduated college. She wasn't even sure if she wanted children, wasn't even sure if she *liked* them. She didn't have time for a child. She had a career to build. "My son?"

"Aye! The one you carry now."

Struck dumb, Diana just stared. This trip was taking a very weird turn.

"You're unaware?" the crone asked, bewildered. She, too, seemed to sense that this encounter wasn't quite going as planned. She grabbed the necklace back from Diana and shook it in front of her face. "This amulet offers great protection to one who will wear it, a descendant of the Solstice Twins. It is a gift from her ancestors, to safeguard the one we wait for."

"The Solstice Twins?" Diana gasped.

"Aye," the crone replied. "It's time to break the cycle."

"Cycle?"

"The cycle that began when another young lass was run through these woods and hunted to her death. She was innocent. It was her sister who set this wheel turning. It was her sister who was a victim of the predator. Her instincts were muddled. She blames herself for things out of her control, and haunts our descendants to their death as a result. She must be stopped."

Diana listened closely. Part of her was captivated by the crone's story, and part of her couldn't wait to report the peculiar happenings of this acid trip to her lover.

"Was this girl one of the Solstice Twins?"

Suddenly a great wind swirled in the clearing, lifting leaves and dust. The trees bent and the ground rumbled. Diana's long, knotted hair whipped about, and she cowered against a tree, holding on for her life.

She was still in the same place, but she could tell—somehow—that she was in a different time. She saw a young girl lying on the ground sobbing uncontrollably. Diana's heart ached. As intellectually driven as she was, her emotions were getting the best of her. She wanted to comfort the girl. Wanted to apologize for whatever had happened. She was being pulled toward her when the very wolf that had chased Diana before appeared and forced her back.

Then the crone stepped forward, arms outstretched as if she were in control of this tempest. All was still again. The wolf and the girl were gone.

"It's time for you to go hunting, child. It is your fate... your work... and your purpose. You have been schooled in the ways that heal for a reason."

"But I don't understand," Diana pleaded.

The crone held the amulet in front of Diana's face again. "Amethyst is the key and must be protected. The predator and the victim return in the mind of every descendant, but there is one we are waiting for, one who has the power to end it all."

The hag closed her eyes. When she opened them again, they glowed red. She spoke:

The wheel will turn, and turn, and turn.
Violence and shame will be the fate of their descendants,
generation after generation.
The water will take them under.
It will take their daughters,
and they will not be redeemed.
Even when the water takes them,
they will not be redeemed.

Then the huntress will have a son,
and her son will have two loves.
The first will be a girl with hair as dark as blood
and scars that go deep beneath the surface.
He will give her the stone that saves her,
and she will give him despair.
When he finds the stone again,
He will find his heart,
and all may be redeemed.

The first and the second and the psychopomps
will follow the Horned God to the underworld.
Amethyst is the key that will open the buried box.
When the spirits are set free,
all will be redeemed.

Look to the twenty-first to find the second.
Find her, and all shall be redeemed.

When she was done speaking, the crone cocked her head to one side and looked as if she were listening to a silent sound. Then she turned to Diana. "The veil is closing, and I have said what I came to say. Life begins in water. Don't let the life of another of my kin end there."

"Are you sure this prophecy is for *me*?" Diana asked. "There's nobody else who can undo this curse?"

The crone's eyes were still embers. "*Whit's fur ye'll no go by ye,*" she whispered with a slithering rasp.

Diana had more questions on the tip of her tongue, but she was struck silent by the appearance of another woman in the clearing. The newcomer was a redhead, tall, with a scar that ran from the top of her cheekbone to the edge of her chin, as if her face had been slashed with a knife.

She walked up to the crone, nodded, and then looked to Diana. "I am Carlin."

Diana flipped through the encyclopedia of folklore in her head. *Carlin. Scottish variant of Cailleach. Another crone—although this woman doesn't look old. Sometimes the carlin is a witch.*

The woman continued, "Look at my face. Remember it, and remember this scar. Find my face, and you shall find the living descendants of the Solstice Twins." Diana focused, trying to memorize Carlin's face.

"Is that all?"

"We are out of time." The crone returned the necklace to Diana's outstretched hand. "But Claire and the others will help you."

"I don't much trust fairies," Diana replied.

"Smart girl," the crone cackled. Then she opened her fist and blew sparkling dust into Diana's face.

Diana's eyes became heavy. They closed—

And just as quickly, they reopened. She blinked,

wondering where she was now. She felt the softness of the pillow beneath her head, and remembered.

"You're back," she heard a soft voice say.

She turned and saw her lover smiling his beautiful smile. As happy as she was to see him and his crazy curly hair, she discovered that she was disappointed to find herself in bed, as if she had never left. The crone, the prophecy, the whole adventure—it really was just the LSD. She let out a sigh. *Oh, well.*

"Take this, Diana. Hydrate."

The water her lover offered her was cool and refreshing. She drank it all, and through the bottom of the glass she noticed a sparkling light coming from the dresser. Hanging from a spindle at the top of the mirror was the amulet.

∞

Diana and her lover were sitting in a doctor's exam room, waiting. "I do like the haircut, Diana. It suits your personality. Short and sharp," her lover said, as he touched her new slick bob.

"Thank you, darling. Those damn fairies traumatized me. I may never have long hair again," she said. "Maybe I shouldn't have taken that LSD."

"And miss your chance to *be* the mystery? You can't be serious."

"That's really more your thing, isn't it? I prefer to keep mystery safely contained on the page." Paper crinkled as she wiggled her bottom on the exam table. "So, how will you feel if the prediction is true?"

He gazed at her with eyes of a deep aqua blue. *A*

son. The thought whirled in his mind like a loose firework. Was it possible that while exploring the numinous temple of her body and mind he had created something so miraculous and pure as a new human life?

"My dear, I would be the happiest man on earth if it were true." He kissed her forehead, and then gently rested his hand on her abdomen.

"You already are the happiest man on earth." Diana smiled one of her rare smiles. He was as naturally joyous as she was prickly.

"But a son!" His eyes twinkled and he grinned like the Cheshire cat.

Diana looked tenderly at the man who challenged her thinking, pushed her toward her calling, and loved her beyond her wildest dreams.

"You do realize our lives would change dramatically. Things can't stay the way they are," she said.

"Honey love, everything is constantly changing anyway. All of reality is a temporary, shifting thought."

Diana allowed herself a gentle eyeroll. "You know what I mean. You're still stirring things up, which is who you are, but it's dangerous. I shudder to think what's in your FBI file. We can't raise a child on the run," she said, trailing her fingertips over his cheeks. "If I really am pregnant, my son must be kept safe."

"I think you really are with child, my love. I already sense the fierce protective spirit of Demeter," he smiled. "My life is malleable, Diana. I see no problem. If you want privacy, then privacy you shall have. We could go to Carbondale for a while and stay with Mother, until we find a place—and a time—to settle."

"Yes, going underground might be safest. I just

couldn't bear it if they took you away from me."

"And *I* couldn't bear for my son to grow up fatherless when I clearly have a choice in the matter."

Diana stroked his face lovingly. "You could care for the baby while I start my research on the Solstice Twins. If we do have a son—if he is part of this prophecy—I need to know how to help him."

He smiled at her thoughtfully. "Oh, of course I would care for our baby. Nothing would bring me more joy." He paused for a moment, reflecting. "Maybe I should change my name…." he smiled.

"That might be a good idea, and it would definitely be fun."

"What do you think of Peter?"

Diana snorted. "It suits you perfectly, my eternal boy."

"We should go out for dinner to celebrate tonight," her lover said.

"We don't even know if we have anything to celebrate."

"I'm thinking Mexican," he mused, as he drifted off into dreamy enchilada oblivion.

"Again? It's a good thing I love you."

"Oh yes, it is a very good thing."

A throat cleared, and they both looked up to see the doctor standing in the doorway.

"Well Mrs. Stewart," the doctor began.

"It's *Ms.* Stewart," she proclaimed proudly.

The doctor gave her a disapproving snare, and then looked back at his chart. "Well *Ms.* Stewart, your hunch was correct. You're pregnant."

CHAPTER NINE

Portland and Champaign, 2010s

Eli stared out the window as his plane took off from Portland International Airport en route to Champaign, Illinois. The sky seemed to reflect his mood: bleak and miserably dull. It was the Winter Solstice, the sun god's birthday. It also happened to be Eli's birthday—his thirty-ninth. It was a day for new beginnings, but Eli was lost in the past.

It wasn't long before a flight attendant offered him a drink, but he waved her on. Stuck in transit on his birthday. Moving forward, yet not moving at all. Eli was not surprised. This had been the paradoxical theme of his life for the last seventeen years.

Eli was bored—utterly, existentially bored. For someone who had grown up surrounded by creativity, imagination, and action, boredom was an abomination. And by now, Eli knew this state well enough to know it would take a powerful outside stimulus to break through this self-inflicted inertia. He also knew that commercial air travel was unlikely to provide him with a suitable diversion.

He continued to stare out the window.

His life hadn't always been hopeless. He had been a happy kid, an only child, only grandchild on both sides of the family, showered with love. His had been an unorthodox childhood—given his background, that was inevitable—and it had given him opportunities and freedoms that most kids never knew.

Eli had grown up in Oregon, where his parents had settled in the late 70s. His father, who went by the name of Peter Stewart, hadn't changed his ornery ways. He was still pushing the psychotropic envelope –and while the FBI seemed to have lost interest in him sometime during the 90s, Peter was so imbedded in the counterculture that he couldn't quite give up his paranoia. Eli's mother, Diana, ignored her husband's delusions of persecution. Eli indulged them.

As a kid, Eli had been thrilled by the idea that his father was a wanted radical, and, when Eli was thirteen, his father even gave him a role to play in his underground intrigues. Peter handed his son a package and a plane ticket, and sent him on his first mission. Eli had been making similar trips for his father ever since.

He wasn't on one of his father's errands tonight, but this in-between time gave him ample opportunity to reflect on the mission that had changed his life forever. For better or worse, Eli still couldn't say.

His father had sent him to southern Illinois in the early 90s. That's where he fell in love for the first time—the only time. Six months later, it was over.

Well, not over. Not really. It would never be over for Eli. He was thinking about the girl he'd lost while he was stuck on this cross-country flight, just as he was pretty much always thinking about her—or trying very hard to find ways to *not* think about her.

When Eli looked out at the gray mist that surrounded the plane, he could see her tear-streaked, defeated face as she made her choice to walk away. His mother had seen it, too, and that fact still colored Eli's relationship with Diana.

After leaving Carbondale, Eli had finished his education at UC Berkeley, ultimately earning a Masters of Fine Arts with a concentration in photography. Eli had had no idea what he was going to do with this degree, but a sailboat he received as a congratulatory gift from his family allowed him to ignore that particular problem for a while. He spent a year sailing with his maternal grandfather, not worrying about what he was going to do with the rest of his life.

When his grandfather's declining health required a return to shore, Eli put his boat in dry dock and embarked on an aimless decade of world travel. Like his mother, Eli had a trust fund that ensured that he never had to work. *Unlik*e his mother, he wasn't driven to work anyway. Oh, he dabbled—he kept travel journals for "inspiration" and he took ridiculously dull photos of famously beautiful places. He tried to do something to fill the void that washed over him at night, but nothing could stop his haunting thoughts of a wild redhead with the longest legs he'd ever seen.

Eli was a photographer who couldn't shoot, and a poet who couldn't write. His muse was gone. Occasionally, he'd sense a trace of her—an angle of light that reminded him of the sparkle in her gray eyes, or a whiff of the fresh strawberries she always seemed to smell of–but then she'd be gone again before he could capture the moment.

Finally, tired of traveling, and of playing hide and seek with a ghost, Eli gave into inertia and ennui. An errand for his father had taken him to a small town in Oregon, and that's where he had stopped. He bought a piece of land, built himself a house, and prepared to spend the rest of his days succumbing to the dull ache of his loss.

Eli had surprised himself by taking an interest in farming—well, farming of a sort. Intrigued by a playful suggestion from his father, Eli had discovered that his little piece of temperate rainforest was an ideal environment for cultivating mushrooms of the mind-expanding kind. The work of foraging and classifying, of coaxing some of the rarer species to flourish, proved to occupy him for hours at a time.

Eli also became an active—if mostly anonymous—philanthropist. Both his parents had taught him to keep a low profile, but they had also taught him to respect the earth. He gave a good deal of time and money to programs dedicated to upholding environmental sovereignty. And, as much as it hurt him to be anywhere near a battered woman, he found himself growing more and more involved with local shelters, providing them with resources and money. It was the least he could do, he reasoned.

The mushrooms were a nice escape, and the giving felt almost necessary, considering the size of his inheritance. In Oregon, Eli forged a small circle of likeminded friends and even found a woman, a sculptor, willing to put up with his gloomy moods and emotional unavailability. And it was almost enough.

The plane began its descent, and the clouds outside his window were replaced by snow-dusted grids of dormant soybean fields, and then by the slightly less regular patterns of suburban neighborhoods. *Almost enough*, Eli thought, resting his forehead against the cold glass.

There was only one person who had ever been enough, and she was practically a figment of his imagination now. He didn't even have a photo to produce as evidence of her existence. He had taken hundreds, but his mother had burned the prints and destroyed the negatives. Because the girl was not a descendant of the Solstice Twins, Diana had no use for her, and she had tried to convince her son that he didn't, either. Eli shuddered at the memory of the burning photos. His mother had always been intense, but it had been a *cool* intensity. There was nothing cool about her that day.

Despite his mother's tyranny, Eli could not forget the girl. She was the only one who would ever be enough for him, and she had been gone for seventeen years—and, for seventeen years, he had gone, too. More or less.

He thought of her still as he rode in a cab through Champaign, where his mother was giving a lecture at the University of Illinois. He could almost see the details of the redhead's face when he closed his eyes and cleared his head. It was hard for him, doing this. It wasn't that he couldn't remember what she looked like—he knew every eyelash, every freckle—but seeing her again was like cooking his own heart over an open flame.

Finally, he shook his head, trying to dislodge the vision. The wild brown curls he'd inherited from his father rustled against the vinyl of the cab's backseat, and Eli tried to think of his mother instead. He hadn't seen her in almost a year, though they lived less than an hour away from each other. She'd been in Scotland, doing research on the folkloric mystery that she had been investigating since before he was born. The Solstice Twins fascinated Diana just slightly more than they failed to interest her son—despite the fact that she had assured Eli that he was a central figure in the prophecy that sprang from their story.

She would only be in the States for a week before jetting off to Greece for a conference. Diana spent a lot of time abroad. Eli was used to it. It had been that way his whole life. He was used to her blithe self-centeredness, too. Case in point: it was *his* birthday, and she had demanded that *he* come to *her* so they could visit before she left the country again.

Eli sighed. He was looking forward to this reunion—she was his mother, after all—but he was also preparing himself for the usual tensions. His mother was too wrapped up in her own obsession to have much patience with his.

∞

Walking through the lobby of a hotel in Champaign, Eli tried to shake off his anxiety. His mother was… herself, and he couldn't help but smile at the prospect of seeing her again. She was a complicated woman: a psychologist, the author of several popular books on mythology, and a compulsive researcher. Eli begged her to slow down, but she vowed that she would only retire when the prophecy she had spent forty years studying was fulfilled. Or maybe when Eli had given her some grandchildren. Both seemed equally impossible.

The mystery of the Solstice Twins was her great quest. She had traced their descendants from seventeenth-century Scotland to Chicago in the early twentieth-century, but then she had struck an impasse. The last descendent she had found, Carlin Fitzgerald, had disappeared at the age of fourteen. Diana had spent more than two decades trying to find out what had happened to her, with no success.

Diana was driven to see the prophecy fulfilled, and not just because she was a stubborn Scot. Diana knew that her peers had little respect for transpersonal psychology—the field to which she and both her parents had devoted themselves. If she could just see the prophecy through to its conclusion, it would justify her own work and that of her parents. She believed that, if she could find the current descendants of the Solstice Twins and help lift the curse that had been set in motion by the death of the first twin, she could present a definitive account of how mythic archetypes manifest in the contemporary world. Diana had assured Eli—more than once—that she was preoccupied with the prophecy because it involved him, but he knew his mother well enough to realize that concern for her son was not her primary motivation. And, at this point, he was also pretty sure that he was old enough to not care. Pretty sure, anyway.

"Eli!" Diana cried as she opened the door of her hotel room. She pulled him into a huge mama-bear hug. Eli bent down so that she could kiss his cheeks and ruffle his wild hair. She couldn't help noticing that there were more white strands than there had been the last time she'd seen him. “Happy birthday and Happy Solstice, darling. How’s my boy?”

“Just smashing, Mother,” he smirked.

“And Rebecca? How is Rebecca?” she asked with a smirk of her own. After ascertaining that Rebecca was definitely not the second woman in the prophecy, Diana regarded her as a nuisance and an impediment.

“She’s as fascinating as ever. She’s working on a new sculpture for Burning Man; it’s a seven-foot wide vagina with twenty-one tiny heads poking out. You simply must see it.” He rolled his eyes and plopped down on the sofa.

“You know, my friend Estella has a freshly divorced daughter. She’s a history professor, no children, drop-dead gorgeous, and just looking for a little fun, like you."

He rolled his eyes again. “No.”

“Oh darling, you may not realize this, but you are so incredibly handsome. You’ve aged well just like your father. It’s such a waste for you to be so lost and lonely.”

“It didn’t have to be this way,” Eli mumbled under his breath.

Diana didn’t miss a beat. “She wasn’t a descendant, Eli. The second love will…”

“If I *just* could have told her who I really was. If you *just* would have let me go after her…” Eli said.

“She wasn’t the woman we’re looking for! There will be another, Eli!”

“I’ll make sure there’s not another, if for no other reason than to spite you,” Eli groused. *Dammit*, he thought. *I hoped we could hold out for more than two minutes before getting into this bullshit.*

"Nonsense," Diana said without much energy. This was a conversation they'd had many times before. Evidently, she was getting a little tired of it, too. "You cannot stop fate."

"Maybe not, Mother, but for all we know, Gretchel still has the amethyst. Even if she has given it away, it doesn't matter, because I'm not capable of loving another woman like I love her!"

Diana stared at her son incredulously, and without a trace of compassion.

"That girl was pregnant and psychotic the last you saw of her, Eli. I don't know if she belonged with that other man, but I do know that she didn't belong with *you*."

"Maybe she wasn't the woman you're looking for, Mother, but she's the only woman I will ever want," he said as his eyes glassed over with ancient emotion.

Diana softened, slightly. She sat down next to him and brushed a lock of curls out of her son's amazing aquamarine eyes. "You were chosen for your role in this prophecy by the fates, darling. We both were. I don't why, and we may never know why. I only know what my father drilled into my head and what I've tried to drill into yours: a Stewart finishes what she starts."

Eli thought of the family crest at Belshire Castle. He thought of his grandfather, Charles Stewart, who completed their sailing trip, despite his declining health. Then he thought of Gretchel and her bruised body. He closed his eyes, and put his head in his hands.

Eli was a million miles away. "She had problems, Mother. Serious emotional scars."

"Which begs the question of why you wanted her so badly to begin with. Did you really love this girl or was it just your mission to be her hero? It's not your duty to clean up someone else's mess, Eli. Take care of your own. In fact, perhaps you should be evaluating *your* intentions instead of mine."

"Don't you analyze me, Mother," he snapped. "You never even tried to see if she was a descendent."

"It would have been a waste of time. I have no reason to believe that the she was a descendant of the Solstice Twins. In fact, she fits the description of the first woman in the prophecy so perfectly that she confirms its truth, as far as I'm concerned. But forget about her, can't you? It's the second girl, Eli. She's the one we're looking for. The second woman wearing that amethyst will be a direct descendant of the twins, and she is the one who will bring you back from this self-inflicted misery." Diana gave her son a hearty thump on the knee, as if to indicate that his problems were solved and this conversation was over.

"What makes you think the necklace is going to just appear out of nowhere on another woman?"

Diana sighed, exasperated by Eli's dull persistence, "My theory is that your redhead probably sold it. That amethyst was one of the deepest, purest stones I've ever seen. It's worth a great deal of money. It may have changed hands many times since you gave it to her. I'm sure it's already working its way back to you. I'm also sure that the next time you see it, you will already be in love with the person wearing it, and then we'll see the cycle of violence that began with the Solstice Twins come to an end. It's not just a story, Eli; it's what I was born to do. I was given a mission, and I won't stop until it's done."

"A prophecy you heard during an acid trip and professional ambition. That's why you've ruined my life,

Mother. Don't pretend it's anything else."

"*The drama*," Diana cried, throwing her head back and waving him off. "Please. You're almost forty, Eli. Grow up."

Eli stared his mother down. "What's it going to take for you to back off, Diana? I don't want to hear any more about the amethyst, and I don't want to hear any more about this alleged second woman. What do I have to do to get that?"

Diana matched her son's basilisk glare. "Oh, just the impossible. Find that which has eluded my matchless sleuthing skills for the last twenty-five years. You find Carlin Fitzgerald's face in a photograph, and I'll never mention the amulet again."

Eli knew that this task really was impossible, and, in any case, he had no intention of trying to complete it. All he really hoped for at this moment was getting through dinner without hearing about the damn prophecy again.

"Deal," he said.

"Wonderful, darling. Now let's eat! I'm famished."

∞

After a quiet birthday dinner, Eli and his mother parted ways. *For such a tiny thing, she is sure a huge pain in the ass,* Eli thought.

He was irritated. He didn't even want to stay the night at the hotel. He wanted to jump a plane and head back to Oregon as soon as possible. He wanted to get back into his quiet, northwestern bubble and have a good sulk.

After seeing his mother to her room, he got back in the elevator, leaned against the back wall, and took a deep breath. Then a quick shiver ran up his spine. The elevator doors were closing, when a pale white hand poked its way in. He reached out to stop the door from shutting.

"Thanks," a girl said. She brushed past him, pressed the button for her floor, and pulled a suitcase and herself into a corner. Eli glanced up, and gasped.

The girl was tall. He was six foot five, and this girl almost stared him straight in the eye. She had thick, wavy, fiery red hair that was twisted into a bouncy ponytail. She had milk-white skin with freckles across her cheekbones, a cute little nose, and bottomless gray eyes. She was a younger version of the woman he had once loved—the woman he *still* loved.

The girl noticed him staring at her. Eli saw her bristle, and then he saw her relax. She cocked her head and gazed back inquisitively. "You seem familiar," she said. "Have I met you before?"

"No. I don't think so." He tried to still the shake in his voice.

"That's weird. You seem really familiar," she practically whispered, looking him up and down.

He wanted to scream out that she looked familiar, too. He wanted to, but he didn't.

"What's your name?" he ventured.

"Ame… with an E. And you are?"

"Eli… with an I," he replied with a grin.

She snickered. "I like your style, Eli-with-an-I. This may sound really weird, but I feel like I am supposed to be right where I am, talking to you, right this very second. Have you ever had that feeling? Like, synchronicity?"

Despite her height, Eli could tell that she was

young. Young, but a precocious thing, just like someone else he used to know. He swallowed hard. "Yes. I have," he said, barely able to get the words out.

She tapped her Ugg-covered foot, while he stared at her in awe. "Are you on Facebook?"

The weirdly quotidian nature of this question snapped Eli out of his fugue state. "No. I'm not really into the whole social-media thing."

"Oh," she said disappointed.

Eli nodded his head awkwardly. He wasn't quite sure how to talk to this girl. He was frazzled beyond belief, yet he felt connected to her in a way he couldn't explain. It wasn't just the similarity; there was something strange at work in the cosmos—or, at least, something strange at work in this elevator.

"Do you go to school at U of I?"

"No," she said and laughed. "I'm just a junior in high school. I came up with my cousin Holly and my uncle to pick up my other cousin, who goes to school here. Brody's on winter break, and my uncle won't spring for a parking pass until he's a junior. I came to check out the campus. I'm working on a volleyball scholarship."

Eli nodded, but couldn't think of anything brilliant to say.

"Well, if you ever happen to get into the social-media thing, and should you ever happen to join Facebook, you should add me as a friend. My last name is Shea. Ame Shea. Ame with an E... it's pronounced *Amy*, but spelled with an E," she laughed, and the elevator stopped at her floor. "By the way, I really like your curly hair," she said and reached her hand out to push a loose spiral out of Eli's face. His heart skipped a beat. He couldn't breathe. He *did* know her. He had felt her kick when she was still in her mother's womb.

The elevator door began to open, and he couldn't miss his chance to ask, although from the last name he already knew.

"Ame-with-an-E, what's your mother's name?"

She shot him an odd glance, and then smiled shyly. "Gretchel."

Eli's shock immobilized him. People were coming into the elevator, and they blocked his view. Finally he saw the red hair again. Ame looked back to the elevator and smiled. Eli could only stare speechless and frozen as she waved goodbye.

Eli was, once again, moving while standing still. But he was soaring on the inside, suddenly released from inertia's cruel pull.

CHAPTER TEN

Oregon, 2010s

Eli woke up nervous on New Year's Day. He had had the same dream he always had: Him holding out the loving cup to Gretchel while she struggled—and failed—to reach it. In the dream, his mother was pulling him away from Gretchel while a snake wrapped itself around his ankle, fangs bared. As recurring dreams go, this one was pretty easy to interpret, but, this morning, he sensed a new message just beneath the surface—a call for help, maybe?

For most of the past seventeen years, Eli had defended himself from despair with the numbing comforts of habit. Any variation from the routine made him a little anxious, and the subtle shift in his response to this dream was especially disconcerting. Already on edge, he decided to do something he hadn't let himself do for days: He logged onto Facebook.

Never a fan of social media—his father had raised him to be way too paranoid to share much online—Eli had opened an account as soon as he got back to Oregon from Champaign. The first thing he did was look up Ame Shea and send her a friend request. Eli had no idea how long it was reasonable to wait for a response, but, after a few days with no reply, he decided that he was tired of feeling like a boy who had been turned down for the prom. Hence the Facebook embargo.

He drummed his fingers and cursed his shitty rural Internet connection as he waited for the site to load. His heart was racing. Eli closed his eyes, and took a deep breath. Feeling slightly calmer, he squinted one eye at the screen.

Ame had accepted his friend request. Looking at her profile picture, he was blown away again by how much she resembled her mother. It was like looking at a ghost.

He skimmed her status updates, which consisted mostly of typical teenage sarcasm and drama. There was nothing about Gretchel. Then he found her photos. He flipped through several pictures of her with friends, with a guy, playing volleyball, with a white horse.... And then he came to a picture that sent a wave of exhilaration through his whole body.

It was a picture of Ame as a child: curly hair, freckles, and a sweet—if not entirely innocent—grin. She was maybe two-years-old and hugging the legs of a pregnant woman. The picture was labeled: "Mama and me (Mom prego with Zach)." He flipped to the next picture and it was two little redheaded kids, Ame and a younger boy with Gretchel crouched between them smiling her big, beautiful smile.

Eli sat back in his office chair, and choked on his own breath. How he had longed to see her face. The picture moved something inside him. He had been a broken man, but now, if only for a moment, he was healed by her image. He was whole. He could almost smell her, taste her, feel her.... The soft skin, the brilliant mind, the wild eyes, the free spirit, the saucy tongue, the fierce soul. But it was even more than that: It was like he was seeing her again for the very first time.

∞

Carbondale, 1990s

After finishing his second year of college, Eli was looking forward to spending the summer taking photographs, playing guitar, maybe even joining the crew of a sailboat. It was not to be. His father asked him to spend a month or two in Carbondale, keeping an eye on his late grandmother's home. Peter had turned it into a refuge for college students with creative talent but little in the way of resources.

"I trust these kids, Eli, but I need you to check on things. If any repairs need to be done, have them done. Make sure the tenants are taking good care of the garden. These kids dance to a different beat, and I have no intention of interfering in their lives, but maintenance is a necessary evil."

"Why can't you or one of your assistants do it?" Eli had no interest in wasting his summer mowing the lawn and calling plumbers.

"You need to spend some time in god's country, son."

"Which god would that be, Peter?" Eli asked.

"Whichever one makes you feel alive," his father replied with a cackle.

Eli sighed. His parents rarely asked anything of

him, but, when they did, it was always something weird, or difficult, or both. Like the amulet his mother gave him when he graduated from high school. He knew about her research into the Solstice Twins, but he had no idea that he was somehow involved in the prophecy his mother had been trying to unravel since before he was born. Then, all of the sudden, she gives him an amethyst necklace, tells him that he's going to fall in love with a red-haired girl with deep scars, and instructs him to give her the amulet in her greatest time of need. Other kids got generous checks as graduation gifts. Eli got a girl's necklace and a predetermined fate.

He had tried to argue that he had free will. His mother told him that fate and free will are not incompatible; it's just that we don't remember our agreements with destiny.

His father told him that determinism and freedom are the balancing energies of the universe, constantly shifting in response to the choices we make. Eli let the subject drop. He hadn't wanted a lecture in spirituality; he just wanted to pick his own girlfriend. But he had taken the necklace then, and he was agreeing to play landlord for his father now.

Peter told Eli that there would be a car waiting at the airport for him. Then Diana got on the phone. "The usual rules apply, Eli. Keep your identity and your background secret. And stay true to yourself. Never forget how important you are."

She sounded strange—stranger than normal, even—almost apprehensive.

"Mother, do you know something I don't about this trip to Carbondale?"

"Your father just has a feeling. Be sure to bring the amulet."

Peter took the phone again. "And I'll have a package for you. Something I need for you to deliver to my buddy, Buddy." Eli sighed again. He was still a messenger boy. Always a messenger boy.

"Dude. Welcome to our humble abode." A tall, skinny kid with shoulder-length, dishwater-blonde hair opened the door of the large, two-story house on Pringle Street. He was half-covered in tattoos and wore baggy shorts, flip-flops, and no shirt. "Another musician. Wicked," he said when he saw Eli's guitar case. "I'm Will, and this is Patty." Will leaned in and whispered into Eli's ear, "By the way, Peppermint here's a lesbian and she is *not* into threesomes."

"Jesus, Will. I'm sitting right here," said Patty. She set a joint in an ashtray, and shook Eli's hand. "Nice to meet you..."

"Eli. My name's Eli."

"Welcome, Eli, and congrats on getting the last room this summer. It's been a sweet gig so far. I've been here three years, and I've never seen the owner. As the most senior resident, I'm queen of this castle and I only have two rules: Pay for your weed and honor the chronic couch." She was a pretty girl with pale skin, long black hair, and a bit of a gothic edge.

"The chronic couch?" Eli asked.

Patty motioned to the battered, sagging floral sofa she sat on. "It's sacred space," she said with a not entirely ironic smile.

Will nonchalantly snatched the joint that was still

burning in the ashtray.

"So help me, Jesus, I am going to beat you one of these days, Will. Quit mooching," she snapped, as Will twisted his wiry body around to avoid a swat and motioned for Eli to follow him up the stairs.

"Want some?" he asked, trying to talk and hold in the smoke simultaneously.

Eli shook his head. "Think I'll wait."

"Patty's got some good smoke." Will opened one of three doors on the second floor. "Here's your room. That's the upstairs bathroom. The can's a little touchy—just jiggle the handle until it stops running. That's Gretchel's room. You're going to kill me for putting you up here with her, but you're the last one, man, so you're SOL."

"Why?" Eli asked.

Will took another long drag off the joint, exhaled, and squinted his eyes. "Because she's crazy, man. She talks to herself constantly—like, lengthy conversations, like she's hearing voices and talking back to them. She has nightmares at least a couple times a week, and then screams half the night. You can hear her all the way downstairs. I've got to keep a fan and a noise machine going just to get a decent night's sleep." Will paused for a moment of reflection. "'Course the weed helps."

"Of course," Eli said dryly, dropping his possessions on the bed.

"It's a damn shame too, because most of the time she's cool as hell. She's an amazing artist. And gorgeous—rockin' bod, legs that don't quit.... Oh, and she's like a Gremlin dude—do *not* give her booze. When she's drunk the bat-shit level increases dramatically."

"Got it. A noise machine, weed, and no booze for Gizmo."

"Attaboy. Come on, dude, I'll show you Pan's garden and let you meet the wild woman—at your own risk, of course."

"Of course."

As they made their way to the garden, Will continued to give Eli a tour of the house. He had no way to know that Eli was familiar with every corner and cabinet. Seeing his grandmother's house filled with strangers made Eli miss her terribly, but he couldn't hold back a grin when he saw the statue of Pan that had watched over the garden since before Eli was born. Penelope had been a religion professor, and Greek mythology was one of her great passions. The other was her garden, which Eli was pleased to see was still flourishing despite her absence. Her prized roses were particularly lush.

"This is where we get a lot of our food," Will said as he gestured toward the neat rows of vegetables and herbs that took up most of the backyard. "It's hard work, but it's worth it. All three of us are paying our own way through school, so this place has been, like, a lifesaver, man. Gretchel claims to be an expert at canning. She's just a sophomore, so she has to go back to the dorms in August, but she said she'll come back and help with the fall harvest. We'll see."

They followed a narrow stone path leading back to the greenhouse. Will hesitated before they went in. "Now, don't get sucked in by her looks, 'cause when she starts screaming tonight, you'll feel like strangling her."

"She shot you down, didn't she?" Eli asked.

"Took an arrow to the chest first day she was here," Will concurred. "She said I was too tame for her wild heart. Can you believe that shit? Me, too tame?" Will shook his head. "Of course she's probably right, freaking nutcase."

"Of course."

When he opened the door to the greenhouse, Eli saw Gretchel bent over a sink. She was barefoot, wearing faded, old Levis that were ragged at the bottom with a Grateful Dead patch on the butt saying *We Will Survive.* Her shoulders and forearms were covered in a field of freckles. She wore a gray tank top and no bra, which revealed every detail of her full chest. Her dark red hair was pulled up in a messy pile on her head. She was extremely tall and toned, and the most beautiful thing Eli had ever seen.

"Hey, Red. This is the new roomie, Eli," Will called.

Gretchel wiped wet hands on her jeans. When her eyes met Eli's she gasped. Eli understood. It was like lightning had struck between them.

None of this was lost on Will. "Why did I bother?" he asked himself as he relit the joint and walked out of the greenhouse.

It seemed like an eternity before Eli could speak, but he forced himself to make words. "I'm Eli, but I guess you know that already," he said, feeling completely tongue-tied.

"Gretchel," she said, holding out her hand, "but I guess *you* know *that*." Their hands were caught in a time warp. After a moment, her fingers loosened and slid along his palm as she let go.

They left the greenhouse, and he took a seat next to her under a big oak tree.

"What are you going to school for, Eli?"

"Photography," he smiled.

She smiled back at him, showing a perfect set of white teeth. "You have my stamp of approval, which I'm sure you've been waiting on," she laughed. "I'm an art student, currently having a love affair with botanicals. How do you feel about getting your hands dirty, Eli?"

"I'm really good at getting my hands dirty." *Doofus!* Eli thought to himself. But Gretchel just grinned.

"Good. This is Pan's garden and we mustn't anger him, lest he slip into our rooms in the dead of night and ravage us silly. He won't hesitate to take a man in bed, Eli. Just warning you. Though he took me once as a young girl, and I rather enjoyed it," she smiled and tapped an index finger to her lip. "On second thought, maybe I *shall* anger him."

Eli laughed and shook his curly mane. He liked this girl's style. "I've tended gardens all my life. I think I can appease the great god Pan."

Gretchel took his hands in hers and looked them over. "Yes. I can see that these hands have played in the dirt quite a bit. This is good. We all need to get our hands dirty to stay connected to the Green Man and the Mother."

"The Mother? As in Gaia?"

"Yes, but not just Gaia. I think there are lots of mothers or goddesses that go by different names, but they're all just a manifestation of the same Great Wild Mother—the feminine energy of the universe. Maybe the goddesses we know are like her children, an extension of herself. And we're her children, too: creative energy birthed from the womb of the Goddess and shaped into carbon-based matter. I was raised to see the Mother as a whole, but also as a triple entity—the maiden and crone emanate from the Mother as the source of all life.

"Then there are the gods—like the Horned One, Cernunnos. The playful man who has the heart of a child. We find him in Peter Pan or Pan himself. I pray to the Horned One as well as the Mother. I often imagine Cernunnos walking beside me, helping me grow spiritually, but protecting me from growing up and from taking myself too seriously. I've entered into a covenant with him that I renew every April Fools' Day.

"Sometimes I pray to Hermes and Aphrodite, too, simply because, together, they make me feel a sensual love for the universe that I can't find anywhere else. When I pray to them I'm completely open to potential, allowing a creative give-and-take to occur."

Having been raised by a transpersonal psychologist and a hippie mystic, Eli had grown used to tuning out talk of archetypes and cosmic energy. But, now, he was rapt. He could happily sit beneath this tree, listening to Gretchel talk like this forever.

"Sometimes I pray for rescue, for a god or a goddess or *someone* to save me from my shadows because I don't have the courage or the strength to save myself."

Gretchel stopped talking long enough for Eli to realize that some kind of response was required. "And what form would this rescue take?"

"Love, of course." Her smile was radiant.

"Of course."

"Yes, I think that love is the only thing that can save me from myself, and I know that the universe is holding that love for me, and anyone else who wants to claim it. Can you imagine a love so pure that it's infinite, Eli? Doesn't that just blow your mind?" He thought about how *she* was blowing his mind.

"I don't know if I can imagine it, really, but I'd like to try."

"I feel closest to that love when I'm outside, in the elements. When I'm connected to the earth, I feel like I'm free, like my wild heart is open, like my bare feet can dance. I feel like I'm truly awake and alive. I guess I feel like I'm home."

"That's beautiful." Eli wasn't sure if he was talking about the girl, her words, or both. "My parents raised me to believe a lot of the same things you believe, but I've never heard them express their beliefs quite so passionately."

"I'm extremely high," she chuckled. "I really do feel like that. I just wouldn't have pontificated quite so, um, expressively if What's-His-Nuts hadn't come out with a joint earlier." Gretchel narrowed her eyes at Eli. "You're not from here, are you?"

"Nope. Pacific Northwest."

"Why are you in Illinois?"

"I have a date with destiny," he said.

She looked deep into his eyes, and Eli felt certain that she could see his soul.

"Gretchel, do you believe in fate?"

"I believe in possibility and potential," she smiled, still looking straight into Eli's eyes. Then she lifted her gaze. "And I do believe I'm falling deeply in love with your curly hair." She reached up and ran a gentle hand through his unruly mop. Her touch raised goose bumps on his arms.

Eli had resented his mother's insistence that her crazy prophecy had anything to do with him, but now he believed. He was meant to be with this girl. If he knew nothing else, of this he was absolutely certain.

∞

It was Sunday night in Carbondale, and Eli was sleeping peacefully in his room when the screaming began. He lay staring at the ceiling, listening to Gretchel's obvious distress, trying to make out what she was saying. After about an hour, he couldn't take it anymore.

Eli tiptoed down the hall and slowly opened Gretchel's unlocked door. He could see her thrashing around in the moonlight. *This is not normal*, he thought. Gently, he sat on the edge of her bed. He didn't want to frighten her, or even wake her. He just wanted to help her if he could. He placed his hand on the small of her back. His touch seemed to calm her.

Eli couldn't see Gretchel's face, but he could tell that she was awake after all.

"Tell me everything's going to be okay." Her voice was a hoarse whisper.

Eli lay down next to Gretchel and wrapped his arm around her waist. His hand found what felt like a rag doll pressed against Gretchel's belly.

"Everything's going to be okay. I promise," he whispered back. She slept quietly the rest of the night.

It was still dark when her alarm clock sounded. Gretchel looked at Eli, who was clearly unsure of what he should do after waking up in Gretchel's bed. She pushed back a tangle of runaway curls, kissed his forehead, whispered "Thank you," and was on her way.

∞

Oregon, 2010s

Eli puffed from a small pipe as he stared at the picture of Gretchel with her children. He hadn't let himself revisit these memories for a long time, but it felt good—like a kind of therapy. He worried, for a moment, that going back to his memories of Carbondale was going in the wrong direction, but he couldn't help himself. He needed to remember that, once upon a time, his life had been beautiful, or the snake that stalked his dreams would swallow him whole.

CHAPTER ELEVEN

Oregon, 2010s

Eli was obsessed. He sat at the computer for days, looking at every picture, reading every post and comment on Ame's Facebook page. His phone rang—calls from Rebecca, his mother, his father, and several friends. He ignored them all.

He was surprised—and pleased—to see that Gretchel was living in her hometown. He had assumed that Troy would have dragged her to the Chicago suburb where he had grown up. That's where she was headed the last time Eli saw her, the day she broke his heart.

Eli watched to see if Ame was using chat. He wanted to talk to her, even if he had no idea what he was going to say. He just wanted some connection—however tenuous—to Gretchel.

In the meantime, he just returned—again and again—to the photo of Gretchel with her children. Gretchel was squeezing them both lovingly, and Eli was sure she was the wonderful mother he had always known she would be.

Other photos were more disturbing. She had aged well, but she looked different. She was too skinny—sickly, almost. She dressed like a soccer mom, and it didn't suit her. When Eli thought of her, she always wore jeans and a tank top, or a wild hippie dress she had made for herself. Eli knew that seventeen years was a long time—he knew that all too well—but Gretchel looked uncomfortable and unhappy in this suburban persona. She didn't look like herself, and Eli got the sense that she didn't *feel* like herself, either. This woman he was seeing—she wasn't Gretchel.

When Eli peered into her photographed eyes, he felt like he was seeing all his fears for her come true. He had predicted this—or something like this—but he still couldn't fathom why she felt she deserved the punishment a life with Troy was sure to bring her.

Gretchel was still the woman for him, though. He didn't care how much she had changed. He would never be able to imagine truly loving anyone else, no matter what his mother or an oracular crone from an acid trip might have to say about it.

∞

Carbondale, 1990s

Gretchel had already left the house by the time Eli got up on his second day in Carbondale. Will explained that she worked for a landscaper who liked to get an early start, and that she always went out for a run first thing in the morning.

Eli holed up in his room all day long, writing to kill time. Shortly after three, he heard singing coming from the bathroom. He closed his notebook and waited for the right moment to approach Gretchel.

Finally, he crept out of his room and walked slowly down the hall. The door to her room was open. He tried to seem casual, but he couldn't help turning to look at her as he walked past.

"Hey, Hermes," she smiled.

"Hermes?"

"The Greek messenger god. I've always pictured him with wild, curly hair like yours."

Eli took a cautious step into her room, trying not to step on anything. Books and CDs mingled with sketchbooks all over the floor. An easel stood in the corner, surrounded by canvases in various stages of completion. Fabric was strewn about near a desk that supported an old sewing machine. An altar sat in the corner of the room, partnered with a prayer pillow. Gretchel's altar tools were carefully arranged on top of a printed, violet piece of fabric.

Houseplants and potted herbs flourished amongst the mess. Gretchel's hippie lair smelled like sandalwood, and Eli noticed the incense burner on her nightstand, along with a rag doll and a tarnished silver cup.

"That's a beautiful quaich," he said. Gretchel replied with a confused grin. He pointed to the two-handled cup.

"Oh, yeah—the loving cup. It's been in my family a long time. A *really* long time, I think. My grand mama gave it to my parents on their wedding day, and my mama gave it to me after my daddy died."

"My apologies," he said quietly.

She brushed at her quilt, smoothing out the

wrinkles. "He's been dead awhile now. It's ancient history." Then she started straightening the pillows on her bed. "Sorry about the mess. I have no great excuse, other than I work a lot, and when I come home I just want to chill. I haven't wasted time like this since I was a kid."

"I love wasting time," Eli said as he took a seat. She scooted herself against two big, fluffy paisley pillows as she dog-eared the book she was reading. He glanced down at the title and smiled. "You like Graham Duncan?"

"I do. I think he's a brilliant god, and I'm hopelessly in love with him." She pretended to swoon. "Have you read any of his books, Hermes?"

"I have."

"I would love to meet the man, just to pick his brain. I'd hitch a ride and follow him across the country like a Deadhead if he ever did a book tour."

"You and every other fanatical reader. He's a complete nutter if you ask me."

"But I didn't ask you," she replied with a laugh. "I wonder what he looks like. I hear he has a birthmark in the shape of a phallus on his ass."

Eli shook his head, trying to keep a straight face.

Gretchel chuckled. "Duncan makes me laugh."

"Is a peculiar sense of humor all it takes for you to fall hopelessly in love with someone?" he asked.

"It certainly doesn't hurt," she said as she coyly batted her eyelashes. "Duncan's words make my own logic seem a little less bizarre."

"He definitely has a unique perspective on reality."

"I like his perspective. His characters are like Alice in Wonderland. They're illogical in a normal social environment, but perfectly logical within the context of the story."

"A trip down the rabbit hole," Eli said. He picked at the beautiful quilt on her bed. "What would you do if you went down the rabbit hole?"

"I don't know. Paint the roses red?" she shrugged. He laughed.

"Actually I would do a lot more than that. I think that more people should explore the depths of the psyche like Duncan does. I think that the psyche holds incredible secrets, and I want to go there on an expedition. Have you ever read the book *Deep-See Diving* by Miranda Stewart?"

Eli had to suppress another grin when he heard his maternal grandmother's name. "Interestingly enough, I have. But most people don't want to go that deep. The psyche is also where universal, archetypal pain resides."

Gretchel stared off into space for a moment, and Eli wondered what she was seeing. "Do you think a person can go there and bypass the pain?"

"I don't know. I think a person should try to go there in order to befriend the pain, to release it and use that transformed energy to create something else, something beautiful."

"Do you think a person could visit their raw pain and survive?"

"Absolutely. I've..." and he stopped himself. He was going too far.

"What would happen to a person if she went into the psyche, unlocked the wrong door, and got trapped by her own ghosts and shadows?"

"Well, I think that person would need a guide, someone experienced, to escort her through the labyrinth," he said. "Have you ever tried mushrooms or acid,

Gretchel?"

She shook her head with a tinge of disappointment in the gesture. "I want to. I'm just petrified by the thought of what I might encounter."

"I've tripped on many occasions," Eli said. *Too many times to count.* "We could do it together sometime if you'd like."

"Can we do it now?" she asked, eyes sparkling with sudden anticipation.

He laughed. "I don't have any acid or 'shrooms right now. Are you in that much of a hurry to meet your shadows?" he teased, and absentmindedly ran his fingers up and down her calf.

"Maybe I'm just trying to befriend my pain," she smiled. He wanted to reply, he wanted to ask her about the nightmares. He wanted to know what made her scream in the night. But the moment passed when she leapt from the bed and grabbed a tube of red paint and a brush. "Shall we paint the roses red?"

Eli sat up. "Huh?"

"I'm kidding." She put the art supplies down and grabbed his hand. "Let's tend to the garden, then I want to show you the fairy ring I found in the woods behind the house." Eli raised his eyebrows again, but he followed her.

He would have followed her anywhere.

∞

Their days developed an easy rhythm. They spent the late afternoons talking on her bed, which led to tending the garden as the sun went down. Then they made dinner. Will could barely boil water and, left to her own devices,

Patty would have subsisted on almond milk, cold tofu dogs, and weed. Gretchel, on the other hand, knew how to cook, and Eli was happy to serve as prep chef.

After dinner, the residents of the house on Pringle Street would retire to the backyard. Gretchel and Patty would sit and listen to Eli and Will play their guitars. When Will and Patty had other plans for the evening, Eli and Gretchel would lie on a blanket, look at the stars, and talk.

When Gretchel went to bed, Eli never followed. He waited until she was asleep, and then tiptoed to her bed to hold her all night. His presence seemed to keep the nightmares at bay.

"Whoa, dude! What the hell?" Will was looking at Eli's guitar, sitting on its stand in the living room. "She painted your fucking *Martin*? Does she know how much that thing cost?"

Eli looked, too. Gretchel had covered his very expensive, carefully crafted acoustic guitar in psychedelic flora. "I think it looks cool."

Will shook his head. "You got it bad, dude, and I can tell you right now this ain't going to end well, but hey, keep doing whatever you're doing 'cause I've been sleeping like a baby since you got here." Will paused for a moment, reflecting. "So what *are* you doing, anyway?"

Eli shrugged his shoulders, and walked out of the room.

It was Friday, and he thought he might ask Gretchel out to dinner. He hopped the steps to the second floor. She was standing in her doorway, waiting for him. She had dried her long red hair and left it down. She was wearing a floral kimono with a wide scarlet belt around her waist—Eli recognized the dress as something Gretchel had made from thrift-store finds. He was stunned to see that she was wearing makeup—her lips were painted a soft shade of red—and not surprised at all to see that she was barefoot, although the deep red on her toenails was also a new development. She was unbelievably gorgeous in jeans and a tank top, but this was too much. Eli couldn't speak. He was bewitched.

"You want to come in?" she asked with a sultry smile, not surprised by his muteness.

He entered the room, but didn't sit on her bed like he usually did. He stood, looking at Gretchel, befuddled. He felt a strong desire to bow down and worship this redheaded incarnation of Aphrodite. Gretchel broke the silence.

"I haven't felt this good in a long time, Eli," she said, coming in closer. "This house has healing energy—really good healing energy. Ever since I moved here I've felt peaceful, and then you came, and it's like my whole world shifted again." She stopped for a moment, her eyes turned down. "I'm not always like this, Eli. I have issues—seriously deep, fucked-up issues. I just think you should know this now."

He reached out, and put his hand on her waist. "Should we talk about your issues?"

She shook her head. "No, but one thing is for sure, you heal me, too." She stood on her toes and kissed him on the mouth. It was a short, wet kiss, and his tongue met hers for only a moment. It was the kind of kiss that just begs to be repeated with conviction.

Eli reached his hand behind him, and shut the

door. "Don't lock it," she whispered. He undid her belt, and the dress flowed loose around her. He put a hand on her face, and kissed her, lingering this time. He worked his other hand under her dress and tenderly grabbed at her backside.

"Eli, it's been a long time since I've had sex sober," her lips whimpered against his.

He pulled his face back a few inches. *What an odd thing to say.* "Then let's consider it making love," he replied, bunching the fabric of her dress in his hands as he lifted the hem.

She pushed his hands back down. "I have scars. I'm afraid for you to see them. It's easier when I'm buzzed."

He released her dress and gently swept her crimson bangs back from the side of her forehead. He kissed the scar that peeked out every now and again. "I think it gives you character."

"That's not the scar I'm talking about," she said. Her voice was sad, and all of the sudden, she was a million miles away. Eli took a step back, letting her go.

"Show me," he said.

Gretchel dropped her head, and then her eyes rose to meet his. Her gaze dared him to watch as she pulled her dress up over her head and dropped it to the floor.

The right side of Gretchel's torso was a map of scars. Eli knew enough to recognize them as burns—serious burns—patched with skin grafts and imperfectly healed.

The sight didn't offend Eli. He was just sad—incredibly, incredibly sad—that Gretchel had endured whatever pain caused these scars. He slid his fingers along them. Her hand fluttered above his, but she didn't stop him. He let his hand slide up to her breast. Her nipple became firm at his touch, and he felt her breath catch. Sliding his hand down her torso, Eli felt more scars. Not burns. These were smooth and regular. Seven cuts, parallel to each other, about an inch in length. He languidly lowered his head to her abdomen and tenderly kissed each scar. The smell of her skin was overwhelming. Strawberries.

Eli cupped Gretchel's taut, deliciously round backside in his hands and nuzzled her midsection. He let his warm breath pour over her skin. She reacted with a quiver. Eli was trying to reassure Gretchel, trying to let her know that she was safe with him, but he felt like he was also honoring a goddess. Her body was more than a temple—it was nirvana materialized. He could have stayed in that spot eternally.

He reluctantly pulled himself away from the rapture and returned his gaze to her freckled profile. His lips grazed hers. "I've seen your scars now. Are you still afraid?"

She wiped away a few stray tears, and then she kissed him, not holding back this time. Soon they were consuming each other.

He moved her to the bed, easing her softly against the paisley pillows. His tongue found a breast and lapped at the stiffness as he tickled her with his mop of curls. His hands slid down her side to find her center, where a hot wetness beckoned him.

He could feel her panting, and then she spoke. "I've been waiting a long time for you, Eli."

CHAPTER TWELVE

Carbondale, 1990s

Summer in Carbondale was turning out to be a blessing—and Eli couldn't help wondering if his father had had some cosmic presentiment when he asked him to look after the house on Pringle Street. Regardless, Eli owed his old man some serious gratitude. He hadn't given sailing a single thought since he first laid eyes on Gretchel.

His days revolved around her. He would watch her get ready for her morning run. He would see her off to work. He was there when she got home. They would fall asleep in each other's arms.

When Gretchel was gone, Eli spent his time writing and taking photographs. When she was around, he was happy to just be near her. Lying on her bed and watching her paint was his idea of paradise.

And she was an amazing lover. Eli was honored that she trusted him, and grateful—boundlessly grateful—for her invention and enthusiasm. He was a lucky, lucky man, and he was smart enough to know it.

They didn't spend *all* their time in bed—not quite,

anyway.

Gretchel started introducing Eli to her favorite wild places. Their second weekend together, they hiked through Giant City and Garden of the Gods. They both carefully maneuvered their way through Fat Man's Squeeze, a tiny crevice in the rock formations, Eli—who wasn't crazy about small spaces—distracted himself by giving Gretchel an impromptu lecture about rites of passage in traditional societies and shamanic journeys to the Underworld. Gretchel, trying hard not to be *too* amused by Eli's nervousness, told him how Aphrodite went down to Hades to bring Adonis back from the realm of the dead.

The beauty of Southern Illinois surprised Eli. His father had been right to call this god's country, although Peter would have been much more persuasive if he had also mentioned a certain redheaded goddess residing there. In fact, Gretchel's presence left Eli feeling content to venture no further than the garden on Pringle Street. As for Gretchel herself, she was restless by nature, but, with Eli, she was learning to slow down. It didn't take them long to find a pace that pleased them both.

They lay in the backyard hammock one summer twilight, her fingers entwined in his. "I'm not big on wasting time like this, but with you, I don't mind. With you, even wasting time is magical," she told him as they swayed back and forth.

"Gretchel, look at that!" Eli lifted his head and pointed toward the woods behind the house. There was a deer gently nibbling at the roses.

Her eyes lit up as they watched it graze. "I love deer. They're so graceful and majestic. They're all over our place in Irvine. You know, when I was a kid my daddy taught me how to bow hunt," she said. Eli was not surprised. He was under the impression that she could do anything. "I shot a buck when I was only twelve. It's hanging at the cottage where I used to live when I was in high school. My daddy, my brother, and Devon, one of our farmhands—they were all so proud of me. I remember feeling bad at first. Guilty. But then I honored the animal's spirit, like I had been taught. I thanked it for the nourishment it would give my family, and somehow the death seemed okay. It seemed right, part of the natural cycle. That's the only time I can remember being at peace with death."

"That's a pretty profound thought for a child," Eli said.

"I grew up in a weird family."

"It can't be as weird as mine," Eli asserted.

Gretchel snorted. "You have no idea. I was raised on a farm and homeschooled until junior high. My mama and grand mama taught us all the normal stuff a kid might learn in public school, but we learned more—so much more. My grand mama has a thing about education. I don't think she had much of one herself–not formal education, anyway.

"We studied history and philosophy, but also mythology and botany. We learned survival skills. I know more about gardening than any girl you've ever met, Eli."

Eli grinned. "I have no doubt in my mind."

"Especially strawberries. God, I love strawberries. I've nearly broken my back cleaning out that strawberry patch of ours. This is the first year I've missed picking season. I'm almost sorry."

That's why she always smells like strawberries. It's become her essence, Eli mused.

"Herbal sciences, spell-casting, and magical correspondences. We worked closely with the elements. And there was dancing—so much dancing. We followed the cycles of the moon, and during major rituals, we would dance like wild things."

"That sounds amazing," Eli replied, and he meant it. His own upbringing had been strange, no doubt about it, but slightly sterile by comparison. Sure, his mother studied transpersonal psychology and was obsessed with an acid-fueled prophecy, and his father.... Well, his father would probably love the *idea* of dancing under a full moon.... Eli couldn't quite picture it actually happening, but he couldn't quite rule it out, either. His parents lived in their own little worlds. They certainly didn't share any intense family traditions like Gretchel was describing.

"It *was* amazing," Gretchel agreed.

Her voice pulled him from his reverie, and he tried to imagine being from a family of witches in a rural, Midwestern community. "But I suppose it wasn't easy. Did everybody know that your family was pagan? What did they think?"

"Well, my grand mama has a good reputation in Irvine. She gets respect for running a successful farm for so long. She's doctored plenty of people—usually for free—and the old-timers like her because they know she doesn't put up with any bullshit.

"Sometimes I wonder, though, if it's not so much respect as fear...." Gretchel's voice trailed off. She watched the deer as it gently decimated the rosebushes Eli's grandmother had once tended.

"What are they afraid of?" Eli asked.

Gretchel shook her head. "The people in town, they think that Snyder Farms is haunted."

Eli smiled, intrigued. "Is it?" he asked.

"Of course," Gretchel laughed. "I think that people in Irvine—especially the older people—suspect that my grand mama is somehow to blame for those hauntings."

"Is she?" Gretchel was usually so reluctant to talk about her past. Eli wanted to know more.

"I don't know. I can tell you that she's a bitchy old thing, but she's never harmed a hair on my head."

Gretchel was quiet again. Eli gave the ground a gentle push to keep the hammock swinging. He wanted to know everything that there was to know about Gretchel, and she had never been more forthcoming.

"I've seen the ghosts, Eli. I've seen them myself. And I've heard them, too."

The deer looked at them for a heart-stopping second, and then it bounded away.

The spell was broken.

"Eli, I'd rather not talk about this anymore. I feel charmed here, in this house, and I don't want to ask for trouble." She paused for a moment. "I kind of have a history of asking for trouble." Eli tightened his arm around Gretchel's shoulder, and he laid a kiss on her forehead. He would never push her to talk about anything. He trusted that she would eventually tell him everything.

The hammock moved back and forth, putting them both into a mellow trance.

She loves me, he thought.

"It's true. I do," she murmured.

Eli was shaken. She had read his mind. He was totally unfazed and completely stunned, intensely gratified and chilled to the bone.

"I love you, too, Gretchel, infinitely."

"I know," she whispered. "And I'll never forget it."

∞

"Hey, Dad, I think I'm going to stay for the rest of the summer."

"Hmmm," Peter replied.

"The house has kind of gone to shit. Little things need fixing, and the roof.... I think the house needs a new roof, maybe?"

The line was quiet for a moment, "Is she pretty?"

"What?"

"I had a new roof put on last year, son." Eli's father laughed.

Busted. Eli gave himself a moment before he responded.

"Pretty doesn't even come close, Dad. I can't explain her. She's everything. Everything I always thought I wanted. Everything I never knew I needed. She's my muse, too. You wouldn't believe what I'm writing, the photos I'm taking..."

"How's the sex?"

Eli sighed and rolled his eyes. There were times when he wished that he had been raised by conservative, suburban types.

"She's a Kegel queen, Dad. A nymph. She does this bouncy thing with her ass that sends me into orbit."

Eli knew that his deadpan tone would be completely lost on Peter. A sense of irony was not—gods bless him—one of his strengths.

Eli strained not to hear his father's response to this information, and tuned in again when it seemed safe to listen. "Your mother's in London right now. I'll see what she thinks about you staying in Carbondale."

"Why would she care? This is what she, wanted, right, for me to meet the girl from the prophecy? This is the girl! She's got red hair and horrible, pitiful scars. Gretchel's the one."

There was an awkward pause. "Just stay there and I'll deal with your mother when she returns." Peter was quiet again. "New love is magical, Eli. Cultivate it well."

"Right," Eli replied, wondering—not for the first time—if there was more to the prophecy than what his mother had told him, "And, Dad... I want to tell her who I really am. I don't feel right lying to her. It's making me feel sick."

"Absolutely not."

"Why? This is the girl I want to spend the rest of my life with."

"No. If something should happen.... Your mother wouldn't want her to be able to trace you."

"What do you mean 'if something should happen?' What aren't you telling me?"

"End of conversation," Peter said, and he abruptly hung up the phone.

Part Three

Pacific Ocean, 1980s

The sky was a canvas covered in brilliant azure, the moon a glowing circle of zinc white at the center. Eli was captivated by its shimmering reflection in the inky black water. He imagined that he could feel the pull of the moon on the gentle waves that rocked his grandfather's sailboat—and maybe he could. Even as a boy of ten, trying so hard to become a man, Eli was sensitive to feminine forces and in touch with his own anima.

Of course, the models of manhood in his world were hardly typical. His father, Peter, was intuitive and poetic and more than happy to let Eli's mother rule their household. And his mother's father, Charles Stewart, was more interested in mythic archetypes than social convention.

Peter and Charles smiled as Eli tried to capture the moon on the water with his camera. They smiled as he sat beneath the light of a swinging lantern to write a few words in his journal. It was a good night, and Peter felt that time was right for his son to come into his inheritance. Diana had been able to give Eli a nearly bottomless trust fund, but Peter had something to offer his boy that money couldn't buy.

Peter knelt on the deck and dumped out the contents of his worn leather messenger bag—several notebooks and a bag of weed. Charles watched his son-in-law with interest.

"And what will you be doing with that?" he asked, a Scottish burr coloring his words.

Peter smiled wide. "This," he said holding the hollow bag before him, "has been with me for many years. Before it was mine, it was my father's—who I never knew, except within my heart."

Eli closed his notebook and turned his attention to his father and grandfather.

Charles smiled, too. He was fond of his daft American son-in-law. "And I ask again, what will you be doing with it now?"

Peter's face assumed what was—for him—a grave expression. "It belongs to the divine messenger. It belongs to the one who is of three worlds."

"So, you mean to give it to young Eli then." Charles had grown serious, too. He could hardly remember seeing Peter without this satchel at hand, and, now that he knew that it was a family relic, he understood what it meant to pass it on—even if he could only guess what Peter had meant by the rest of his speech.

"You're giving it to me?" Eli asked, panicking at the responsibility of caring for something so important.

"Yes, Eli. This is yours now."

"But Dad, you use it all the time, I couldn't," Eli protested.

"You must."

Eli was quiet. He took the bag from his father's

hand, and set it in his lap. Peter was rarely adamant. He believed in the power of choice and free will. Eli trusted that his father would only insist if it was important. He tried to feel equal to the occasion.

Eli ran his fingers over the fine cracks in the leather. "It's so old," he said. He closed his eyes and felt like he was sinking into the past….

His father's voice pulled him back to the present. "Take good care of it, son. It's special. Just like *you're* special."

Despite the awesomeness of the occasion, Eli couldn't suppress an eyeroll. He had been hearing about how special he was… forever. Peter saw his son's sarcastic look, laughed, and tousled Eli's crazy curls.

"I guess it's a good place to keep my camera and journals," Eli acknowledged.

"For now, son. You'll discover what it means to be the messenger soon enough."

Eli dozed for a while, but the subtle change in rhythm as they pulled into harbor rocked him awake. He shook off sleep and took up his usual post in the prow, the mooring line in his hand. As Charles guided the boat toward the dock, Peter looked at his son with a mix of love, pride, and wonder. Then he saw all the color drain from Eli's face, and he watched as the boy dropped the rope from his shaking fingers.

"What is it?" Peter gasped, racing toward Eli. His urgency caught Charles's attention, too.

Eli pointed at the dock. Both men turned to look, but there was nothing there.

"What is it, Eli?" Peter asked again.

"It was a woman. I saw a woman on the dock."

Peter wrapped an arm around Eli's shoulders. "Why did that frighten you, son? Why were you scared of this woman?"

"She looked so angry," Eli whispered. "And hateful. And I knew that she shouldn't be there. I could tell that she *wasn't* there—not really."

"What did she look like?"

"She had red hair and a rotten dress. She was soaking wet. The dress looked so heavy, like it was made out of wool."

CHAPTER THIRTEEN

Irvine, 2010s

It rained the day of the funeral. Cold, freezing, sleety rain. The wake the day before had been almost unbearable. Troy was not only a fantastic car salesmen and manager of the biggest car dealership in the county, but also a school board member and a country club trustee. Everyone who was anyone in Irvine stood in line to shake hands with Troy's widow. Ame kept threatening to puke on the shoes of the next person who told her what a great man her father had been.

But that hadn't been the worst. Having to keep up an appropriate façade while surrounded by Troy's family had been torture.

The funeral had been smaller, but now that it was done, her house was full of people: family, friends, neighbors, and enemies.

Gretchel stared blankly at the wall of her massive living room. It was white. For ten years, she had wanted to paint that wall a cheerful pale green—the color of the cottage's living room—but she had never done it. Why hadn't she? Because Troy told her it would decrease the value of their home if the interiors were anything other than white or beige.

"Gretchel..."

What was that color called? "Haven?" Yes, it was "Haven." She had liked the name as much as she had liked the color itself. She thought she still had that paint chip somewhere. Maybe it was in her closet, stashed away with all her other ideas and dreams. After everyone was gone, she was going to find that paint chip, and she was going to paint that wall green.

"Baby Girl?"

She kept staring at the blank wall, which housed a fireplace that had never been used—again, Troy was worried about resell value. Expensive scented candles—also pristine—and pictures of a family pretending to be happy rested on the spotless mantle. Those would go, too. Gretchel was going to toss the candles and take some *real* photos of her children. She was also going to build a damn fire, and she might just burn everything that reminded her of Troy.

"Gretchel? Gretchel!"

Or maybe I'll just leave everything exactly the way it is and sell this place. I have never liked this house. Never. Gretchel didn't notice that everyone around her had gone silent.

"Somebody get her a glass of water."

She moved her gaze from the white wall and looked around the room. The furniture could go along with the house. She looked at the brand new beige sectional. She didn't even notice that it was crowded with people.

"Give her some Scotch," Michelle said.

"No!" a group of voices called out in unison.

Gretchel felt a warm, thin arm wrap around her. It was her mama. Ella's soft touch and gentle voice pulled her daughter out of her reverie. "Gretchel, I know you're hurting, but Troy's parents are preparing to leave. Bea wants to talk to you before they head back to Chicago."

Gretchel's eyes focused, and she noticed the house full of people that she hadn't seen just a few minutes before. Her mother-in-law was putting on her coat in the foyer.

"I'll see them out."

She could feel eyes on her as she walked toward the front door and grabbed an umbrella. Troy's father, Edward, was already outside, and Bea didn't stop moving. Gretchel followed her. Edward got in the car without saying goodbye, and Bea stopped halfway down the drive.

"We've taken care of the funeral expenses." She cleared her throat and continued. "I'll want Zachary for spring break. And after he finishes the school year, he'll come stay with us."

Gretchel stared at this woman who had hated her from the moment they'd first met. "What do you mean? Like for a week or two? Or for the whole summer?" Gretchel asked.

"I mean he'll be living with us from now on. He can play sports at a better high school, and we'll see to it that he attends college, maybe eventually law school. Unlike his father, he's got a good head on his shoulders. We're not going to let him waste his potential like Troy did," the older woman spat.

Gretchel stared at her in disbelief. "I don't think so. Zach can stay with you for a week or even the summer, but you're not taking my son away from me."

"My dear, it's not a good idea to pick a fight with a family full of lawyers." Bea paused for a moment. "But you've never really been known for good judgment, have you?"

Gretchel was wide-eyed. "Why did you even come here? You never loved Troy. You never gave a good goddamn about him," she fumed.

"Watch your tone with me, Gretchel." There was steel in her voice.

"Why are you doing this to me?"

"Because you're a blasphemous whore, and I won't let you ruin my grandson like you ruined my son." Bea's thin lips stretched in a tight smile. "You can keep the girl. She's ruined already."

Gretchel stood, dumbstruck, as her mother-in-law slid into the waiting car. She watched as her father-in-law sped away.

This could *not* be happening. Bea had *not* just threatened to take her son away. Gretchel lingered in the driveway, trying to collect herself before she went back inside.

'Er hearts as black as the Earl of Hell's waistcoat!

Aye. And it be a dreich day to shoogle the lass.

Haud yer wheescht! She needs a guid shakin'. This was the Woman in Wool.

Gretchel moaned.

Teddy, who had been observing Gretchel and Bea from the window, watched in horror as Gretchel started slapping at the side of her head. She looked like someone who had been at the beach all day, but Teddy knew it was voices—not sea water—his friend was trying to get out of her ears.

"Uh-oh," he mumbled.

"What did that wicked old woman do now?" Ame asked, scooting in next to Teddy to look out the window.

"Maybe your mom's finally going to get what she deserves," Michelle whispered into Zach's ear as she put an arm around him.

"She didn't do anything wrong," Zach said, and pushed her away.

The mourners watched Gretchel come into the house. Only Teddy, standing close to the front door, saw the look in her eye. He'd seen that look before. "This is not going to be pretty," he muttered.

Gretchel stopped for a moment and swung her head like a bear scenting danger. Her mad gaze landed on a display that Bea had set up before the funeral: Troy's golf bag, leaning against an easel that held a blown-up version of the studio portrait that graced his business cards.

Gretchel seemed almost calm as she glided across the room. Nevertheless, Michelle pulled Zach and Ben toward her, and Teddy held Ame when she made a move to intercept her mother.

Standing in front of the golf bag, Gretchel considered several clubs before she made her choice: a driver. Nano-technology titanium face. Gold-plated. Imported from Japan. It cost more than she earned in three months when she was doing landscaping in college.

Gretchel hefted it in her hand, feeling its weight, and, once again, the crowd fell away. All she could see was her next target: a curio cabinet in the dining room. It was filled with religious figurines, all from Bea. They were ugly and insipid and uninspired, and Gretchel knew that Bea had known that she would hate them. They weren't gifts. They were insults. Everyone cleared a path as Gretchel strode toward the cabinet.

"Gretchel, please calm down," Ella begged.

"Give 'em hell, Baby Girl!" Miss Poni cackled from the couch.

"Get back, everyone!" Gretchel's brother, Marcus, yelled.

The neighbors and country-club chums, congregating around the tastefully nondescript dining-room table Troy had chosen, scampered away in fear as Gretchel strode toward them, driver in hand.

She paused before the curio cabinet, raised the club like a baseball bat, and swung with all her might. Then she swung again, and again. Cold cuts and casseroles were covered in a shower of broken glass, crystal fragments, and porcelain shards.

"Everybody out!" Ella ordered.

∞

Marcus, Teddy, and Cody finally managed to get a kicking, screaming, bleeding Gretchel up the stairs and into the master bedroom. Her sister-in-law, Cindy, ran after them, brandishing a bottle of pills. "Give her one of these."

"What is it?" Teddy asked.

"A sleeping pill."

"No," Teddy said.

"It'll help her sleep. She has to sleep. She's going to hurt somebody. She's going to hurt herself."

Teddy knew Gretchel had been pushed past her breaking point. With the amethyst gone, the wild woman was stirring, and with Michelle in the living room a catfight was inevitable. Gretchel would win, of course, and Michelle had surely earned it, but Teddy had to consider what was really best for Gretchel. Reluctantly, he took the pill from Cindy.

Gretchel took it from him without a struggle. Marcus excused himself to start cleaning up the mess—just like he'd always done after one of his sister's outbursts—while his wife tried to clean the tiny cuts on Gretchel's face and hands.

Ella held her daughter and rubbed her back while she sobbed.

"Honey, what did that horrible woman say to you?" Teddy knew all about Gretchel's relationship with Troy's parents.

Gretchel was crying so hard she could barely breathe. "She's going… she's… going... she's going to take Zach. She's going to take away my son." Gretchel looked up and saw Cody standing in the doorway. His eyes were wide. "Cody, you can't let it happen."

"I won't, Baby Girl. I promise I won't."

Teddy rushed toward him. "Don't promise her anything, you spineless twat." He pushed Cody out, shutting the door in his face.

Teddy took a deep breath before he spoke to Gretchel again. "Look, Baby Girl, Bea's hurting, too. She's lost her son. She's not only lost a son, she lost a son she barely knew, a son she never really loved. She's grieving, and she's probably dealing with her own shadows. I don't know what she said to you, but she can't touch you. Be here, right now. You're with people who love you."

Ella nodded her head in agreement, but, truth be told, she was glad to see her daughter angry. It was a sign that there was still some fight left in her, that her spirit—though badly injured and frail—was still intact. It was a sign that the real Gretchel was coming back.

"Oh, Baby Girl. You are my daughter, and you're a beautiful wild witch, and you're free now."

"And you'll never, ever have to play golf again," Teddy whispered in her ear. "Now just think the most splendid thought you can conjure, and hold yourself there until you fall asleep."

Gretchel's eyelids were already drooping. She turned on her side and nestled into her pillow as her mother covered her with the comforter. Teddy kissed the scar on her forehead, and left the room. Cindy went with him.

"Rest, Baby Girl." Ella stroked her daughter's back. Then she began to sing quietly.

Gu robh neart na cruinne leat
'S neart na grèine
'S neart an tairbh dhuibh
'S àirde leumas....

Gretchel listened to the words of the lullaby, *May you have the strength of the universe, and the strength of the sun…*

As she drifted further into sleep though, it was another voice she heard. It was him. She could smell him; she could feel his arm around her, and his curls tickling the back of her neck. She was back in Carbondale.

"Everything's going to be okay. I promise," he whispered as he pulled her closer. She couldn't remember ever feeling as safe and loved as she did in his arms. Just as the sleeping pill overpowered her, she turned and looked into his aquamarine eyes. Then there was nothing. Just dreamless darkness.

CHAPTER FOURTEEN

Irvine, 2010s

The bath water was lukewarm. The lush bubbles that had covered Gretchel like a down duvet were reduced to tiny little swirls. She watched them circle around, creating a moving, aquatic version of Van Gogh's *Starry Night.* It was soothing to watch. The swirls flowed calmly around each other, peacefully disassembling and reassembling as Gretchel's breath moved across the water's surface. They weren't fighting the flow; they *were* the flow.

She felt herself being lulled, and she instinctively shook her head and rubbed her eyes, trying to chase away the grogginess and apathy that she had grown to hate. She was afraid of becoming numb again. It was much better to feel things fully—no matter the intensity—than to not feel anything at all. No, that wasn't right. It wasn't better, but it was truthful, and she was craving truth.

A knock at the bathroom door startled Gretchel from her reverie and destroyed the wispy remains of her bubble bath.

"Gretchel, it's me. I'm coming in." It was Teddy.

"Come on. I'll dry you off." Gretchel got up, and let her best friend envelope her in one of the enormous, Egyptian cotton bath sheets Troy had stocked the linen closet with. "You're so beautiful, Gretchel. Sometimes I'd swear that you're Aphrodite incarnate."

"Cut the crap, Teddy," she growled.

He stuck his tongue out at her, and then he spun her around to give her hair a good toweling.

"Wow," he said. "I haven't seen this thing in a long time. It's still breathtaking, Gretchel."

"What are you talking about?"

"Your tattoo."

Troy had told her that tattoos were trashy, and he had insisted that Gretchel keep hers covered in public. She had learned to not even think about it when she wasn't buying clothes.

It was a phoenix, stretched across her shoulder blades—a replica of a painting she'd done a long time ago, a painting she'd left behind with so many other pieces of her past when she left the cottage.

"This is you, Gretchel, You're going to rise above all of this. You're going to soar from the ashes and be reborn."

"I think I need to sit in the flames until I'm purified."

Teddy exploded. "You've been through the flames already, Gretchel!" He looked at her scars, but he was also talking about the last seventeen years. "How much more purification do you need? How much more do you need to punish yourself?"

Gretchel flinched, and Teddy felt terrible. The last thing Gretchel needed in her life was another angry man.

He wrapped her in terrycloth and guided her toward her bedroom.

Gretchel dropped the towel and lay down on the bed. Teddy squeezed out some lotion, warmed it in his hands, and rubbed it over her back. Now that Gretchel's husband was dead—and now that she had given away the amulet that made her numb—he felt comfortable being honest with his friend for the first time in a long time.

"Troy didn't just hate your tattoo because he thought it was tacky, Gretchel. He hated it because it was your artwork, and he didn't want his wife to be an artist. He hated it because he wasn't quite dumb enough to not know what it meant—the last thing he wanted was for you to rise up. And he hated it because he knew that Eli paid for it, and he knew that Eli was the man you should have married."

Teddy felt Gretchel shudder beneath his hands. "Say his name again," she whispered.

Teddy hugged Gretchel against his chest, and whispered in her ear. "Eli."

"I dreamt of him this morning." Teddy eased Gretchel back onto the bed. "I was near a body of water, wearing a beautiful ivory dress embroidered with gold. I felt like a child—like Persephone, maybe. I was waiting by the edge of the water, and then I saw him. He appeared to me as Hermes, flying with those crazy winged shoes, showing me which way to go."

Teddy smiled and kissed her shoulder. "You always called him Hermes."

The bedroom door opened with a blast of cool air. "Who's Hermes? Whoa! Jesus, Teddy, she's been a widow for less than a week and you're already switching teams?

Only my mother could turn a man as gay as you are straight."

"What do you need, Ame?" Gretchel tried to keep her voice mellow. She knew that Ame's relationship with Troy had been horribly complicated, and she also knew that Ame might be grieving in ways she couldn't understand.

"I just came in to tell you that Zach and I are back in our normal routine tonight. He has basketball practice. I'm going to work. We'll see you later." Ame kissed her mom on the cheek. "Hang in there, Mama. This is all happening for a reason. Dad's karma finally came back around to kick his ass, but as far as we're concerned, I know that things are going to be okay." Ame turned as she was headed back out the door. "And, by the way, the grandwitches have arrived."

Gretchel nodded, and slowly rose from the bed. Teddy marched her into her closet and helped her pick out clothes. She was finally awake, and he wasn't going to let her slip back into the oblivion.

∞

The Shea family was broke.

Gretchel had always left their finances to Troy; as if she had a choice. It seemed like they were fine—better than fine. But it turned out that their comfortable life was just as illusory as Troy's public persona.

Gretchel had known that their cars belonged to Sunset Auto. It just made sense that a luxury dealership's top salesman and manager should drive something new and expensive, and the same went for his wife and daughter. And Gretchel had known that their house was mortgaged. She hadn't known about the additional loans Troy had taken against the house, though, and she had no idea that the crash in the real estate market meant that they owed more than the house was worth. The allowance Troy gave Gretchel every month hadn't changed, so she had no idea that they were basically living paycheck to paycheck. Savings account, retirement accounts, the kids' college funds: all wiped out. Troy had left his wife and children with a modest life insurance settlement, negligible assets, and a pile of debt.

Gretchel went through the mess of paperwork in front of her one last time, even though she had given up hope of unearthing any buried treasure. *Thank the gods and goddesses we have the cottage*, she thought. *At least my kids aren't homeless.*

Her kids… Ame was mature enough to handle this, if only because she had grown up expecting disaster. Zach was going to have a much harder time adjusting to this new reality. Gretchel cursed Troy for doing this to them, and she cursed herself for letting her kids down yet again.

Everything was going to have to go.

Cindy was clearing out the gargantuan entertainment center.

"DVDs?" Cindy asked Gretchel.

"Take them home to Holly."

"DVD player?"

"Sell."

"Blu-Ray?"

"Sell."

"What is this, a VCR?" Cindy seemed perplexed by the black box in one of the entertainment center's cabinets.

"I'll keep that." Cindy gave Gretchel a funny look, and then put the VCR in the appropriate box.

"Do you want these old VHS tapes, too?" Cindy asked. Gretchel jumped up and quickly looked through the labels. Golf. There were six tapes from the 90s. All of them records of Troy trying to perfect his swing. Gretchel had seen all of them, more times than she liked to remember. She flung them across the room, one at a time, smashing a photo of Troy with each throw. The video tape she was looking for had nothing to do with golf.

"Quit breaking stuff!" Teddy shouted from upstairs.

"I need to break stuff!" Gretchel shouted back.

"Baby Girl, just sit your ass down," Miss Poni barked.

Gretchel glared at the old woman, and then plopped down onto the sofa. "I'm tired of this already," she complained.

"You ungrateful little shit," Miss Poni muttered, slamming her cane against the floor.

Marcus came in the house as the insult landed. "That's enough, Grand Mama. Leave her alone."

"You coddle her like she's a goddamn fairy princess," Miss Poni growled at her grandson.

Marcus slapped his ball cap on the sofa in frustration, but he held his tongue. It wasn't smart to talk back to Miss Poni. Then he grabbed Gretchel's hand and pulled her toward the stairs.

"Just use your best judgment for a while," Marcus

told the women in the living room as he led Gretchel up the stairs to her bedroom.

She crawled onto her bed and grabbed her old rag doll. She had slept with it since Troy's death, just like she used to do before she married him. She held the doll close to her body, the hair of red yarn spilling every which way.

Marcus was entranced by the doll. He couldn't look away. He was stuck in a time warp and was, for a moment, rendered speechless.

"What do you want, Marcus?"

The spell broken, Marcus turned to his little sister.

"What the hell's going on with you, Baby Girl?"

She sighed. "I never thought I would be rid of him, Marcus. *Never.* And now that I am… I guess I just don't know how to behave or act. I'm torn between the old Gretchel who was wild and the Gretchel who's been a broken woman for so long. I don't know who I am or who I want to be. I'm a mess. What do I do?"

"Well, first you slow down, and quit driving everyone nuts."

She pursed her lips, and gave him the eye.

He stared at her without speaking, clearly thinking about what he was about to say next.

"I took the shotgun to the house on the hill and locked it in the gun safe. I have the only key," he finally said, and Gretchel cringed. "I don't know what the hell you were doing with the gun anyway, but you're lucky Troy didn't have the chance to turn it on you."

"I'm lucky, Marcus? How have I *ever* been lucky? Do I look like I'm lucky now?"

"You're lucky just to be alive, after everything you've been through. I swear to the gods, you've got more lives than all my farm cats put together," he chided.

Her lip began to tremble, and Marcus sighed. He rubbed her arm. "Look, Baby Girl, Mama's told me exactly what you've been going through. We're all grateful to see the old Gretchel coming back, and we understand how hard coming back must be, but your mood swings are about to drive everyone over the edge. Mama said she heard you talking to the voices again, said you were mumbling crazy shit like you used to. Did a voice in your head tell you to get the shotgun?"

"No. It was just there —in my car."

Marcus eyed her cautiously.

"I swear, Marcus! I have no idea how it got there."

He was inclined to believe her. He didn't like to think that there were malicious spirits roaming the property, trying to stir up trouble, but he knew Snyder Farms too well to dismiss the possibility.

"I notice your necklace is gone. Did the voices tell you to take it off?"

"No."

"Did *anyone* tell you to take off the amethyst?"

"It wasn't so much that I heard someone as much as it was a *feeling* that I heard someone," she said quietly. "I just knew it was time."

Marcus gave his sister another long, considering look.

"Well, it's good to have you back, Gretchel, but you've got to keep it together. You've blocked out the voices before without help from booze, medication, or magic amulets, and you can do it again. Otherwise you're going to end up back in the loony bin."

"You wouldn't let them take me, Marcus. You

wouldn't!" There was real panic in her voice.

He lifted his hands in defense. "Baby Girl, I didn't want you to go the first time, but what the hell were we supposed to do? You've got to take care of yourself. Get yourself into therapy," he said and eyed the rag doll again. "You need to start talking about things."

She shook her head vehemently. "I'm not ready."

"Not ready? It's been over two decades, and that's too long. You've got to start letting go."

"She won't let me."

Marcus took a deep breath, trying to contain his frustration. He had mourned the loss of his wild-woman sister during her years with Troy, but he had forgotten that the old Gretchel wasn't exactly an easy person to deal with. "Who won't let you?"

"The Woman in Wool."

Marcus rubbed his face hard with his hands. "So you're seeing her again, too?"

"I saw her on New Year's Eve."

"Describe her to me, Gretchel. You've never told me what she looks like."

Gretchel gripped the rag doll tightly. "She's a young woman, but old."

Marcus sighed. "How's that, Gretchel?"

"Well, she's young but her aura is old… *really* old. Her hair is a rat's nest and her clothes…. She wears this horrible wool dress. It's practically rotting off her. She looks like a beggar, a peasant. She's barefoot and dirty, and she reeks of brackish water."

Marcus didn't know what to think.

His mother and Miss Poni never talked much about the Wicked Garden when he was growing up, but the farmhands told ghost stories. He had never seen or sensed anything especially alarming himself; at the same time, it wasn't as if he had been raised to discount the supernatural. Marcus practiced the same faith as his family, but he was essentially a well-educated dirt farmer who had inherited some idiosyncratic traditions and mediocre psychic abilities. All he wanted to do was tend his land. He did *not* want to deal with a dead brother-in-law, teleporting firearms, and the return of the Woman in Wool. He sighed again and put a hand on his little sister's shoulder.

"You just make sure you tell people when you hear things, Gretchel. Don't try to go it alone. We're all here for you, and remember that you've got Ame and Zach to think about, too. Maybe everything will get better when we get you moved down to the cottage. I know Troy's death hasn't been easy on you, but it's not like you loved the man. Moving on might be easier than you think."

Gretchel wiped a few tears away, nodded in agreement, and even managed a weak, but wicked, smile. "Say, Marcus. I don't suppose you have any new farmhands?"

Marcus frowned and shook his head. "Oh no, no, no. No more farmhands for you, Baby Girl."

Aye. The tart's seen more pricks than a secondhand dartboard, a voice whispered in Gretchel's head, and a mass of cackling followed.

CHAPTER FIFTEEN

Irvine, 2010s

Work was slow that Friday afternoon. Despite the promise of a sixty-percent-off post-holiday sale, Ame hadn't had a single customer.

The fresh blanket of white snow probably had something to do with it—people were either enjoying the weather outside or determined to stay inside. What they most certainly were *not* doing was venturing downtown to buy fairy figurines, Tarot decks, or esoteric paperbacks at the metaphysical bookstore where Ame had a part-time job. She sighed as she watched the last rays of daylight bounce off the icicles hanging just outside the window. She was stuck there 'til eight, customers or no customers.

Ame left her post at the cash register to wander down the crystal aisle. As always, it brightened her mood. The stones spoke to her. She read their vibrations with ease. She could tell the difference between rose quartz and smoky quartz with her eyes closed. She recognized them as living entities, buzzing with energy—not just sedentary chunks of earth.

She touched a beautiful piece of blue lace agate, and suddenly she felt compelled to pull out her laptop. It wasn't as though there was much to do. The bookshelves were in perfect order, and Ame had dusted everything there was to dust. Anyway, Ame knew that the owner, Claire, was far too impressed with her talent with stones to much care what she did during a lull.

She logged onto Facebook and checked to see if any of her friends were available to chat. She saw that the guy she had met in Champaign was online. She kept meaning to ask her mother about him—she was curious about their connection—but it just never came up. He seemed like an all right guy. On a whim, she sent him a message.

Eli heard the tiny bleep of an instant message, and nearly fell out of his chair. He was stoned again. He hadn't smoked pot like this in years. He was acting like he was in college again. Worse yet—he was acting like his father.

Eli's heart raced when he saw that is was a message from Gretchel's daughter.

Hi! Remember me?

Hi! Yes I remember you. How's it going Ame?

I'm ok. We're survivin. But it hasnt been fun. Mom's losin her noodles.

What do you mean?

My dad died New Years Day.

Eli sat stunned. His buzz fizzled, and exhilaration worked its way through his nervous system. Troy died? Troy was gone? He didn't like the idea of relishing another person's death, but… But this was Troy. Then it occurred to him that Troy was this girl's father, and he felt like a ghoul and an asshole.

I'm so sorry Ame with an E.

Dont b. He was a horrible person. I hated him.

I'm sorry about that too.

This was too much for Eli. He knew the day Gretchel walked away that Troy was going to not only destroy her life, but the life of her unborn child. It seemed that everything he had feared had come to pass. It made him hurt for this beautiful girl.

So how do u know my mother?

I dated her in college. Please don't tell her we're talking.

Y? My predator instincts r startin 2 kick n.

Eli sighed. He felt like the biggest jerk that ever was, messaging a teenage girl and asking her to keep it private. *At least Ame* has *predator instincts, unlike her mother*, he thought. Ame had sent another message.

I HATE SECRETS! Prove 2 me how U know her.

We both went to SIU in the early 90s.

Any1 could have known she went 2 school there N then.

Eli ran his hands through his thick curls. He was becoming really uncomfortable with the turn the conversation was taking, but he couldn't back out now. He thought for a moment, typed in a new message, and sent it before he could change his mind.

She has scars from third degree burns on the right side of her torso, from the top of her right breast to the bottom of her hip. She has cuts on the other side of her torso. She also has a huge phoenix tattooed on her back. It was a 19th birthday present from me.

U do know her! Not many ppl have seen those scars or the tat.

Please promise me you won't say anything until I say it's OK.

Y?

Because what we had didn't end well.

She's never tlked bout U. I'm dying 2 ask her bout U now.

Please don't. Not yet.

OK. G2G. I'd like 2 tlk 2 u again. I get online every nite @ 10pm.

I'll be here. Glad we met Ame with an E.

Glad I met u 2 Eli w/ an I. L8R

∞

Troy is dead.

Eli was on his fifth one hitter. He had been sitting in front of a blank computer screen for three hours, thinking the same thought over and over again: *Troy is dead.*

What should I do? The initial rush of energy he'd felt when he learned the news had quickly been met by an equally powerful sense of paralysis. He could almost—almost—laugh at the irony. He'd been waiting seventeen years for something, *something* to propel him out of his sad, pointless, torpid existence, and, even now—even after learning that the primary obstacle between him and Gretchel was gone—he had not a fucking clue what to do about it.

Eli rubbed his bloodshot eyes and tried to clear his head. He needed to think about something else for awhile. Also, it had become essential that he consume large quantities of salty snacks immediately.

After depositing an entire bag of tortilla chips and a jar of salsa on the coffee table, Eli walked to his bookshelf. He grabbed a favorite—*The Dharma Bums*—and opened it as he moved toward the sofa.

Something fell out of the book and landed on the floor.

It was a postcard. Rebecca had sent it to him while she was on a tour of Italian museums. It was—somewhat predictably—Botticelli's *Primavera.* Eli had barely looked at it when he had first gotten it, but now it caught his attention. That figure in the center—*Venus, right? Aphrodite?*—had stirred a memory. It was her gown. White with gold trim. Eli closed his eyes, and he saw Gretchel in an ivory dress, moonbeams bouncing off golden embroidery.

∞

Irvine, 1990s

The Summer Solstice approached. It just so happened that this was also Gretchel's birthday. Ella insisted that her daughter come home for the weekend. Gretchel's last visit had been spring break. Teddy missed her; her nephews missed her; her whole family missed her. So, dragging her feet all the way, Gretchel took Eli to Snyder Farms.

"These are phenomenal," Eli said as he sifted

through the stacks of paintings Gretchel had pulled out of the bedroom closet at the cottage. He had already gone crazy over the poppy painting in the living room, and now he was in a state of bliss. "I know dealers out west who would pay big money for these."

Gretchel rolled her eyes and snorted.

"Seriously. You should be proud of your work."

"So, you rub elbows with art dealers out west, do you?" She grinned at him.

He had said too much. He covered his unease with a smile, said nothing, and continued sifting through the treasures Gretchel had unearthed.

"Mama's going to be pissed if she knows that we've been down here without stopping at the house on the hill first. I just wanted you to see the cottage before we go up. It's weird, because there was a period of my life when I hated this place so bad, but I've missed it. It feels oddly good to be back. Bittersweet. I hate to sound clichéd, but it feels like I'm home again."

"There's nothing wrong with being home, Gretchel. It's the most universally sought-after feeling there is. Everyone's trying to get back home—if not to a physical place, then to a psychological equivalent."

She smiled and Eli melted. He continued flipping through the canvases, and then he gasped when he came across the phoenix. "Gretchel this is the most amazing thing I've ever seen."

She looked thoughtfully at the painting. "I remember I started it early in the morning, because I've always gotten up early—farm life does that to you. I sketched the outline at sunrise, and finished it the same night. Adding all that detail was the best part of the experience. I always feel good when I'm painting, and I've always incorporated mythic elements in my work, but this was… I don't know. It was like I was channeling something beyond me, something bigger than me. I was fifteen or something. I wasn't talking much then. Wasn't doing much of anything. Just painting.

"You finished this is less than twenty-four hours?"

"My teenage years were pretty fucked up. Mental issues," she said, swirling her finger around the side of her head. "Anything I could do to help me escape, I did. Not much has changed."

"I've never seen you out of control," he said.

She ignored his comment, and touched the painting. "It is pretty, isn't it? The phoenix rising out of her own ashes, reborn as another version of herself. Transformed. That's how I feel since I've met you. Like I've become a better version of myself."

He watched her mindfully. "We'd better go see your family, but I'm going to leave this painting out. I have an idea."

Pulling up at the house on the hill, they saw a couple of cars and several trucks parked across the huge yard. There were enough picnic tables pulled together to accommodate a banquet. Balloons and streamers hung from the trees. Children ran across the grass screaming, while grown-ups chatted in groups. Eli looked slightly stunned. He hadn't expected quite so many people. His family wasn't into big gatherings. Or small gatherings, for that matter.

"Welcome to the country," Gretchel laughed. "Hey, you know why cowgirls are bowlegged?" she asked.

Eli just shrugged. "Because cowboys eat with their hats on."

Eli chuckled and shook his head. His father would absolutely adore this girl. "They've really gone all out for you."

"They're afraid I might slice my abdomen in two or try to knock myself off again."

Eli was taken back by her words, and by the matter-of-fact way she said them. Apparently, something had happened on her birthday, something very bad. Eli felt so close to Gretchel—closer than he had ever felt to anybody—but there was so much that he didn't know about her.

He held her hand while they walked toward the crowd. Teddy was the first to reach them. He grabbed Gretchel, swung her around, and showered her with kisses. Eli knew that Teddy was not a competitor, and he was happy to see she that had such a good friend.

"You haven't called me in weeks," Teddy scolded.

"I've been a little preoccupied." Gretchel smiled in Eli's direction. "Teddy, this is Eli. Eli, this is the infamous Theodore Wintrop: best friend, personal stylist, and secret-keeper extraordinaire."

"It's nice to meet you, Eli. A relief, actually. When Miss Poni said that Gretchel was bringing a guy home, I thought for sure it was Troy." Teddy turned the full force of his disapproval on Gretchel. "I see you've finally come to your senses."

This was the first Eli had heard of an ex-boyfriend named Troy, but, judging from the glare that Gretchel was directing at Teddy, Eli sure as hell wasn't going to inquire.

Teddy wove his arm into Gretchel's and the three

of them continued toward the awaiting crowd. At the front of the pack stood an old woman supporting herself with a cane. She was tall—frail, but indomitable. She stood next to a woman who had to be Gretchel's mother. Her hair was cut short, but Eli recognized that it was the same red as Gretchel's, faded slightly by age.

Eli could not help but notice that he was being scrutinized intensely by both women. The older of the two motioned for Eli to step forward.

He reached out his hand and she took it. Her grip was surprisingly firm. He realized that it had been a mistake to assume that this woman was frail in any way.

"Could you please remove the spectacles, my dear boy?"

Eli felt embarrassed to have forgotten his manners. He used his left hand to take off his sunglasses and his ball cap—his right hand was still captive.

The old woman looked into his eyes, and he felt a shiver go down his spine. Then she smiled, with a satisfied look. Confused, Eli stole a glance at Gretchel. Her face was rigid. After a few tense seconds, she snapped.

"Grand Mama, stop staring and acting like a crazy old lady."

"It's good to see you too, child, and be careful who call you crazy," she replied, without taking her gaze off Eli.

Gretchel rolled her eyes, and couldn't help but let out a snigger. "Eli, this is my mean-ass Grand Mama Epona, more commonly known as Miss Poni, and this is my sweet mama, Ella Bloome." She hugged her mother. Miss Poni had yet to release Eli.

"Mama, I think you're about to break the poor

boy's hand," said Ella gently.

Miss Poni finally let go. "Enjoy the midsummer festivities," she smiled. She waved as she walked away. She flicked her wrist with a flourish, and the pyramid of timber in the middle of yard burst into flames. The solstice bonfire had begun.

"Showoff," Gretchel muttered.

It took Eli a moment to realize that what he had just seen was either an amazing parlor trick or a piece of honest-to-god magic. He turned to Gretchel, wide-eyed, but she just laughed and pulled him toward the thick of the party.

It was a nearly perfect afternoon. Eli tried to avoid Miss Poni—he found the thought of another encounter with her mildly terrifying—but he did have a chance to chat with Ella. He also met Gretchel's older brother, Marcus, and liked him immediately. He was as tall as Eli, and had the same gray eyes as Gretchel, but only hints of red in his sandy brown hair. He hadn't tried to intimidate Eli, but he had let him know that he had best not hurt Baby Girl, as everyone called Gretchel.

Marcus' wife, Cindy, was quite pregnant, but it didn't seem to slow her down as she chased after two-year-old Blake. Her four-year-old, Brody, attached himself to Eli, following him around like a miniature shadow. Brody was especially fascinated by Eli's guitar. Eli showed the little boy how to hold it properly, and let him strum the strings.

Gretchel introduced Eli to the farmhands—three grown men and two high-school boys—as well as their families. If they had any misgivings about working for witches, they didn't show it. All of them spoke fondly of their employers, and, more than once, Eli heard about the miraculous efficacy of Miss Poni's home remedies. The older men looked on fondly as Ella showed their small children how to make protection pouches to be thrown into the bonfire later that evening.

The food was amazing. A couple of farmhands had roasted a pig. There were homemade breads and bounteous summer vegetables, and, of course, freshly picked strawberries.

Eli tried to not look startled when Miss Poni chose to join him and Gretchel at their picnic table.

"I could eat my weight in this stuff," he said, trying to be a good guest.

"Have you tried the strawberries?" Miss Poni asked.

"The best I've ever had," Eli replied.

Gretchel smiled. "I told you they were good.

"Baby Girl used to make the best strawberry shortcake this side of the Mississippi."

Gretchel's face instantly turned sour. Once again, Eli was slightly confused. There was clearly more to this conversation than he could possibly understand.

Miss Poni shook her and ladled another spoonful of strawberries onto Eli's plate. "She'll make it again someday."

"Over my dead body, old woman," Gretchel hissed. Eli was taken aback. He had never seen Gretchel like this.

Ella pursed her lips, and handed her daughter a protection pouch. "I don't want to hear another word about dead bodies, and if you speak to your grand mama like that again you'll be camping your ass here tonight while Eli goes back to the cottage by himself. Do you understand me, Miss Bloome?" Ella's voice was quiet, but stern.

Eli could practically hear Gretchel grinding her teeth, but she didn't say anything else. He turned his attention to his plate and kept it there. It was clear that Gretchel, her mother, and her grandmother were talking about something without actually talking about it—and that Gretchel didn't *want* to talk about it. He could guess that it had something to do with her "issues," but that was all he could guess.

"Well, I'm ready for my presents," Gretchel finally croaked to keep herself from arguing with her elders.

Around sunset, Gretchel bowed out of the party, and promised to return to the house on the hill for breakfast. Eli made his goodbyes, too. Just before they left, Marcus pulled Eli aside and asked him to keep close watch over his sister that night. When Eli asked if there was something he should know, Marcus paused for a moment and then confided in him that their father had passed away on the Solstice. Eli was shocked, but this certainly helped explain the tense undercurrent he had sensed between Gretchel, Ella, and Miss Poni. Eli thanked Marcus for telling him.

Ella gave Gretchel a stack of fresh linens while one of the farmhands loaded a basket of food into the trunk of Eli's car. Then they were off.

Eli had assumed that they'd be going straight to the cottage, but Gretchel surprised him by rolling a four-wheeler out of a shed. He was mildly terrified, which

Gretchel found hugely amusing. He clung to her waist and tried not to scream as they raced through a mile of farmland, around a lake, across a levy, and down to the Kaskaskia River. Eli said a prayer of thanks of his own when Gretchel stopped to offer a silent prayer and make an offering to the water. His sense of gratitude was short-lived. The ride back was just as frightful as the ride there.

"Do you always drive like that or were you just trying to scare the bejeezus out of me?" he asked, running a hand through his nappy curls and turning his SIU ball cap backward. He tried to ignore the fact that his knees were shaking.

"A little of both," she said with a grin as she ditched her sandals and ran after a firefly. Eli smiled as she chased the fluttering spark of light, and he was surprised to see her stop—suddenly—when the firefly flew into a patch of land overgrown with weeds and wildflowers. He saw an old pickup truck, burnt-out and rusted, with a thorny locust tree growing against the passenger-side door. He thought about the burns on Gretchel's body and felt faintly ill.

Gretchel was frozen, immobile. Eli shook himself and walked toward her. He tried to sound cheerful. "Are you ready for one more gift?"

His voice seemed to revive Gretchel. Her face was pale as she turned to smile, but her eyes lost their haunted look as she walked toward him.

Eli had already given Gretchel several birthday presents. At the family party, he had given her a nice set of paints and a roll of canvas. Gretchel had been appropriately appreciative, but she had lost it when she tore away the giftwrap—yuzen paper printed with strawberry blossoms—to find a signed first-edition of the latest Graham Duncan book, *Hermes In Heat.*

"How did you get this?"

"I work in the publishing industry, so, you know, I pulled some strings." He tried to forget about the fact that he was lying to her—again—by focusing on her joy.

His remaining present was in a pocket of his khaki shorts.

Hand-in-hand, they walked to the lake. Eli hadn't had a chance to notice when they were flying on the four-wheeler, but there was a causeway that led to a little island. It was fenced all around with a pretty wooden railing. Gretchel led him past a pentacle made from railroad ties and almost overgrown by herbs and wildflowers.

There was a small, antique wooden boat bobbing against the shore on the far side of the island. Gretchel led Eli aboard, and he rowed them to the middle of the lake. They floated under the light of the moon and an umbrella of stars. *Perfect*, Eli thought. He reached into his pocket.

"I haven't wrapped this last gift, but I have a feeling you won't mind."

"You're spoiling me, Eli. I was happy with the white roses you picked from the garden in Carbondale. It was enough," she said with a smile. Eli could tell that she meant it.

He pulled out a bag of mushrooms, and her eyes grew twice their size. "We're going deep-see diving!"

"Yes, but it's not just for shits and giggles, Gretchel. This is not recreational to me. Don't leave my side, not for a second."

Gretchel laughed. "We're in a rowboat, in the

middle of a lake. Where am I supposed to go?"

"I'm serious, Gretchel."

Chastened, Gretchel apologized. "I'm just a little nervous, but I'm not afraid. I'm ready. I have you to guide me."

Eli's whole body went rigid as he was overwhelmed by a déjà vu. He felt a sense of foreboding, but he couldn't explain it and he didn't want to disappoint Gretchel. He gave her a handful of fungi. He had been planning to take the second handful himself, but, at the last minute, he decided against it.

Gretchel watched him for a moment. "Aren't you coming with me?"

"I'll be with you, Gretchel, wherever you go. That's the only place I want to be."

Satisfied, Gretchel leaned back against a faded cushion in the prow as Eli settled in to watch over her.

"Eli, I can hear the lake. The ripples in the water…. They're humming." Gretchel spoke with quiet awe. Eli smiled. Even in his utterly sober state, he was enjoying the way the moonlight made the surface of the lake shimmer. It was mesmerizing. He leaned over the side of the boat to trail his fingers in the water, and instead of his own shadow, he saw a beautiful face looking back at him.

Well, that's odd, he thought.

Suddenly, a hand reached out of the water and grabbed his wrist.

"What the fuck!"

He jerked back, and the boat rocked. Gretchel just managed to catch herself before she tumbled into the water.

"Holy shit, what are doing, Eli?" she screamed.

He grabbed the sides of the boat to stop the rocking. "I'm sorry. There was a hand. A fucking *hand* just came out of the water, and grabbed my wrist. I saw a face, too." He stared into the water, but now there was nothing but a few wild wavelets and innocent moonlight.

He turned back to Gretchel and she was wearing a different dress. It was ivory, old-fashioned, with ornate golden detail. Her hair was down and flowing around her. "I'm not afraid. I'm ready. I have you to guide me," she said softly.

"What the *fuck*?!" he repeated.

"Eli, what the hell is wrong with you?" Gretchel cried.

Eli saw that she was, once again, wearing a soft green, cotton sundress, and her hair hung in a braid over her shoulder. He shook his head. "There was a hand… and a face… and you were… I mean, I didn't even take the 'shrooms, and I'm still tripping!" He had never been more frightened in his life.

Gretchel, however, was surprisingly relaxed. "Oh, I forgot to tell you that this lake is haunted."

Eli just stared.

"I probably should have told you."

A variety of responses went through Eli's head before he chose one. It wasn't the first, and it wasn't the most obvious one, but Snyder Farms was turning out to be a whole lot weirder than he imagined—and he was capable of imagining some serious weirdness.

"Gretchel, maybe you could have chosen somewhere else—anywhere else—to try psychedelic drugs for the first time, rather than *while floating in a tiny, ancient boat on a haunted lake*?"

"Well, Mama gave me a protection pouch. I guess we should have made one for you, too. Here, you can have mine."

Eli took it from her hand without thinking. Then he closed his eyes for a moment, trying to pull himself together.

When he opened them, Gretchel was leaning over the side of the boat, staring into the inky depths. "I'm going in."

"No, Gretchel!" he said. "Take the pouch back. Take the fucking pouch back!"

He forced it back into her hand, settled her into the prow, and rowed with all his might back to the shore.

Once they were back on dry ground, Eli started to feel a little less freaked out. He held Gretchel's hand, and let her lead him wherever she wanted to go.

Eli had noticed the barn when they had visited the cottage earlier in the day, but it was only as they got close to it that he noticed that it was falling apart.

"Did you keep horses here?" He had no idea where this question came from. Gretchel didn't seem to notice the catch in his voice.

"Yeah. I rode all the time when I was a kid. We had several. I used to have a black mare named Pixie," she said quietly. "After the accident, she got sick. Marcus thought she got into some snakeroot or something. She's buried in the Wicked Garden." She pointed to the patch of weeds and wildflowers that had seemed to trouble her earlier. "I've never been able to connect with a horse again. They hate me, and I'm scared of them."

Eli wasn't sure what to say. He couldn't imagine any creature hating Gretchel.

Not far from the barn was the truck he had noticed earlier. They were close to it when Gretchel dropped to her knees and fell silent. Eli didn't want to disturb her. It looked like she was praying.

"I *am* praying," she murmured.

"What?"

"I *am* praying," she said more loudly.

Eli was, once again, unnerved, "How did you know what I was thinking?"

She turned and looked at him oddly, *because I heard you say it,* she thought.

But I didn't *say it,* he retorted.

Well, I heard it, she replied.

Is it the mushrooms? Wait, I didn't take the mushrooms! What is happening, Gretchel?

Weird things happen at Snyder Farms, Eli.

Eli had been raised by an expert in transpersonal psychology and one of the world's most famous hippies. He had been raised to expect the weird—to *seek out* the weird—but he still felt unprepared for the weirdness of Gretchel, her family, and Snyder Farms.

He reached out a hand and helped Gretchel rise.

Wait just a minute. He was still hearing her voice in his head. She walked to a pile of large stones that were conveniently—almost religiously—stacked several yards away. She picked one up, and launched it at the truck.

Wow, Eli thought, *she must have played softball.*

No, I've never been much of a team-player. She threw another stone, knocking glass from the back window. There was a bull's-eye spray-painted on the tailgate. She took another rock, threw it, and hit the target square in the center.

Jesus! Eli thought.

You should see me shoot my bow, she replied.

I'm getting hard just picturing it.

It always had that affect on the farmhands too, she replied.

CHAPTER SIXTEEN

Irvine, 2010s

Evening had descended on Irvine. To Gretchel's great relief, everyone had left. She loved her family. She appreciated their help, but the day had left her drained. She took a shower, threw on pajamas, and collapsed into bed.

"Hey, Mom," Zach said from the hallway.

"Hey, Baby Boy. Come talk to me."

"Did you know that our phone's not working?"

"Yeah, we had it turned off along with everything but the gas, electricity, and water. No landline. No internet connection. No satellite TV."

Zach shook his head in disbelief.

"Sorry, kid, but things are going to be tight for awhile until I figure things out. And, hey, we're moving soon anyway."

"I can keep my cell phone, can't I?" Gretchel could tell he was panicking, because all of the sudden he sounded like his voice had never dropped. He sounded like a little boy worried about losing his security blanket.

"For now," she smiled.

He wasn't exactly mollified, but he was willing to let the topic go.

"Cody dropped me off. Guess I'm still allowed to talk to him and Ben?"

"I have no problem with you associating with Cody and Ben. Just keep your distance from Michelle. I really don't have to tell you this do I?"

"No. She's a dumb bitch. I've never seen anyone as nosy as she is. Every time I go over there she's asking about you. Ben has to sneak me up to his room just to avoid her."

Gretchel was about to chastise her boy for calling any woman—even Michelle—a "dumb bitch" when he surprised her by crawling into bed with her and burrowing into her embrace. She couldn't remember the last time he had done that.

Zach closed his eyes and let his mother stroke his shaggy ginger-red hair for a few moments. Then he looked around the room and Gretchel felt him become tense.

"You're cleaning out his closet?" His voice had gone small again, and she could tell that he was struggling not to cry.

Gretchel couldn't hold it in anymore. Tears cascaded down her face.

"I had a bad day, Baby Boy," she cried. Zach turned himself around, hugged her and began sobbing into her chest. Gretchel held him close and let the teenager grieve with her.

"I miss him. I miss him a lot. But I was scared of him, too. I couldn't stop him from hurting you and Ame. He was too big for me, and every time I tried, he would beat me, too. I hated him! But he was my dad. I'm not supposed to hate my dad!"

For the first time since she had taken off the amethyst, Gretchel craved its numbing power. She didn't know how she would ever learn to live with this, what she had done to her children. She thought that, maybe, if they knew the truth about her life, they would understand. But she also knew that, if they knew the truth about her life, they would turn on her. She *knew* they would.

"Zach, I won't lie. I hated him, too."

Zach pulled himself away and looked into her face. "Then why did you marry him? Why would you marry someone you hated? And why would you *have kids* with someone you hated?"

Gretchel struggled to come up some kind of response for her son—not a lie, but not the whole truth, either.

Zach's face twisted into a scowl, but not before Gretchel saw the disappointment there. She was letting him down again.

"You know what? Never mind. I've got homework to do." He jumped off the bed and out the door before she could reply.

"Why did I screw everything up?" she asked the empty room.

Shoulda stayed outta the tavern. Ya knew he'd find ya, lass.

Aye! He knew the lush'oud show up eventually.

Gretchel wiped more tears from her face, not surprised to hear the annoying prattle of the Scottish voices mouthing off in her head.

"You're right," Gretchel replied. "Troy had me figured out. If I would have just stayed away from the booze all those years ago, it would have changed everything."

She curled up on the bed and embraced her rag doll, shuddering at the memory of Troy tracking her down in Carbondale.

If she had just had more time at the house on Pringle Street with Eli, things might have been different. She wondered if Eli ever thought of her the way she did of him. Doubtful. He was too good for her, and the Woman in Wool had made sure she never forgot it.

∞

Irvine, 1990s

Eventually, Eli was able to guide Gretchel back to the cottage.

Gretchel thought that Eli was acting kind of strange. Of course, being attacked by a ghost was probably a new experience for him, and maybe telepathic communication wasn't something he shared with every girlfriend. Also, given that she was on 'shrooms, she probably wasn't in the best position to judge strange behavior.

In any case, she forgot about Eli as soon as she walked into the cottage. The colors! The green of the painted walls, the honey-gold of the oak paneling, the deep burgundy of the sofa.... They weren't just abstract properties anymore. They were living entities, with personalities and distinct physical attributes. Gretchel felt like crying. *She was an artist! She should have known!* She followed the colors into the bedroom, and sat on the edge of the bed to watch them.

After awhile—a few minutes, a few days, a few centuries—she remembered Eli. Where was he?

That was when she noticed that he was sitting right next to her.

Gretchel smiled and leaned into his shoulder.

She turned toward the window and saw the moon in full bloom. She heard a howl from deep in the woods.

Eli shuddered. *Is that a wolf?*

Yes, she thought, and he shuddered again when he heard her voice in his head, answering his silent question.

Do they ever come close? Have you ever seen one? The hair on the back of Gretchel's neck rose, and she couldn't tell whether it was because of the wolf howl or the electric vibrations of Eli's thoughts.

I see a lot of things. She laughed internally, and she knew that Eli wouldn't know what she was laughing about. Then she laughed aloud. The sound of laughter massaged her body. She fell backward onto the bed. Eli still had no idea what was so funny, but he loved seeing Gretchel like this, and soon he was laughing with her.

Eventually, Gretchel wiped the tears out of her eyes and pulled herself together. Eli crawled over her on all fours and stared into her eyes.

She reached up and touched his cheek with the tips of her fingers. His face hung above her like the full moon. Everything else fell away. Gravity didn't seem to make sense anymore. When his lips touched hers, waves of lust rolled through her body, crashing over her with a longing she'd never felt for any other man.

He leaned in to kiss her on the neck. She slowly unbuttoned his grungy plaid shirt and pushed it back off his shoulders. Her hands moved over his taut, tan chest.

An orgasm swept over her before he was even inside her. The moment he penetrated, Gretchel thought that he would come quickly—and he did—but he didn't stop. Each thrust provoked a different feeling, but each new sensation was part of the same endless climax.

She moaned underneath him and then on top of him and then while he took her from behind and then she didn't know what was happening, exactly, because she hadn't opened her eyes from that first moment of orgasm.

Are you with me, Gretchel?

Yes. I'm not afraid. I have you to guide me, Hermes.

She was in a state of extended rapture, and she knew that Eli was, too. She could not only hear his thoughts; she could also feel what he was feeling. It was as if they were no longer two, but one.

And she could see Eli, even though her eyes were closed. He was looking down at her lovingly, and they were no longer in the bed. They were on the delicate petal of a poppy.

Then Gretchel saw things she couldn't name, heard sounds that she couldn't define, and felt sensations that she could only recognize as bliss while everything around her faded to white. Floating in a luminous cloud, they held each other within their psyches. They were the God and Goddess. They were creation, and they were love, and above all, they were truth—the source of all and all that ever would be.

Eventually, Gretchel opened her eyes to find Eli sleeping next to her and the phoenix painting hovering in the middle of the room. She reached out her hand to touch it, but, instead of brush strokes and dry paint, she felt feathers. With a great flutter of wings, the flame-red bird took off in flight, and Gretchel felt she had no choice but to follow. She took one last glance at Eli's sleeping face, and knew that, where she was going now, he could not guide her.

Gretchel followed the phoenix through a limitless emptiness until it disappeared into a field of poppies that stretched as far as she could see. She walked into the field until she was surrounded by orange blooms. A woman appeared from out of nowhere. She was pale and beautiful, with gleaming black hair flowing over her shoulders. Her face was luminous, but her clothes seemed to change in front of Gretchel's eyes. One second, the stranger looked like she was dressed like a fairy-tale princess. The next, she seemed to be draped in robe of cobwebs and dry grass. Without preamble or introduction, she said, "Follow me."

Gretchel did.

The raven-haired woman led her to a clearing, a barren patch of earth in the ocean of poppies. She sat down, and motioned for Gretchel to do the same. Everything was still.

A snake emerged from the poppies and slithered toward Gretchel. She was unafraid. She had seen this creature before, in another form. She knew him, and she knew that he loved her. She let the snake coil around her arm.

More stillness.

There was a thundering in the distance, and all three entities sitting in the circle of earth turned toward it.

Gretchel felt a fluttering in her belly as the ground shook. The flowers parted, and a white horse emerged. It stopped and reared at the edge of the clearing, shaking its mane. When it stilled, Gretchel saw an amethyst glowing in its forehead, like a third eye. Gretchel smiled and laughed in delight. She knew this creature—or at least who this horse had been in another life.

"I've missed you," she whispered. "I've missed you so much."

The horse scratched at the ground within the clearing, then she moved—slowly, gently—toward Gretchel, reaching down to nuzzle her neck. Then the horse turned and walked away, back into the poppies.

"Please, stay with me just a little bit longer," Gretchel pleaded. The horse turned for a moment, and then it was gone.

A sob wrenched Gretchel, and her tears fell on the barren ground. She wiped her eyes.

The raven-haired woman was gone. In the spot where she had been sitting, there was nothing but a shovel. Gretchel picked it up and started to dig. The snaked slithered in a circle around her. She dug until she was six feet beneath the surface, and then she hit something hard. She threw aside the shovel and clawed at the earth until she uncovered what seemed to be a box.

She brushed the dirt from its top and saw that it was decorated with an intricately detailed eternal knot. She knew this pattern, and it was familiar, too—just like the snake and the horse. She felt like she had seen it many times before. She knew—without knowing how she knew—that the more lines there were in the knot, the more protection it offered. This design was so intense that it was almost—almost—chaotic.

She kept digging.

When the box was free, she tried to open it. She

couldn't. It was locked, and she had no key. Reluctantly, she decided to leave it behind.

At this moment, Gretchel realized that she was at the bottom of a deep hole, with no obvious means of escape. She tried climbing, but each hold she took crumbled beneath her fingers. Her sense of panic mounted. In her frenzy, she loosed great clumps of dirt and then the walls of earth around her gave way. She was being buried alive.

"Help me!" she screamed.

Skeletal hands reached through the shower of dirt and clutched at her.

"Let me go!"

Gretchel, I'm here.

She heard the words in her head, although no voice spoke.

You can't go there yet, Gretchel. Come back to me. It was Eli. He had come looking for her, and he had found her.

Free us, a chorus of voices sang in her head.

I don't know how! I don't have the key! Eli, help me!

Then suddenly an instinctual warning ran through her awareness. She looked up toward the moonlit sky, and the Woman in Wool began pouring water into the hole.

Gretchel screamed as water filled her lungs and the hole collapsed into blackness around her.

"Gretchel, I'm here!"

For a moment, Gretchel had no idea where she was. Then she looked around and realized that she was in the old pickup truck. She screamed again.

"What the hell are you doing here?" Eli shouted as he pulled her from the cab.

Gretchel kicked and wailed as he held her. Her

eyes were wild. Afraid of hurting her, Eli let her go.

Gretchel ran as fast as she could, away from the truck, away from the Wicked Garden.

When Eli caught up with her, she was in the cottage kitchen, drinking a glass of water. "What was that all about? Did you really not realize you were in the truck?"

"I didn't. No one but Grand Mama is supposed to go into the Wicked Garden. It's forbidden," she said, chugging more water.

Gretchel didn't realize that she was naked, filthy, and dripping wet until Eli wrapped a blanket around her.

"I don't understand what happened, Gretchel. I thought you were having a good trip. I'm so sorry."

Eli looked so scared and sad that Gretchel was quick to reassure him. "I *did* have a good trip. For a while, it was the most beautiful and real thing I have ever experienced," she said trying desperately to catch her breath. Then she walked to the bathroom and began furiously brushing her teeth. She could still taste dirt.

He watched her cautiously. "You were screaming again, Gretchel. Like you used to. I should have stayed awake and taken care of you. I'm so sorry."

"You were there. I heard you."

Eli held his head. "I *was* there. I dreamt that I saw you in a hole, and you couldn't get out. It's what woke me up this morning. What does that mean? I remember poppies and a hole. What were you doing there?"

Gretchel gave him an exaggerated shrug. "Maybe I have a death wish."

"Don't say that!" Eli couldn't help thinking about Gretchel's scars—the scars that she had inflicted on herself. He shuddered.

Gretchel changed the subject. "I have a horrible headache."

"That's not uncommon after a trip." Eli found some ancient aspirin in the medicine cabinet in the bathroom.

"The phoenix came to life, Eli."

He stared at Gretchel as he handed her the aspirin bottle. "The one from the painting?" She shook her head. "I saw it, too, in my dream. I watched you follow it. I don't remember everything, but I remember sailing, flying over the ocean, looking for you."

She smiled and touched his face. "Most of the trip was beautiful, Eli. And amazing. Do you remember being on the poppy?" He nodded and smiled back at her. Gretchel cleaned herself up a bit and got dressed. She called to Eli from the bedroom. "I'm ready for breakfast. Have you ever had biscuits and gravy?"

"Yeah, in Carbondale, at Mary Lou's."

"Ah," she replied, "But you've never had mine."

Gretchel zipped around her mother's kitchen like she was playing tag and the ghost was it. Eli sat quietly at the table, drinking his coffee.

"You still get up and run, Baby Girl?" her mother asked as she walked toward the coffee pot. Gretchel glanced at the clock; it was barely six in the morning.

"I do, Mama. I don't always run, but I rarely miss greeting the dawn." Her mother gave her a sad smile. "Besides, I have to get up early for my job," she said, and continued stirring the gravy.

"I'm so proud of you. You've come a long way,

Baby Girl."

"Stop it. You're embarrassing me."

Miss Poni slowly walked into the kitchen. "I thought I smelled sausage gravy."

"Eli never had it before he moved to Illinois, Grand Mama. Can you believe it?"

Miss Poni sat across from Eli at the table, and locked him in her gaze. Gretchel saw him squirm. "Grand Mama, please stop staring. He's taken," she said with a forced laugh.

Miss Poni turned her steely eyes on her granddaughter. "You opened a door last night."

Gretchel focused on the cast iron skillet in front of her. "Let it go, Grand Mama."

"Yes. I see that's what you're trying to do." The old woman paused for a moment, considering. "Just be careful, Baby Girl, you're messing with powers you can't control."

Gretchel spun away from the stove to glare at Miss Poni. "I said *let it go*."

Unperturbed, Miss Poni turned back to Eli. "Something very special happened last night." Eli choked on his coffee as he blushed an astonishing shade of violet-red.

Gretchel slapped a dishtowel against her leg. "*Let it go*, Grand Mama!"

The old woman ignored Gretchel's outburst. "Do you have something for her, Eli?" she asked.

"What do you mean?"

"Another gift. You have another gift for her, a very important gift," she said.

Eli sputtered. Miss Poni was undoubtedly the

most unnerving woman he had ever met—and that included his mother. "Well, yes.... If Gretchel wants it, I'd like to buy her a tattoo." Eli turned toward Gretchel. "The phoenix. It would look fantastic on your back, Gretchel. I'm sure Will can use the money, and I know he'd do a fantastic job. You've seen his work. He's really good."

"But that would cost a fortune."

"No." Ella was adamant. "No tattoo."

"Mama, I'm nineteen-years-old. And when have you ever been able to stop me from doing what I want, anyway?"

Ella gave her daughter the icicle eye. "Never, but that won't stop me from trying."

Miss Poni rejoined the conversation. "Are you sure there's nothing else you have for her?"

"Enough!" Gretchel shouted, slamming a casserole dish full of gravy in the middle of the table.

Miss Poni gave Gretchel a laconic glance before addressing Eli again. "Son, can you do an old woman a very small favor?"

"Of course. How can I help?" he asked.

Miss Poni pulled an old notebook from the pocket of her chenille robe and handed it to Eli. "The pages seem to be stuck together." Eli took the notebook and flipped through its pages with no trouble at all. All the women in the room—Gretchel, Ella, Miss Poni—watched him with curiosity. He began to feel foolish.

"Here you go, ma'am. It seems fine now," he said as he handed the notebook back to Gretchel's grandmother.

"I guess you had the magic touch," Miss Poni said with a smile.

CHAPTER SEVENTEEN

Oregon, 2010s

It had been a couple of weeks—long, slow, painful, weeks—since Ame had gotten in touch with Eli. He had stayed close to his computer anyway, just in case, stepping away occasionally to eat, use the toilet, and dip into his stash. He was well and truly stoned throughout most of this period, but he still retained enough self-awareness to realize that he was behaving in an obsessive manner. *Jesus,* he thought, *I've turned into my mother.*

He was pretty sure that he had scared Ame away. Every creepy thought he could imagine she might be thinking was rolling through his head. He was having trouble focusing on anything else. He knew he was projecting, but he also knew that he was probably right. He knew, furthermore, that his situation was getting kind of messed up. He hadn't been out of the house, or taken a call, or seen Rebecca while he waited to hear from Ame. The situation was… not cool.

So, one Saturday morning, he finally put down the one-hitter, shut down his laptop, and made the scenic, hour-long drive to his parents' place. The estate seemed quiet as he rolled up the long, meandering driveway. Of course, the estate *always* seemed quiet. Eli's parents were big into quiet.

"Eli!" his father called from the living room. Peter was perched on the coffee table, arranged in lotus position. "I was just thinking of you, and here you are. Our prince has returned."

Eli repressed a sigh and ran his hand through his hair as he tried to dispel some of the tension he could already feel constricting his head. *Why the coffee table?* After reciprocating a very enthusiastic embrace, Eli stepped back to take in his father's pink paisley bathrobe. "You look ridiculous, Peter."

"You don't say?" Peter gave his attire an appraising glance as if it was the first time he had seen it. "Well maybe I should just get rid of this silly thing, then," and with that, he dropped the bathrobe to reveal that he was wearing nothing underneath.

Eli had seen his father naked so often and in so many circumstances that he might have gotten used to it, but…. No. No, he hadn't. Eli picked up the discarded robe and held it out to his father with an imploring look.

Peter grinned, and resumed his pink paisley finery with a flourish. As he twirled, Eli got a fresh glimpse of his father's many tattoos, all various depictions of the Arcadian goat god Pan.

Peter claimed that he was a descendent of Pan, and Eli was convinced his father actually believed this. Which made sense, really, since Peter was the horniest person Eli had every met, and he was quite capable of causing panic among even the calmest of people.

Eli eyed the long growth of hair on his father's chin. "What's with the facial hair? You look like you're channeling Lane Staley."

"Was going for more of a ZZ Top thing, if I can hold out that long," Peter said itching the long, grayish, brown beard. "Think I can braid it yet?"

Eli shook his head—*no, no, no*—as he made his way to the dining room, where a Lego village stretched out from wall to wall. He knelt down, picked up a couple of pieces, added them to a building, and then turned back to his father. "How was Greece?"

"Magical, as always."

"Right. Stupid question. Is mom here?"

"You've actually caught her at home, son. It's a rare treat indeed. You know where she is."

They passed the first-floor bathroom as they walked toward the east side of the house, and Eli nearly gagged. "You ate Mexican last night, didn't you?"

"*Si, señor*, and I savored every last morsel," his father said with a devilish grin.

"I thought mom banned Mexican food."

"I enjoy breaking rules. Bring on the punishment, and I'll enjoy that, too."

"You might be enjoying your punishment, but I don't think Mom's enjoying *this*," Eli said as he sprinted down the hallway, stopping at a set of double doors.

He hadn't passed through this threshold in a long time, and he wasn't eager to do it now. *What am I doing here?* he asked himself. *I'm trying to escape my own obsession, and I'm walking right into hers.* He opened the doors anyway.

"Eli!" Diana called. She ran and hugged him, then backed up and on tiptoe slapped him on the side of the head.

"What the hell?" he yelped.

"*That*, son, was for screening calls from your mother. I've been trying to get in touch with you for two weeks! Answer your phone when I call, damn it."

Eli rubbed his head and collapsed on a sofa. He regarded his mother. She was dressed in black cigarette pants, a printed black and white silk blouse, and towering black heels. Dressed to the nines even at home—an obsessive perfectionist if ever there was one. "I'm much easier to track down than you are, Mother. I can't believe you're even here."

"I have been here for you anytime you've ever really needed me," Diana insisted as she scooted Eli's legs off the sofa to sit down next to him

"What about Dad? Don't you think he gets bored without you here?"

Peter roared with laughter. Diana cackled. "Darling, in our forty-two years together, I have never—and I mean *never*—known your father to be bored. *Really*, Eli."

"Perhaps Eli's too miserable to think clearly, Diana," his father laughed.

"You think my misery is funny?"

"A little, yes," Peter smiled, grabbed Eli's face, and gave him a big kiss on the forehead. "Lighten up, son."

Diana shook her head, still chuckling, "What brings you out of your seclusion today, Eli, and why the hell have you been hiding out anyway?"

Eli stammered, "Uh, I've just been busy."

Diana snorted. "That hardly seems plausible. What have you been doing—traveling, writing, taking photographs…?"

"Sure…. I've been…." *Damn it!* Eli realized that he had committed a grave tactical error. He was not a busy man, and his mother knew it. What *Eli* knew, however, was that, at the first mention of the Solstice Twins, Diana would forget everything else. "Say, Mom, can you explain these numbers to me?" He pointed to a dry erase board covered in numbers and notes.

Diana took the bait without hesitation.

"The thirteens follow a pattern. All the descendants of the twins that I've been able to trace were thirteen when they lost their fathers."

"You know Gretchel lost her father young," Eli said.

"And remind me again how old she was, Eli?" Diana bristled at any suggestion that Gretchel was part of the prophecy.

"I don't know."

"And her mother is alive, yes? And her grandmother, too?"

"They were seventeen years ago."

"Exactly. None of the women in this bloodline lived past the age of forty. Every one of them committed suicide by drowning. It would take an incredibly strong woman to break this kind of cycle. What was Gretchen's grandmother's name?"

"Her name is *Gretchel*, Mother, and they called her grandmother Miss Poni."

"Sounds like a hillbilly. And her mother's name?"

"Ella," Eli said quietly. "Her name is Ella." He descended into memory for a moment before he pulled himself out of it. "What does the twenty-one mean?"

"Surely you remember this from the prophecy, son. *Look to the twenty-first to find the second. Find her, and all shall be redeemed.* I'm certain that 'the twenty-first' refers to the twenty-first descendent, but it might also mean the twenty-first century. And the second, of course, is your true love."

Eli looked at his father and both men shared a dramatic eye-roll. Eli tried to avoid engaging with his mother when she mentioned this aspect of the prophecy, but he was feeling feisty. "Gretchel's birthday is June twenty-first, on the Summer Solstice," Eli said.

Diana looked at her son. "You never told me that."

"You never asked. You never cared about anything concerning Gretchel," he shot back.

Reluctantly, Diana when to the dry-erase board labeled *Gretchen.* Her name was written across the top in big letters, but there was very little written underneath. She jotted down this new information. Eli stepped up behind her, erased the N with his finger, and replaced it with an L. He returned to the couch.

"I never cared about Gretchen because the Cailleach specifically said that the second woman to wear the amethyst would be the descendant. Gretchen was the first, Eli, and she's not the one! I've told you this a million times. And she betrayed you! I don't want you to have anything to do with that woman. I won't have your heart broken again."

Eli looked to his father for support, but Peter was smiling at something no one else could see. "What are you doing?" Eli asked him. Peter didn't respond. He let out a chuckle, as his eyes followed some invisible delight. Eli shook his head in frustration.

"Mother, I've told you that Gretchel's family is Scottish, right?"

"That doesn't mean they are descendants. It will be the second woman to wear the amethyst, Eli!"

"Well, they were witches, too. Miss Poni had advanced magical skills. I saw her start a bonfire with a flick of her wrist."

Diana looked at him skeptically. "Were you stoned, Eli?"

"No, mother, I was *not* stoned." Eli rubbed the vein in his temple that was beginning to throb. He sounded like a teenager, he *knew* he sounded like a teenager, and he hated it. When the throbbing subsided somewhat, he managed a slightly more mature tone. "I saw that at Gretchel's nineteenth birthday party. Does that matter at all?" Diana turned her back to him, and, somewhat grudgingly, added a note below Gretchel's name. Eli could tell that she wasn't sure it *didn't* matter, and that she was slightly perturbed by that fact. He suppressed a triumphant grin, but just barely.

Eli stood up again. He went to the board that traced the descendants of the Solstice Twins from the 1600s—when the first twin had burned—as far as Diana had been able to trace them. He counted the names. There were only sixteen. "So, Miss Poni would be seventeen, Ella eighteen, Gretchel nineteen, and Ame twenty."

"Ame? Who the hell is Ame?"

"She's Gretchel's daughter."

His mother stared at him a moment.

"And how do you know that Gretchel gave birth to a daughter?"

Busted.

"I met her. Entirely by chance. We've chatted online a couple of times."

Diana was clearly torn between upbraiding her son for having any kind of contact—even vicarious contact—with Gretchel, and trying to figure out what, if anything, this new data meant. She couldn't resist the pull of the whiteboards. She scanned them for a full minute before saying, "Let it go, Eli. This Ame is irrelevant. Gretchen is not the one."

Eli felt rage stirring in his chest. "What, exactly, are you planning to do when I find this promised girl? What is your role in this mystery, anyway—besides playing pimp for your son?"

Diana let that last remark go. "Once you lead me to the second girl, I'll listen to her stories and try to help her and her family. I don't know exactly what's going to happen, but I do know the amethyst pendant is the key that will unlock a box, and that opening the box is the next step in ending the cycle of violence that has plagued the descendants of the Solstice Twins."

Eli wondered if his mother knew how absolutely insane she sounded. Doubtful. Both his parents lived in some kind of parallel universe. It was a wonder he wasn't in a padded cell by now.

"The amethyst isn't the key, honey love."

Eli and Diana had forgotten that Peter was even in the room, but there he was, curled up in the Eero Aarnio ball chair in the corner, lighting a bowl carved from a piece of stag's antler.

"What do you mean it isn't the key?" Diana's affection for Peter was limitless, but her patience with him was not, and the Solstice Twins were *her* territory.

"For a transpersonal psychologist, you have a pronounced tendency towards literalism, Diana." Peter smiled at his wife while she scowled at him. "But I truly believe that the key works figuratively. I'm not saying that the key isn't real. I'm just saying that the amethyst might not be a physical tool that opens a mechanical lock. Maybe it's a symbol, a sign, a metaphor...." Peter's voice trailed off as he took a hit.

Diana shook her head—once, decisively. "No. You're wrong. Carlin said the amethyst was the key. I heard it with my own ears. The amulet will open the box."

"What box?" Eli asked.

He was ignored.

"The amethyst may open the box, but it isn't a key like the one that unlocks our front door. I'm just looking at it from a different perspective."

"You don't know anything about this, Peter. I've been researching this for forty years. You've caused enough trouble by encouraging your son's useless, destructive hope." Diana turned to Eli, "And *you*, you leave that girl—that Ame—alone. Her mother ripped your heart out once, and she'll do it again if you let her."

So much for telling her I was thinking about flying to Illinois, Eli thought forlornly.

Diana grabbed her coffee cup and marched out the room. Father and son watched her go without saying a word until she slammed the door. Eli was surprised to note that her hands were shaking when she reached for her mug.

"Your mother's hitting the caffeine a little hard these days. She's a bit on edge," his father remarked. Given how high-strung Diana was *without* stimulants, that was really saying something.

"She's pissed now. Why did I even come?" Eli asked.

"Because you're still hopelessly in love with Gretchel, and you want your mother to back the fuck off so you can go after her," his father answered. "Did I come close?"

"Dad, is it wrong for me to still want her after all these years? Is there something wrong with me that I can't move on without her?"

Peter blew out smoke rings that danced around the sunlit room. Eli felt a stoned disquisition coming on. He eased into the sofa and made himself comfortable. This could take awhile.

"You saw yourself in Gretchel; that's what love is, son. You were drawn to her because, in her, you saw some aspect of yourself that you thought was missing. You're still trying to recapture that recognition. You don't think you'll be complete until you find her.

"But I'm not sure that's true, Eli. You're complete now and you always have been; you just don't recognize yourself anymore. Gretchel helped you see yourself and your true potential with open eyes. When you were with her, you were wide awake. When it ended, you fell into a deep sleep—metaphorically speaking. You've convinced yourself that getting her back is the only way to wake up again, even though you know that's not the case. Your upbringing might have been deficient in some respects—" Eli was shocked to hear this admission from either of his parents—"but, at the very least, you had a solid education in opening the doors of perception." Peter paused to relight his pipe. He offered it to Eli, who declined. Peter had access to weed of truly astonishing quality. The contact high was enough for his son. After an impossibly long inhalation, Peter continued.

"That said, I have to admit that there is no more joyful way to live a life knowing the self than being in love with a beautiful woman who fills up your world with vibrant light and truth. So, I say go after her. Devil may care. Let's say she breaks your heart again. So what?"

Peter paused again to make sure that he had his son's attention, and he looked more serious than Eli had ever seen him look. "But if she *is* going to break it again, son, make sure she does it in a way that makes you feel so utterly insane that just the shock of it wakes you up and makes you cry out for change. If she's going to break your heart, at least give it your all. Go in with open arms. Reach out and embrace the insanity. Dance in the flames of her desire. Run through the fields of her ecstasy. Go in like a beginner, as if you've just met her for the first time. Be a fearless child and ask to be taught. If she cries, cry with her. If she laughs, laugh with her. Jump up and down and shoot a million sparks out your ass. Let the sparks engage the wick of the explosive that will *wake you up*. Who cares if she breaks your heart again, if that pain turns your pitiful pining into action? What better way is there to know you're alive than to feel love and pain so deeply?"

Peter paused again. This time he availed himself of the opportunity to take another hit. "But what if she *doesn't* break your heart? It's quite possible she has an ongoing hard-on for you, too. Have you considered the possibility that she's waiting on you to finally grow a pair and chase her down the rabbit hole?"

Peter took one more draw on his pipe and blew out a few contemplative smoke rings. "I'm not saying I know the answer, because there isn't one. There are an infinite number of ways this scene could go down. But I *do* know this, Elliot: You have got to quit whining about Gretchel, because you're totally fucking up my flow."

Eli's heart swelled with tenderness. Peter was a flipped-out, eternal child who claimed to be friends with a fairy named Claire. He lived on the edge of a dream—and he was a genius. Now Eli knew why he had come back home. He needed this—this advice, but, more generally a dose of familiar insanity from his reliably crazy parents. What could be more comforting than listening to his pink-paisley-clad father talk metaphysics while smoke from the stickiest bud the Pacific Northwest had to offer scented the air? Eli felt like a kid again—but, this time, in a good way. He stretched out on the sofa and stuffed a pillow under his head.

"If I do find her, can I tell her who you are? Who I really am?"

"Devil may care, son. Let the FBI take me."

"The FBI doesn't give a rat's ass about you, Dad," Eli sighed. This conversation also had a soothingly well-worn quality. "You're an American institution, or you belong in one. In any case, your legend has surpassed your paranoia."

"Maybe. Ah, what does it matter anymore anyway? Devil may care." Peter stretched his legs and then rearranged himself in his cocoon-like chair. "You know, I fought the devil once, in the late 70's. I was on peyote. I pinned his scrawny ass to the ground and made him my bitch. You'd be surprised to know who the devil really is.

Not who you think. Not who you think at all. It would knock your Technicolor socks off to know that little nugget of truth, but you're not ready to face that epiphany. Not yet."

Eli had heard this anecdote before, too. It was practically the little brother he had never had. His thoughts, though, had turned to more immediate matters. "Mother is never going to agree to any of this, though."

"She's a protective thing. She thinks you're a gift from the gods, and she believes what Gretchel did was unnecessary."

"She doesn't have a fucking clue."

"Maybe not, but do you? Do you know why Gretchel broke your heart?"

Eli was speechless. He had never known, and he still didn't know.

Peter patted his son's knee and brought him back from the throes of self-pity. "If Gretchel's as smoking hot as you've always said she is, I may just come out of exile and shag her myself, you little pansy-ass mama's boy."

"That's not even remotely funny," Eli fumed.

His father cackled. "Jealousy doesn't become you, son. Detach yourself from ego. Manifesting a desire shouldn't be such hard work. Stop resisting."

Eli pulled a folded printout from his back pocket. "This is an old photo of Gretchel with her kids. Ame's almost seventeen now."

Peter looked closely at Gretchel. This was his first glimpse of the woman who had captivated and then devastated his son. *Hot damn,* he thought. Then he studied the little girl, and he grinned.

He pulled a bag of mushrooms from the pocket of

his pink paisley bathrobe. "Let's take a trip together, son, for old time's sake."

Eros who is love, handsomest among all
the immortals
who breaks the limbs' strength
who in all gods, in all human beings
overpowers the intelligence in the breast,
and all their shrewd planning....

Peter was lying on the floor, quoting Hesiod. Eli was still stretched out on the sofa.

He closed his eyes and tried to find a happy place before the psychedelic alkaloids kicked in....

Carbondale, 1990s

Eli thought back to Carbondale, of course. He drifted right into the backyard of the house on Pringle Street. The garden was all lit up. A feast of food and three kegs sat next to the greenhouse. Revelers where scattered about the backyard, celebrating the end of the summer.

This particular party was in Gretchel's honor. She was only a sophomore and school rules said that she had to move back to the dorms. Eli had already enrolled for the fall semester at SIU without his mother's permission. He tried not to think about Diana's impending fury as he watched Will hold a cute blonde upside down for a keg stand.

"So help me Jesus, Will. You're going to drown her," Patty yelled. She helped Will get the girl upright again, at which point the cute blonde spewed beer everywhere. Eli pulled a clean handkerchief from his back pocket and helped her dry herself off a bit. Excessively, drunkenly grateful, she leapt into Eli's arms, wrapped her legs around him, and tried to give him a kiss. When Eli resisted, she giggled and patted his curls instead. "Your hair's all bouncy," she laughed.

"Bouncy. What a great description," Gretchel said, taking her place beside Eli. He set the little sprite down as gently as he could, and she ran off to join her friends at a picnic table.

Gretchel shook her head at Eli playfully. "I can't leave you alone for two seconds. You're a chick magnet."

He grabbed her, buried his face in her neck, and shrouded himself in her beautiful red hair. She smelled, like always, of fresh strawberries. "Where have you been?"

"I had to lay down for a bit. I started feeling really sick, like I was gonna barf. Think I'm nervous about leaving."

"I don't know how I'm going to be able to sleep without you by my side every night," Eli said, but he was more worried about how she would sleep in a dorm room without him there to quiet the screams.

"I promise I'll be here every weekend, and some weeknights, depending on my work schedule."

"You don't have to work, Gretchel."

"Really?" she asked sarcastically. "You're *really* going to support me and pay for my education? Can you start paying back my student loans while you're at it? And I've *love* a new car...."

It was killing him to not be able to help her. He had the money, he had the time, he had everything. "I have some money saved. Whatever you need, I can give you. You don't have to work."

"You're silly." The anger in her voice was gone. "I'm a bottomless pit, Eli. Once I got started borrowing money from you, I wouldn't stop. I'd be spoiled, and you'd be broke in a month."

Not likely, he thought as he led her away from the keg. She was eyeing it way too much for his liking. After three months together, he had still never seen her drink, and he didn't want their last night in the house on Pringle to be the first.

"Who's that girl hanging around Will?" Gretchel asked. Eli noticed that Gretchel had become very protective all of the sudden. The girl was pretty, and looked like she had arrived via Grateful Dead caravan. As if she could tell that they were talking about her, she turned and made eye contact with Gretchel. Eli watched Gretchel jerk back.

"That's Ginnifer. She's moving into your room tomorrow," Eli said, still watching Gretchel's reaction to the girl's gaze.

Ginnifer returned Gretchel's puzzled stare with a calm smile. Silently, the two women seemed to come to some sort of understanding. Ginnifer waved and turned away.

"What was that all about?"

Gretchel turned back to Eli. "She's moving in my room?" Evidently, she wasn't interested in telling Eli what that was all about. "The owner doesn't waste any time does he?"

"How do you know it's a he?"

"I spoke to him on the phone when I called about the place in May. Wish I could meet him to say thank you. Staying here has been the best thing that's ever happened to me. *You* are the best thing that's ever happened to me."

Eli kissed her long and hard. He didn't want to let her go. There had to be some way to bend the housing rules. Maybe he could convince the powers that be that her nightmares were a mental handicap, and that she needed to stay off campus. It was a thought.

Gretchel and Eli came up for air just in time to see a local band start their second act. The crowd began to cheer.

Gretchel jumped up and began dancing, her bohemian dress twirling around and around. Eli was enchanted. He watched intently, unable to move his eyes away from the divine sight of Gretchel dancing freely against the light of the bonfire. She motioned for her loving cup on the ground. He picked it up, and held it out to her. Déjà vu struck him in the chest as she moved forward, took the cup, and sipped at the fresh water. He shook off the eerie feeling and joined her. They danced and danced and danced.

"I love you infinitely," Eli whispered into her ear. "Please don't ever forget that Gretchel."

She whispered to him, "I love you, too. Please don't ever forget that… that... that.... Eli... Eli... Eli..."

The memory was beginning to skip. He couldn't see her anymore, but he could feel her presence and her hand in his. The 'shrooms had kicked in—*way* in.

With her attitude in check and an aluminum bottle of water instead of coffee, Diana opened the doors of her office suite to find Peter naked, wrapped up in the drapes quoting Rimbaud:

…one evening I sat Beauty on my knees

And I found her bitter
And I reviled her.

Eli was spread out on the floor. "Not again," she mumbled to herself. "Eli. Eli. Eli," she called, and poked him in the side with the point of her Jimmy Choo.

...Eli...Eli...Eli...

"Way to go, Peter. Your son's a goner." She glanced behind her, and saw that her husband was now lying spread-eagle on the floor.

Before they took the mushrooms, Peter had put Phish on the turntable, and as the sound of the garage band in Carbondale drifted away, it was replaced with "Bouncing Around the Room." Eli could hear the music, but he felt like he was underwater. It was a pleasant feeling. Then it was as if two memories were merging into one. He was deep-sea diving—or was it deep-*see* diving? *What body of water am I in?* he wondered. He knew that Gretchel was drifting away, but, at this moment, he could sense her near him.

Then his head began to echo. His whole being was the echo.

Eli heard someone speaking. It was a woman. Was it Gretchel? Was she still there with him? He lifted his head, but couldn't open his eyes. He lay back down, releasing a little, bubbly chuckle. He gazed up through the depths and saw a group of redheads waving at him. He felt odd, but cheerful for the first time in a long time, and perhaps a bit like his hair—bouncy.

Peter saw Eli in his own hallucination, and thought: *Why in the hell is he laughing at all those skeletons? And why are they screaming to be set free?*

CHAPTER EIGHTEEN

Irvine, 2010s

It was Saturday night. Ame was working. Zach was with Ben at a hockey game in St. Louis. Gretchel and her kids had been packing, organizing, cleaning, and moving house for two weeks—all with the help of Ella, Marcus, and Cindy. Gretchel could hardly remember the last time she had been alone.

And now she was—inside and out.

She lay down on her bed, fresh from the shower, and let out a long overdue sigh. The voices had been just a murmur for the past six days. Now that Gretchel was fully awake and capable of feeling emotion, she was capable of feeling lonely. At least the noisy Scottish broads kept her company.

Old thoughts began rolling around in her head. The shower had been hot. She was sweating even though the temperature outside was subzero. She took off her robe and lay back down. The thoughts in her head started taking shape, and she began having feelings she hadn't felt in a long time. Lusty feelings.

Closing her eyes, she thought of Eli. It was painful. He was the only man that she would ever truly love. He was the only man that could bring out the life in her, revive the spirit that had been broken when she was teenager. He was the only man who had ever been her equal in so many ways. The only man she wanted to give herself to, for he had given her everything she had always wanted and needed.

But he was gone, and he was never coming back. That was the harsh reality. She had burnt that bridge a long time ago.

She thought of other men, other connections severed. She had patched things up with Devon, eventually, but that was over, too. There *was* someone else, though.... Not Eli—no one would ever be like Eli, ever—but she knew that this man from her past had never quite gotten over her. She could tell by the way he still looked at her.

He had sent her a dozen texts in the last two weeks, and she had ignored every one of them. Once upon a time, he had been one of the hired hands at Snyder Farms. He started working there when she was barely a teenager. He had turned into a handsome man, and—if memory served—he was a decent lay. Better than Troy, certainly, though Eli still had them both beat by a wide margin.

Quit thinking about Eli! she yelled at herself.

Her feelings were beginning to get the best of her.

Cast a spell, and he'll come a runnin', the Woman in Wool whispered sweetly.

"And suddenly you want to help me? I don't trust you. Go away," Gretchel said aloud.

Gretchel hadn't had sex in three years. Her body had healed from Troy's torture, but he had wanted nothing to do with her after that, and she would have beaten him off her if he had.

Cast a spell. The scared li'l rodent'll come, the Woman in Wool insisted.

"Oh, I'm sure he'll come, even if he is scared. As long as he's scared stiff, he'll do," Gretchel said aloud. As she laughed at her own dirty wit, she discovered that she was inclined to take the advice that had been offered her. What could it matter, really, if she called this man to her? She wasn't using him. She was just giving him what he wanted.

Gretchel wandered around the house, gathering what she could find for an attraction spell. It had been so long.... It occurred to her, as she rooted through drawers and looked in cupboards, that a text message would work just as well, but she didn't want to text. She wanted to do some magic. She wanted that at least as much as she wanted to get laid.

Once she was settled into the cottage, she would build a new stock of herbs and implements, but for now.... She found a pink birthday candle, a pack of matches, and a red Sharpie in the kitchen junk drawer, and a galvanized bucket in the basement. She knew she had a notebook on her bedside table, so she headed back upstairs.

Gretchel carried everything to her walk-in closet, the one place in this house that felt like her space. She surveyed her supplies with a critical eye: not exactly ideal for the type of magic she had in mind. She would just have to do her best with a powerful intent—and maybe some good lingerie.

She sorted through the clothes that hadn't been boxed up and carted off to the cottage, and settled on a pair of diaphanous black panties and matching bra. She decided to give her hair a blow-out, brushing it until it was a shining wave of flame-red flowing down her back. She found a lipstick she hadn't worn in ages—a brilliant matte red. *Now we're getting somewhere*, she thought. She still felt lust, but now that feeling was united with something else: a sense of power.

A fire began burning within her, but this was more than lust. It was control, and it felt odd and slightly unsettling. Paradoxical, even. She was preparing to exert her will over another human being, but, at the same time, as she moved into the spell work, she felt driven by a force beyond herself.

Gretchel grabbed a soap dish from the bathroom and took it to her closet. She lit a match, melted the bottom of the pink candle, and stuck it to the dish. Then she used the red marker to write two names on a piece of paper. She wrote the names three times, going over her writing again and again until they were a nearly-indecipherable blur of red. Then she lit the candle and held the paper over it while she chanted.

Light the flame,
Bright the fire,
Red is the color of my desire.

She held the burning paper until it almost singed her fingers, then she dropped it in the metal bucket. She focused all her intent on the tiny point of light. As it sputtered out, Gretchel felt her longing surge through her whole body and then fly out into the world, toward the man she wanted—or, at least, the man she wanted right now.

Gretchel took a deep breath, savoring the feeling of a spell well cast. Then she looked for something to wear while she waited.

The living room was dark and a little chilly. Gretchel thought about throwing a fleece jacket over the gray cashmere sweater she had put on, but that wasn't exactly the look she was going for. All the furniture was gone—given away or sold—so she simply stood by the window, looking out on the silent January night. She didn't expect to be waiting long.

Fifteen minutes passed.

Gretchel began to feel extremely cold and slightly impatient.

Be still, ye randy tart! He's comin'.

"Shut up," Gretchel muttered.

Then she heard a knock at the back door. She took her time answering it.

"Hey."

"Hey." His voice frosted the air. "Can we talk?" He couldn't help looking around to see if anyone had seen him.

Gretchel was well past caring what her neighbors might think about anything. "Sure." She moved aside to welcome him in, but not so far aside that he didn't have to brush against her as he entered.

He followed her from the kitchen to the living room. Gretchel could feel the invisible cord that had pulled him to her. It was a connection made of momentary need—nothing like the soul-deep union she had had with Eli—but it was real enough for now. She knew that, at this moment, he would follow her anywhere.

She turned to regard him. She saw him all the time, but she hadn't really *seen* him in years. She touched her neck, as she looked him over.

Tasty, one of the voices cackled appraisingly.

So tasty, Gretchel agreed internally.

He was looking her over, too, but he felt compelled to play the role of old family friend. "How are you? How are you doing? I've been worried about you."

"I'm sick of talking about how I'm doing," Gretchel said.

"Do you need anything?"

Gretchel looked around at the empty room and laughed a mirthless laugh. "I need *everything*."

He blew out a sad sigh, and Gretchel almost felt bad for laughing.

Enough. The spell had done its job, now she had to work her own magic. She tossed her flaming hair and stepped forward until her bare toes touched the tips of his boots. "Your wife..."

"...is in Kansas City," he answered.

Gretchel nodded, and began ascending the stairs.

"I have something that needs fixing. Can you help?"

He followed her. He would have followed her anywhere.

The Gretchel he had known—the wild Gretchel, the crazy Gretchel, the Gretchel he had loved—was back. He wanted her, just like he had always wanted her. He wanted to give her whatever she needed. *Oh God*, he prayed. *Let me fix what's broken, whatever it is, just let me fix it.*

Gretchel slid out of her leggings as soon as she reached the bedroom. Then she took off her sweater and let it drop to the floor. She turned to face him, her hands clasped behind her back. Moonlight glinted off her scars, which were just as awful as he remembered. Actually, they looked even worse now that she was so frightfully thin. He stepped into the room, kept walking until he was pressed against her.

"You don't miss him at all, do you?" he whispered in her ear.

"Who?"

He pushed her onto the bed. His forcefulness surprised him, but he felt driven by something he didn't understand and didn't care to question.

"We need to be together, Gretchel. I'll get a divorce," he said, assaulting her neck. "We'll move out of town, out of state. Let the secrets come out, we won't care, we'll be gone," he said burying his face between her breasts. "We'll take the kids—your kids, my kid.... I'll make it all good, Gretchel. Just give me the chance."

When he threw her to the bed, Gretchel knew that her spell had maybe worked a little too well. All that pent up power, all that suppressed energy.... She had unleashed it, and she was not going to be able to control what she had wrought.

Shut up, man. Now's no time for talkin' the Woman in Wool growled.

Gretchel's fingers worked at his fly.

"Run away with me, Baby Girl. I love you. I've always loved you."

"But I don't love you. Right now, though…" She found his hard cock and wrapped her hand around it. "Right now," she whispered in his ear, "Right now, I need you."

A guttural moan escaped his lips.

"Forgive me, Gretchel. Ask your gods to forgive me."

The Woman in Wool hissed.

"How dare you?" Gretchel screamed, flinching away from him.

She was hurled back in time, and she watched that night unfold in reverse order: the fire, the accident, the blood, the beating, the gun, the sex, the barn, the warning, the prediction. Then her memory moved into fast forward... and she saw headlights.

"That burden is mine to carry. This is my punishment, not yours." Her voice was a husky rasp in his ear. "Punish me."

He looked in her eyes, and it wasn't Gretchel he saw looking back at him—or at least it wasn't *just* Gretchel. He knew that she was no more in control than he was. "No."

"You coward," she hissed.

She got off on Troy beating her. She liked being punished, he thought. "No, Gretchel. No." He had felt compelled to go to Gretchel, and he hadn't fought it. But now he resisted.

"They're dead because of me. Punish me you, fucking coward. You left me there, you fucking coward!" she screamed.

He lost the power to fight her. She was pulling him into her madness, into their past.

He raised himself above her, and with a tear-streaked face, he cocked his hand back and smacked her hard. He hovered above her, a grown man crying desperate tears.

"I'm sorry," she said. "Thank you." Then she arched herself up against his rock hard member. He flipped her over, grabbed a handful of her hair, and rode her like he knew it was the last time.

CHAPTER NINETEEN

Oregon, 2010s

Eli was drunk. He hadn't meant for it happen. Rebecca drove him home, undressed him, and helped him into bed.

"I gotta pee," he said, pulling down his boxer shorts before he reached the bathroom. They fell around his ankles. He tripped and fell into the wall.

"Wait, wait, wait," Rebecca called, pulling the shorts out of the way, and letting him lean against her while she led him to the bathroom.

She turned her head while he did his thing. She leaned up against the wall, regretting the decision to get back together with him after his long period of being incommunicado. She thought a night out might cheer him up, might distract him from the weird funk he'd been in. She thought maybe he'd smoke some pot, or have a few drinks. She hadn't counted on this train wreck. She'd counted on his best friend, Andy, being able to talk some sense into him.

"All done. Would you be a doll and help me?" he

slurred. Rebecca shook her head in disgust.

"There's nothing worse than a drunk when you're sober," she mumbled as she helped him to his bed.

Rebecca undressed. It was past midnight and she resigned herself to staying the night. He wouldn't like seeing her there in the morning, but that was too damn bad. She was exhausted from babysitting him all night.

"She won't chat. Why won't she chat?" Eli asked.

"Who won't chat?" *It's happening*, Rebecca thought. *He's found someone else.* She knew it was inevitable, but she liked to pretend that they were a happy couple. She could pretend all she wanted, but, deep down, she knew she was just a replacement for the one that got away.

"Ame. Why did she come into my life and then just disappear? She's just like her mother. I don't get it. I just don't get it. Did I scare her away?"

"You're drunk, Eli. Go to sleep."

"She looks just like her mom. She looks just like her, Rebecca. You just wouldn't believe the similarity."

"I don't care, Eli. Go to sleep," she cried, tears sprouting at the corners of her eyes.

"Will warned me that Gretchel was crazy when she drank. But she loved me! I know she loved me!"

Rebecca couldn't take any more. She jumped out of bed and pulled on her clothes. "Enjoy your reminiscing, Eli."

"Buh-bye now, Becca," he replied.

Eli could hear her stomping through the house as she left. He sat up and yelled, "Don't let the door hit your ass on the way out." Then he collapsed on the bed, and began giggling hysterically. Then his laughter dissolved into a frustrated moan. "Why? Why?" he repeated until he drifted off to sleep, and saw the redhead peeking out of the shadows.

∞

Carbondale, 1990s

Gretchel had only called once the first week of school. She'd told Eli she was swamped: classes, homework, and her new job downtown. By the time she got back to the dorm at night she was too wiped out to come by, but she promised Eli she would be there on Saturday.

Saturday came and went. Sunday passed, and she hadn't called or answered his calls. Another week went by. After trying to catch her before and after class, before and after work, after trying to reach her by phone, he had given up the fight. He couldn't wait any longer.

He was at her dorm by 10:30 in the morning, the Saturday after her second week of classes. He marched down the hallway of the top floor and saw her roommate with a laundry basket. "Hey," he called, "is Gretchel in there?"

"Yeah, but she's sleeping," the girl said. "Thank god. The only time she doesn't freak out at night is when she's passed out drunk. I don't know how long I can take this."

The alcohol helps keep the nightmares away, too, Eli thought.

"I'd like to see her if you don't mind."

"No problem. I'm heading out anyway. Can you get her to clean up the puke? It's getting rancid in there." She opened the door, dropped the laundry on her bed, and left.

The smell hit Eli like a cloud of putrid regret. He made a mad dash to open the window and turn on a fan. Then he looked at Gretchel and the smell no longer mattered. His heart leapt at the sight. She was sprawled out on her stomach, diagonal across her bed, naked but for the white bikini underwear that made her backside look so tight and perfect that he was sure that, if he flipped a quarter against it, it would bounce back into his hand.

Gretchel's left arm was hanging off the bed, her fingers almost touching the vomit on the floor. Her hair was stringy and matted. It spread out around her like the flames of hell. The phoenix tattoo that stretched its wings across her back was vibrant against the paleness of her skin. If she weren't so pathetically passed out, he might have thought her body lying there, with the rays of midmorning drenching it with light, was the most beautiful thing he'd ever seen.

After cleaning up the vomit, Eli tried to wake her. She wouldn't budge, so he lay next to her, and watched her sleep. He had never seen this side of her. He fell asleep until it was afternoon. He woke when the phone rang. It was right next to Gretchel's head, but she didn't stir.

"Allow me," Eli mumbled, still half asleep. "Hello."

The other end of the line was silent for a moment, and Eli got a really bad feeling.

"Who the fuck is this?" an abrasive male voice inquired.

"Who the fuck is this?" Eli retorted.

"This is Troy Shea. Who is this, and why are you answering Gretchel's phone?"

Eli's heart dropped. The ex-boyfriend. "I'm her boyfriend, so I think that gives me a few privileges."

"Really? So you're the hippie that the dirty whore was trying to lie about."

"Don't you dare call her a whore."

"Well she is a whore, and if you could have seen her last night you would have known just how dirty she can..." Eli slammed down the phone. He began to shake. He tried to breathe—he tried to regain his composure—but there was a rage building inside of him, unlike anything he had ever felt.

"Gretchel, you have to wake up and talk to me." He reached for her shoulder and gave her a shake.

"Ouch," she moaned.

He had barely touched her. He looked at her, apprehension building, and then he gently turned her over. He gasped.

There were three circular burns at the edge of her old scars, and a new row of cuts—jagged and raw—alongside the cuts that had healed long ago.

"Gretchel, wake up," he yelled in her ear.

She jumped. "What?"

"Where in the hell did these burns come from?"

"Where am I?" she asked looking around the dorm room.

"Are you serious?"

She went to the bathroom, and when she returned, Eli studied her body. It looked as if she'd gained a few pounds. She wrapped a bandana around her head, and fought to zip up her old Levis with the Grateful Dead patch. She winced when her hand grazed one of the burns.

"Oh, crap! I'm late for work," she said.

"Gretchel, where did those burns come from? Did that Troy asshole do that to you?"

"I need water. I'm so thirsty," she said. She went to the mini fridge, pulled out a gallon jug, and put it to her lips.

"Where did the burns come from, Gretchel? Did you burn yourself or did Troy do it?" Eli demanded, becoming angrier by the second.

She slammed the jug down on her nightstand. "Troy did it. Yes, yes, yes. Troy did it. He found me last weekend, on The Strip. I went out, just for a couple of drinks with some old friends, and he was there. He was waiting for me to show up, and good old predictable alcoholic Gretchel was busted. One of his friends saw you and me together this summer and told him. He confronted me about it last night after he bought me all the beer I could drink and countless shots. He burnt the hell out of me with the cigarette lighter from his car until I confessed I was sleeping with you. Is that what you wanted to hear? Well, that's what happened. That's how I got the fucking burns."

Eli didn't know who this person was. Her eyes were wide and wicked, her face was tired and pale. She looked like she had run into the devil himself. Maybe she had.

"I'm calling the police."

"No!" She grabbed the phone out of his hand, slamming it back down on the nightstand. "This is none of your business. It's a waste of time anyway. His dad's a high-powered lawyer in Chicago. It'll only make things worse if you get involved."

"I'll take you away from here. He won't be able to

find you. Gretchel, I can keep you safe. I can put you through school. I can take care of you!"

"You need to leave, Eli. I have to get ready for work. And if Troy finds out you've been here, things will get worse. I know what he's capable of."

"He already knows I'm here. He just called."

"Shit!" She grabbed her head, and paced around the room in a manic flurry.

"I'm not afraid of him, Gretchel. You don't have to stay with me, but I'll be damned if this guy's going to hurt you again."

"*You. Have. To. Leave.*" She pushed him out of the dorm room. Eli stood in the hallway wondering what had just happened. Deep inside, he knew it was officially the beginning of the end.

∞

It was Halloween. Eli hadn't seen Gretchel in weeks. Teddy had agreed to come down to help talk some sense into her. As much as he dreaded being in Carbondale on Halloween again, Teddy made the trip to Pringle Street. Eli tried to convince Marcus to come too, but Cindy was about to give birth to their third child, and he wasn't leaving Irvine.

"Dude. I know this sucks, but you've got to move on. He's a predator, man. He's sucked her in but good, and here's the thing: Gretchel's the only one that can make the decision to get away from him." Will was sitting on the chronic couch with his arm around the new roommate, Ginnifer, who listened intently.

"I hate to admit it, but he's right, Eli," Patty

added.

"I can't stop trying."

"No, you can't. You're the best thing that's ever happened to her, and I won't sit around and watch Troy destroy her," Teddy said. "She does that just fine on her own."

"Why is she so self-destructive, Teddy? What happened to her?"

Teddy twitched nervously in his seat. "I'm bound to secrecy."

"Oh come on, man. This is her life were talking about," Eli cried.

"I'm sorry, but I won't betray her trust. I'll stay loyal to her until the end of my days."

Eli threw his hands in the air, and paced the living room. "Was he like this when she dated him last year? Did he abuse her?"

"I knew he was a monster the moment I first laid eyes on him, a year ago today exactly. He's sociopathic, and after what happened last winter...." Teddy started to get choked up.

"What happened last winter?"

Teddy shook his head. "I can't say."

Eli clenched his fists and seethed.

Patty shook her head, and spoke up, "Please don't take this the wrong way, Eli, but I think you're making it worse. She's a prize to him, and he's not going to let go of his trophy. Not to you, not to anyone. He's a rich little brat with nothing better to do. His parents probably sent him down to Southern Illinois to get rid of him. I know his type. He causes his parents a bunch of hell, and mommy can't tolerate his antics, so she ships him off to a school far enough away from her social circle that he can't be an embarrassment, yet he still gets a decent education. It's so predictable."

Eli paced, wishing he could tell Gretchel who he was. Then he could take her away. She could go to any school in the country, she could have anything she wanted. But it wasn't going to happen, and he couldn't turn to his mother for help. She was only giving him one semester in Carbondale as it was. He had to get this settled as quickly as possible before he lost Gretchel forever.

"We're going to find her tonight," Eli said. "We'll bring her back here before she gets drunk, and talk some sense into her." The plan was good in theory, but so was the bologna, peanut butter, and jalapeño sandwich Will had dreamed up the last time they were all stoned immaculate.

"Take my bong, baby," Will said to Ginnifer. "I have some frat ass to kick."

∞

The Strip was already packed with people when they arrived. Eli had no idea what he was thinking. He had a feeling there was going to be a fight, and he had little faith in his back-up.

The three men walked into one of the bars Gretchel frequented, and Eli could see her across the room. She was sitting against the wall with several girls, staring into space.

"Keep your eyes out for Troy. Here's money. Get some drinks and act cool," Eli said.

He struggled through the crowd. When Gretchel saw him, her eyes grew wide, and she quickly downed the rest of her drink. She walked toward the bathroom, and then quickly made her way to the front door and slipped out into the crowded night. Eli grabbed her arm gently, and pulled her down the street.

"What are you doing here, Eli? He's going to kill you."

"Let him try."

He stared into her bloodshot eyes, and Eli could see the pain of a million lifetimes swimming in the tears that were about to fall. "I miss you, Eli. I love you, and I'm sorry, but this is over. *We're* over."

"Don't tell me that."

"It's too complicated. I'm stuck and I can't get out."

"Yes, you can. All you have to do is take my hand and we'll walk away right now. Together," he said, putting his hand on her face.

"Things have changed, Eli. If I walk away from him he'll hurt me again, and.... I'm... he..." Gretchel choked back a sob. "I'm pregnant, Eli. I was pregnant all summer and didn't know. I can't risk him hurting the baby," she began to cry. "I can't lose another baby. I just can't."

Eli couldn't breathe. Gretchel was pregnant. She was pregnant with Troy's baby.

Gretchel blew out a tense sigh and the smell of the alcohol hit Eli like a fist.

"You're pregnant, and you're drinking?" he said through gritted teeth. "Are you crazy? If Troy doesn't kill the baby, you will. Are you out of your goddamn mind?"

Her tears came faster, and Eli's eyes began to water as well.

"I can't stop. I need it. Besides you, it's the only

thing that makes the pain go away," she cried. "Save me, Eli. Save me from Troy and save me from myself. Be my hero, Eli."

Eli was about to pull Gretchel into an embrace when he saw a look of terror on her face. He heard his name being called, and as he turned around, a sucker punch sent him straight to the ground. Several men, including Troy, were gazing down at him. Eli tried to get up, but Troy kicked him in the face.

He caught a glimpse of Will throwing punches before he had to dodge another kick from Troy.

"Somebody help him!" Gretchel screamed out into the crowd. Then Teddy appeared from nowhere. His fist barely connected, but it was enough to throw Troy off balance. Eli just avoided another shoe to the head, and grabbed at Troy's feet. He pulled him down, but it didn't take long for Troy's friends to incapacitate Eli.

Teddy pulled Gretchel aside, away from the melee. A couple of guys were holding Will back, though he fought as hard as he could to free himself. Eli was still being held down as Troy proceeded to beat him ruthlessly.

Within moments, cop cars were sounding off, and then an ambulance. "No!" Gretchel screamed and clutched her head in agony. Teddy was still holding her, trying to cover her ears.

Troy's friends had scattered. Will was kneeling beside Eli, who, in the worst pain he'd ever felt in his life, rolled his head around on the ground and saw Gretchel screaming for him, and trying to fight off Troy. Teddy tried to push him away, but Troy shoved him to the ground. Eli could only watch as Troy grabbed Gretchel by the back of the neck and directed her down the sidewalk.

Eli flipped himself over, and tried to claw his way after them, but the paramedics interrupted his pathetic rescue mission, and the fight was over only moments after it had begun.

CHAPTER TWENTY

Irvine, 2010s

It was Ame's first afternoon off in forever, and where did she decide to go? Work, of course. She could live without a lot of things, but Internet access was not one of them. She had a term paper due the following week, and she needed the net's infinite resources. So, to the bookstore she went.

Even though it was the weekend, Ame had been up for hours by the time she packed up her laptop and headed out. She was an early riser like her mother. She cherished the calm and the quiet. In the morning, Ame had time to be still. She had time to pray to the Wild Mother and her beloved Horned God. After praying, she knew without a doubt that she would not make the same mistakes her mother had.

Those moments of serenity were a necessary relief from the rest of her day. Ame was a seriously overbooked teenager. There was school, where she took honor classes in everything. She worked at the bookstore Monday, Wednesday, and Friday. Volleyball practice was Tuesdays and Thursdays, with tournaments every other Saturday and Sunday. And, when she wasn't at a tournament, she was on college volleyball recruitment trips with Teddy and Marcus.

During Ame's job interview, Claire had raised a dark, perfectly-shaped eyebrow when Ame described her volleyball schedule. "You must be quite passionate about your sport to devote so much time to it."

Usually, Ame faked the role of a die-hard team-player, but, for some reason, she felt like she could be—or *had* to be—honest with Claire. "I'm six-foot-three and freakishly athletic. I was born to play volleyball, and I'm going to need a scholarship if I want to go to college."

Troy had never wanted her to succeed at anything, and her mother was naïve to think that he would help a daughter he loathed. Even before the revelation about her drained college fund, Ame had known that she was essentially on her own. She had always known that.

"Well, Ame, what *are* you passionate about? What do you want?"

Once again, she felt compelled to tell Claire the truth. "I want to work on the family farm and grow a garden with my mother and can the vegetables we grow. I want to ride my horse. I want to dance under the moonlight. I want time to read and write and just think. I want to learn the old ways—everything my grandmother and my great-grandmother can teach me, but I think there's a lot I need to learn on my own, too. That's why I'm here. That's why I want this job."

Claire had found this answer satisfactory, and she had been pleased with Ame's work, which is why Ame was free to make use of the store's Wi-Fi connection on her day off.

Ame was thinking back to everything she had told Claire at her job interview as she pulled a thermos of coffee and her decrepit laptop from her backpack and settled into the Barcelona chair in the back office. The move from the house to the cottage would definitely help her achieve some of her goals, but she couldn't slack off on school or volleyball. College was a must. She was never going to be dependent on a man like her mother had been, and she was never going to be any man's victim. She had met the predator in her dreams, but she refused to be his prey.

She sighed. Even if she were living at Snyder Farms, she probably wouldn't have much time to take advantage of it. She hadn't even been able to find time to see Peyton for a couple of weeks. She barely had time to respond to his texts and messages. She definitely wasn't going to find time to dance under the moonlight.

Peyton. He was a sweet guy. Smart. Strong. Incredibly hot. She had met him on a trip to SIU. Ame gave herself a minute to check out his Facebook profile before she got down to research.

She noticed that she had nine messages waiting for her on Facebook. She smiled, until she realized that they were all from Eli. Before she had a chance to look at them, there he was, ready to chat.

Ame. Please forgive me for being such a pest. How is your mother?

Hi Eli with an I. Wow. Jeez. Sry I haven't been online. My dad left us in a bit of a financial mess when he kicked it. No internet access. We had to move to a little cottage on my great grand mama's property. I love it; my brother hates it. Mom is losing touch w/ reality & it's all just a big f'ing mess.

The cottage will be good for her. How is she behaving?

She talks 2 herself a lot & dnt even get me started on the nightmares. I haven't had a decent nite sleep in almost 2 months. Have u been 2 the cottage?

Yes, I've been to the cottage. When I met her she was having nightmares quite often. You make it sound as if it's something new.

I've never known her 2 have nightmares. It started New Year's Eve, the nite before my dad died.

What the hell? Eli thought.

Does she need money? Please be honest with me.

Well of course she needs money. She's not working.

I can send you whatever you need.

Ame sat back, sipped at her coffee, and considered this new information. This guy was too good to be true, and Ame knew that anything too good to be true was almost certainly a lie.

What's your motive Eli with an I? What exactly r u tryin 2 do here?

I just want to ease her burden. I can send you a couple grand to start.

We'll talk college another time. It would be my honor to finance your education, anywhere you want to go.

U don't even know me. Why did u and my mom break up? What happened that she chose a d-bag like my dad over u?

She waited for an answer. She waited a long time. Finally a response popped up on the screen.

She was pregnant with another man's child. That child was you. I had every intention of raising you as my own. Things got very complicated. That's all I can say.

Ame was perfectly still, her mouth wide open, a mug of coffee in one hand, the other hand resting on the keyboard. She looked like a sculpture of the Great Coffee Bean Goddess of the Twenty-first Century. She was contemplating what her life might have been like if she had been raised by a father who wanted her, a father who loved her.

Give me ur phone #. I can't take ur money, but I do want to kno more.

DON'T TELL HER WE'RE TALKING!

What r u afraid of Eli with an I? My dad's dead.

It's complicated Ame with an E.

Look I have to meet my family for dinner in an hour & do research on a term paper b4 then, but ur going 2 start explaining things or I WILL go 2 her.

Give me a mailing address and your phone number, and I'll tell you what I can.

∞

Ame couldn't concentrate on her research. She gave up, and drove to the local Mexican restaurant to wait for dinner. She was sitting on a bench out front when her phone chirped. It was a text from Eli. He was sending a package—next day air—to the cottage.

"If he turns out to be an ax murderer, I'm fucked," she mumbled. She didn't have time to respond to his text, before she saw her uncle Marcus walking across the parking lot.

"Are the grandwitches bringing Mom?" she asked.

"Yeah. Cindy and Holly are picking up Zach. They'll all be here shortly," he said. He sat down and put an arm around her cold shoulders. "How's it going?" he asked.

"Okay," she shrugged. "I'm just really busy. I feel like I should be spending more time with Mom. Zach's been staying at the Browns' every night because of her nightmares. I just feel like we leave her alone too much."

"Those damn nightmares. I thought they were over," Marcus said under his breath.

"What do you mean by that?"

"She used to have them all the time when she was younger. Post-traumatic stress," he explained.

"Why don't I know any of this?" she asked. "Do you think Dad dying set her off again?"

"No, I'm pretty sure it happened a little before then. She's had a hard life, Ame. If she starts acting strange—and you'll know what I mean when you see it—please tell me. It's absolutely crucial that you tell me."

"What happened to her, Uncle M? I know your dad was killed in the truck accident and Mama was in the truck when it happened. No one ever talks about it, though. What happened and why is it a big secret?"

"It's a long story, and I'm not at liberty to elaborate."

"You know I haven't had the easiest life either, but I'm not insane because of it."

"No one said you've had it easy. We all tried to get your mom away from Troy. Hell, I spent a week in jail when you were just a baby, because he beat your mom up and then I proceeded to beat the shit out of him. But she never left him. We tried, Ame, but you cannot help somebody who doesn't want to be helped. She blames herself for things that are beyond her control." Marcus thought for a moment, deciding what to say next. "She doesn't like herself all that much, in case you haven't noticed."

Ame nodded. She'd noticed.

"Did you know an Eli?" she asked.

A shocked expression erupted on Marcus's face, then he eyeballed his niece suspiciously. "How do you know about Eli?"

"Long story, and I'm not at liberty to elaborate," she smirked. "Was he a nice guy?"

"He was a great guy. He was the best thing that ever happened to Baby Girl."

"He was a *happening?* Why didn't they stay together?"

"Troy. He manipulated and controlled your mother. She was in love with Eli, and he was good to her."

"That just doesn't make any sense."

"What doesn't make sense?" Gretchel asked. She was walking toward the restaurant with her mother, grandmother, and assorted relations.

Miss Poni gave her great-granddaughter a sly grin, as if she could read the girl's mind.

"Nothing," Ame said. She sighed and Marcus rubbed her back again.

"Well, are you coming?" Gretchel asked.

Ame glared at her mother. "No, I'm just breathing hard."

Marcus turned his head and spewed out uncontrollable chuckles.

Gretchel just shook her head. "Shameful. Let's go, birthday girl."

CHAPTER TWENTY-ONE

Oregon, 2010s

Eli was glad to have something to do. After mailing a money order, he drove home in silence. It was a long drive back to his house in the woods. He didn't mind, because it gave him time to think. He remembered another long drive, a drive from Carbondale to the cottage.

∞

Carbondale, 1990s

Eli had tried to contain his sense of urgency, but the speed limit on the two-lane highway that took him to Irvine was more than he could handle. As soon as the officer who had issued his ticket was out of sight, Eli was racing down the road again.

It was Thanksgiving break. Eli had been packed and ready to leave for Oregon when he got a call. Teddy explained that Gretchel had taken a train to Irvine to see her newborn niece Holly, and to tell her mother that she was pregnant. Gretchel was at the cottage, alone. Troy hadn't gone with her to break the news. This was Eli's last chance, and he wasn't going to miss it.

By the time Eli arrived at the cottage, it was nightfall. He could see lights on inside, but there was no answer at the door. As he paced around the cottage, he saw a figure moving near the lake. He took off in a dead run.

"Gretchel!" he yelled. The figure moved more quickly "Stop running from me! I'm not the one you should be running from!"

Eli didn't give up. He sprinted toward Gretchel, and she finally stopped. When he caught up with her, she closed her eyes and wiped tears away. He pulled her to him and caressed her back. He could feel the swell of her belly against his body, and it filled him with a hopeless joy.

"I'm not running from you," she whispered.

"The hell you're not."

"I want to be with you, Eli, I do. I want you more than anything in this world. Almost…" she corrected.

"Almost?"

"I want redemption more. I have to pay my debt. Troy is my punishment. I have to go with him. This is how it's supposed to be. I have to let you go. It's my punishment," she rambled. She was making no sense to Eli. If she only knew that she was the girl in his mother's prophecy. If he could only tell her they were meant to be together.

"We're heading to Chicago for Thanksgiving. I'm meeting Troy's parents and we're going to finally tell them about the baby. We'll probably transfer to a school up there. He keeps telling me to stop worrying, but I have a really bad feeling in the pit of my stomach."

"You *should* have a really bad feeling, Gretchel. That's

your intuition telling you to run for your life. Are you insane?"

She smacked him hard across the face. He backed up, shocked.

"Yes, as a matter of fact. You have no idea what kind of person I really am, Eli. I'm no good. I never have been. I've been rotten since the day I was born, and I've never changed. I cause people pain no matter what I do. I can't fight it anymore. Troy is my fate."

"Why would you say these things?"

"Because I'm a wicked little witch who doesn't deserve any better," she said and stormed off past the lake.

"Don't do this. I don't care what kind of issues you have, Gretchel. You said it yourself: I heal you. And I can't live without you because you bring out the best in me. We bring out the best in each other. You make me want to get up in the morning and live. You inspire me to go deeper, to love deeper, and feel deeper. And I know I do the same for you. I don't care what you've done in your life, because I know there's nothing that can't be forgiven, but you have to learn to forgive yourself. You're my goddess, Gretchel Bloome. I can't sit back and watch you do this to yourself."

"You don't have time for me to get better, Eli."

"Baby, I've got all the time in the world for you. I'll wait. Come away with me. I'll take care of you. I have the resources, Gretchel. We can get you well, but you have to give me the chance."

She closed her eyes and shook her head back and forth. "How are you going to take care of me when you're struggling to get through school, too? Are your parents going to foot the bill? You know, your controlling mother and the lunatic father you've told me so much about?" Now she was angry and sarcastic. "I'm sure your father and I would get along quite well, since he's crazy and all."

"You *would* get along well, Gretchel, and I mean that in a positive way. Look, I haven't been honest about who I am, and there's a good reason for it. I can't tell you about my father—you'll have to meet him yourself—but I can tell you that my mother and my grandparents have powerful resources that can help you."

"You're lying," she said and darted off down a worn four-wheeler path in the woods.

He grabbed her, they fell to the ground, and he held her there. "Please stop running from me. I'm not the one who's going to hurt you. If you stay with Troy, he's going to keep abusing you. He could kill you. Is that what you want? Do you really have a death wish?"

"Maybe," she said and finally stopped fighting him. She tucked her legs underneath her on the dirty path and cried into her hands.

"What about the baby?" Eli whispered, and tears began falling from his face. Gretchel began to sob. He wrapped his arms around her. "Let's go to Oregon, or we can even stay in Irvine if you want, but let's raise this baby together. I'll treat it like it's my own. I swear to you, I will love you both until the day I die."

She slowly pulled herself back, then touched the spot on the edge of his face where stitches had been sewn only weeks before. He reached up with his mouth and kissed the inside of her wrist. She shuddered, and then she put both hands on his face. He drew her in and kissed her fully. She finally pulled back. He studied her face as she looked over his shoulder into the woods. Then she grabbed at her head and howled in pain as she ran back to the cottage.

Eli took his time walking back. He could taste the alcohol in her kiss. In addition to being sad and confused, he was also pissed beyond belief.

When he got to the cottage, he found Gretchel huddled in the corner of the master bedroom, her hands on her ears, rocking back and forth. He wanted to reprimand her for drinking, but he bit his tongue. Instead he bent down and wrapped his arms around her. He didn't force anything. He just held her.

"You make the voices go away better than the booze," she whispered.

"The voices?"

"The ones in my head, especially the angry one. She yells at me, tells me what a no-good, worthless whore I am."

Eli looked up at the ceiling. He needed his grandmother, and he needed her badly. He wasn't qualified to doctor the little girl inside this woman. The only thing he was capable of doing was listening to her and loving her unconditionally. He said a silent prayer asking for guidance, then did the best he could.

"Gretchel do you see things?" he asked. She nodded her head yes. "Have you been seeing the ghosts again?"

"Yes," she whispered through a sob. "And sometimes I see animals—animals that nobody else can see. I've seen them since the accident. Sometimes it's worse than others. Right now it's really bad."

"What kind of animals?" he asked. She didn't answer. He pulled himself away from her, and reached out a hand.

She let him pull her up, and he laid her on the bed and snuggled up next to her.

"A wolf mainly, and lots of deer," she finally answered, "Sometimes I see a snake and a massive stag," she continued. "Since I've been pregnant I keep seeing a white horse beckoning me in my dreams and a black horse in my nightmares," she said, and nestled her head on his chest.

"Do they mean anything to you?"

"It seems like they should, like I already understand, but at the same time I don't."

"Do you think they have anything to do with the truck and the Wicked Garden?" he asked.

She nodded again. He tried to process this information. "Gretchel," he started as tenderly as he could, "is Troy the first man to hit you?"

She shook her head no.

CHAPTER TWENTY-TWO

Oregon, 2010s

Eli stood, staring at his suitcases, still not sure about whether or not he was going to load them into his trunk. It was the last week in March. Ame had sent him a message thanking him for the package he'd sent, but he hadn't heard a word from her since.

Going to see Rebecca had not helped. Not at all. She had chewed him out about the night he'd gotten drunk and started talking about another woman. It was pretty clear that their relationship—such as it was—was finished, so Eli had left without staying the whole weekend, and they both knew he wouldn't be coming back.

Spending time with his friends hadn't done him a whole lot of good, either. Rappelling down mountains, camping in the wilderness, going to shows, getting baked on the beach—none of it was sufficiently distracting anymore. Not even the thought of sailing—once his greatest passion—could pull him out of his renewed obsession with Gretchel.

He thought about taking the suitcases back inside,

unpacking them, and getting on with the rest of his life… But he just couldn't. His chance encounter with Ame gave him hope that he would see Gretchel again, and everything he had learned since that first conversation in a hotel elevator assured him that Gretchel needed him. He was ready to go, as soon as the time was right.

In the meantime, he really needed to get his shit together.

Eli was reading—trying very hard to avoid both Facebook and weed—when he heard a knock at the glass door that led to the patio. It was Andy, Jim, and Rick. Eli sighed and walked, reluctantly, into the evening air to greet them. Andy sat a cooler on the patio and handed Eli a bottle of beer.

"You're really starting to creep us out, man," Rick said. "What the hell's going on?"

Eli took the beer, twisted off the top and, with the cap between his thumb and middle finger, he snapped it across the patio, directly into a zinc bucket already half-filled with bottle caps.

"He's still got it," Jim said, attempting the same thing, but watching his cap take a wrong turn, ricochet off the house, and come back to hit him in the leg.

"I'm just like my mother. I'm obsessed. I can't for the life of me get Gretchel out of my head."

"Well, this was going to be an intervention. Guess you're not in denial, so what next. Andy?" Rick asked.

Andy glanced at his best friend. Eli had been there for him through everything. He was the best man at his wedding, the first one to visit after they brought both kids home from the hospital. Hell, Eli was his kids' favorite babysitter, and he had provided all kinds of money and resources for Andy's disabled daughter. When Andy was determined that he could start an olive farm in the Pacific Northwest, Eli had gone in as a partner. And he wasn't just a financial backer, either. Eli had worked as hard as anybody to make sure the farm was a success. Andy was indebted to his friend, and he knew that his friend would never ask for or expect any kind of repayment.

Andy tipped back his own beer, but he had nothing to say.

"So, why did she leave you hanging in the first place? Did she have daddy issues or something?" Jim asked.

Eli thought about the truck that sat in the Wicked Garden. "Yeah, I'm pretty sure she has some serious daddy issues." He took a long pull of his beer.

"Ought to go well with your mommy issues," Rick mumbled, and Jim snickered, spraying beer involuntarily.

Eli chuckled, too. He knew it was the truth.

"You know, there's a gaggle of women from here to Portland waiting for you to ditch Rebecca."

"I already did."

"Thank god. She wasn't your type, dude," Jim said. "What's Gretchel look like?"

Eli pulled out his wallet, and showed his friends the picture of Gretchel with her kids.

"Holy hell," Jim whispered.

"Good god almighty," Rick agreed.

Eli looked to his best friend for answers. Andy took another drink of beer while he considered what he should say. He had no right to not tell Eli what he really thought. It would be selfish. He had to do it.

"Go," Andy said.

"What?"

"Get the hell out of here, Eli. Why are you still here? *Why are you still here?*"

Eli shrugged his shoulders. "My mother."

All three men face-palmed in unison.

"Look. Eli, everyone knows Diana could make a lumberjack piss down his leg with just a glare, but this is your life, man. You've got to do what you've got to do. Go to Illinois."

∞

Eli had the blessing of his friends. It still wasn't enough to convince him to leave. So, he made a call to the maniacal genius who would give him the final push.

"Is Mom in the house?"

"Yes, sweet boy, but she's sleeping. What's on your mind?"

"Dad," Eli began clenching his fist, "Gretchel's husband is dead. I've been communicating with her teenage daughter through Facebook, but I haven't heard from her in weeks. They're living at her family's cottage."

"The dirtbag's dead?" Peter asked.

"Yes."

"You know where Gretchel is, and haven't gone to see her yet?"

"No."

"What kind of pussy are you?" Peter bellowed into the phone.

"But Mom..."

"Cut the cord already, Oedipus. You're almost

forty years old. Oh, for the love of all that is orgasmically grown. How long do you want to live like this, Eli? Because you're the one that makes that call, not some fucking prophecy. I love your mother, son, but we've never seen eye to eye on this 'second love' issue. If there is such a thing as fate, I'll tell you one thing for sure, its only job is to set the pattern; it's your job to make the choices of how you will arrive. To your mother, you'll always be those fluttering swallows in her belly, the sweet baby that she had to protect from the world. But you're a grown man, Eli. Go out and live your life! I'm driving to your house tomorrow, and if you're still there I will personally kick your ass from here to Timbuktu, which is an interesting enough place to visit, but I'd think you'd much rather be in Illinois."

"Are you done?" Eli asked.

"Oh, I'm just getting started, son. You are an abomination before the god of love."

"I'm just waiting for Gretchel's daughter to let me know it's all right to come. I haven't heard anything from her in weeks."

"You're waiting on a teenage girl to give you permission to live? Are you serious? Go out into the woods of Illinois and make life happen, Eli. Get your ass off the sidelines, and dive head first into the abyss. Life is malleable, son. What do you have to lose?"

Just my mother's trust, love and respect, he thought.

CHAPTER TWENTY-THREE

Irvine, 2010s

Gretchel was bored. It was the first of April, and she was hoping someone—anyone—was planning a joke. Maybe boredom was the April Fools' gag the universe had in store for her. She hoped not. Boredom was dangerous for a recovering alcoholic—or a not-quite-recovering crazy lady.

She'd already done all the laundry, cleaned the cottage from top to bottom, mapped out a garden on paper, and planted what she could. She had paid bills, balanced the checkbook, and tried not to faint when she saw what was left in the bank. She had piled up the trash for Ame to burn, tried to start the mower (unsuccessfully), washed down patio furniture, repainted two Adirondack chairs sage green to match the cottage, filled bird feeders, mulched every flower bed around the property, and trimmed the hedges. She had organized her closet (twice), brought in firewood, and planned meals for the next month. She practiced some spells and she sewed an intricately detailed dress—the first time she had sewn in ages. She finished turning the nursery off the master bedroom into a studio, and she tried to paint.

She tried, but she wasn't ready. She was far from ready.

Maybe she'd call Teddy. No. He was swamped at the salon. Cindy? No. She was busy helping Marcus in the fields. Maybe she could help with the farming. No. She needed a job, but working on the farm would be her last resort.

She paced the living room, and Suzy-Q–who hadn't left her side since she returned to Snyder Farms—paced with her. Gretchel stared up at the buck on the cottage wall. She remembered the covenant she used to renew with him every year. She laughed to herself. It had been ages since the thought even crossed her mind. Maybe it was time to renew the agreement. It was April Fools' Day after all, and she was definitely a fool.

Instead, she plopped herself down into the big storybook chair. Suzy-Q settled on the floor next to her. Solitude made her anxious, and she certainly didn't want to be left to her own thoughts, since her thoughts did not tend towards the placid or the happy. When she was busy, she was able to keep her worst thoughts at bay, which also meant that the voices were mostly silent.

There was more to her sense of unease than her fear of bad thoughts and the voices they conjured, though. She felt like she was waiting for something, but she didn't know what.

"I can't take this," she said to the buck.

The silence became overwhelming, and she gasped for breath as if she were resurfacing from a deep pool of water. She clutched her heart, and realized for the umpteenth time that the amethyst was gone.

What had it done to her? *It saved me*, she thought. But it also numbed her in a way that was unexplainable, and she was still ambivalent about feeling again. She was a girl that had felt too much. As a child she had felt everything; she could read a room in seconds and know just what was about to take place just by the aura the inhabitants gave off. Maybe it was safer not to feel. Yes, it was safer, but it made her whole life meaningless.

She thought about the man she had conjured with her spell, and she shuddered. That had been a mistake. He had called again just that morning, but she was determined to keep ignoring him.

Two hours after that screened call, Gretchel had taken delivery of a dozen white roses. She stared at them as they sat on the dining table, wishing that they had been from Eli. They could paint them red together. She smiled. Then she thought of the man in town again.

She stared up at the buck. "What am I going to do with myself? How am I going to survive without a hero or a magic jewel around my neck? I don't think I'm going to make it this time," she told the inanimate object. "Please give me a sign. Show me that this punishment is almost over."

Nothing. The buck remained quiet. Did she really expect him to talk to her? Maybe? She *was* crazy, after all. She sunk deeper into the chair, and something dug into her backside. She sat and up pulled a book from between the seat cushion and the back of the chair. A gasp escaped her lips. It was the Graham Duncan book Eli had given her on her nineteenth birthday. She thought she had lost it long ago. Gretchel smiled at the buck and whispered, "Thank you."

Graham Duncan's books had changed the way she saw the world. It was as if the author knew her, as if he could reach inside her mind and pull out wisdom and insights that had always been there, if only she could have seen them for herself.

She flipped through *Hermes In Heat*, and saw a passage that she had underlined. *What is it you really want, and what illusion are you willing to sacrifice to claim it? Chew on that for a while.*

Gretchel felt goose bumps rise on her arms. She eased back into the big, comfy chair, and she began to read.

CHAPTER TWENTY-FOUR

Irvine, 2010s

Across town, in a tidy and secure subdivision, Ame and Holly sat in the Brown family's driveway.

"I'm always waiting on this little shit," Ame told her cousin. "Come on already. I don't have time for this." She honked the horn, and then she saw Zach motioning for one more minute from a second-floor window.

"Ame, can I tell you something?" Holly asked.

"What's wrong?" Ame panicked. This was *not* the kind of thing she liked hearing from her slightly psychic cousin.

"I've had a bad feeling all day. Something's going to happen."

"What is it? Tell me," Ame insisted.

"Whit's fur ye'll no go by ye," Holly whispered.

Ame was speechless. She'd heard Holly spout out predictions, but she had never heard her speak gibberish.

"What the hell does that mean?"

"I don't know, exactly. I've heard Miss Poni say it, but I've never quite understood it. I keep hearing it, though, in my head. And I can't see what's going to happen—I can only feel it. It's something big."

"What *are* you talking about?"

"I don't know," Holly whispered in frustration. She turned to her cousin. "I'm sorry."

"No sweat. Now, if you had the answers to next week's physics test and you suddenly went blank, well, then I'd be irritated."

Holly chuckled.

Ame turned on the dome light and started digging around in her backpack. She pulled out a book and handed it to her cousin.

"You got the new Graham Duncan!" Holly said, eyes lighting up.

"The day it came out. I'll get it to you when I'm done. Shouldn't take long."

"I'll buy my own, thanks," Holly beamed. "He's my hero. He's a hero to anybody who rejects mediocrity."

"Yes, but you've missed his whole philosophy. *You're* supposed to be your own hero, Holly."

Holly thought for a moment. "Yes, Ame. You're right. That *is* his point."

"Chew on that for a while," they both said simultaneously, and laughed.

Then a knock at the window nearly sent Ame flying into the back seat. She turned to see Cody staring at her.

"Stalk much, Brown?" she snapped.

"Sorry. Hey, Holly. How's your mom doing, Ame?"

Ame grimaced. She was sick of answering this question. "She's nuts. She talks to herself all the time, and the nightmares are just too much."

Cody shook his head, taking in the information. "What does she think of Zach staying here every night?"

Ame looked at him incredulously. "What do you think she thinks? She'd rather strangle your wife than look at her. I understand Zach can't sleep with the nightmares, but give me a break. She's managing. *We're* managing."

"Does she ever tell you what the nightmares are about?" he asked.

Ame looked at him funny again. "No. She won't talk about them at all. She never talks about *anything.* She never has. You've known her forever, right? You must have a lot of stories to tell. Has she always been crazy?"

"Yeah, I used to work at Snyder Farms, but Gretchel and I were never close. I don't really have anything to tell you." Cody sounded nervous.

"Bullshit. You're hiding something. *Everybody's* hiding something. I'm sick of the secrets. I'm the one who has to live with her and take care of her, but I have no idea how to do that because I'm clueless as to what she needs. Start talking, Brown. Now."

God, she's just like her mother, Cody thought, *Impossibly gorgeous and completely terrifying.* He was still struggling to formulate some kind of response when Zach walked out of the house carrying two duffle bags and a suitcase. Cody pulled himself away from the driver's side window, thankful for the distraction.

"Pop the trunk," Zach yelled.

"I'll pop your trunk if you don't hurry your ass up," Ame grumbled back. Then she shouted, "I'm not done with you, Brown," at Cody's back as he scurried into the house.

"What was that about?" Zach asked, jumping in the back seat.

"Nothing. I can't believe you're coming home tonight. You're doing a good thing. Mom will be very happy," Ame said, backing out of the drive.

Zach was quiet for a moment. "I need you to stop at the Irvine Hotel."

"Why?" Ame asked.

"Just do it," he growled. He turned his face to the window. "I'm so sick of this town I could puke."

"Eat a cracker," Holly said sweetly. Ame snickered.

"Doesn't matter. I'm leaving soon," he said, "I'm going to stay with Grandma and Grandpa Shea. Michelle thinks it's the best thing for me right now."

"You can't be serious," Ame said.

"I am. I've already talked to Grandma."

"They're both just using you to get Mom all riled up, and that's the last thing she needs right now."

"Well I'm sick of worrying about what Mom needs. I'm going to take care of what I need."

"Auntie G will never let you go," Holly said.

"That's why I'm not telling her. I'm leaving tonight. Grandma Shea's at the Irvine Hotel right now."

Ame looked at her brother in the rearview mirror. She shook her head back and forth, and did her best to fight back tears. "You're going to kill her. You're going to send her right over the edge."

"She's *already* over the edge, Ame. She's psychotic and I need to be around normal people. Normal people with money."

"You're such a selfish little fuck."

"Maybe so, but this selfish little fuck is heading for the Windy City."

Ame was disgusted with her brother, but she was also tired of being the grownup. She didn't see how she could take care of her mother and keep Zach from running away to Grandma and Grandpa Shea if he was determined to do it. She turned to look at Holly. But Holly's face was enigmatic. Ame took a deep breath and drove toward the Irvine Hotel.

"Give this to Mom," Zach said as he passed an envelope from the backseat. "She'll be all right. I know how to bullshit people."

Ame grabbed the envelope, with tears rolling down her face and anger boiling in her belly. "You learned from the best."

After he grabbed his bags and shut the trunk, Ame put the car in gear and roared out of the parking lot, just missing a rental with Missouri plates as it pulled in.

∞

Ame's feet felt like lead as she walked toward the cottage. She hoped against hope that her mother was already in bed.

She wasn't. When Ame opened the front door, she saw that Gretchel was curled up in the storybook chair, her long legs dangling over the side. Avoiding the inevitable, Ame clutched at a distracting detail.

"Who are the roses from?"

"A misguided admirer," Gretchel's face was impossible to read.

Ame tossed her backpack on the couch and sat down across from her mother. "You're reading one of my Graham Duncan books? Good for you Mom. I think you'll like him."

Gretchel smiled at her daughter. "This is *my* book, Ame. Take a look."

Gretchel showed her daughter the inscription, and enjoyed the look of awe it produced. "Where did you get that?"

"It was a gift. I lost it when you were a baby and I just found it today."

"Seriously?"

"Yes, seriously. I didn't know *you* read Graham Duncan," Gretchel smiled.

"I love him."

"Me, too. He's my hero," Gretchel said.

Ame couldn't help but sigh. *Why does nobody get the man's point?*

Gretchel's smile widened. "I used to have the biggest crush on him. I would fantasize about what he looked like, and I imagined us running away together. I was just so enamored with his writing. It moves me in a way that's difficult to explain."

Ame sat on the edge of the couch. She silently cursed her brother. It wasn't fair that she had to be the bearer of bad news, just when her mother was finding something to hang on to. "I hear he's a bit of a nutter," Ame said with an unhappy laugh.

Gretchel grinned, remembering someone else referring to her precious Duncan in the same way. "And quite horny, to tell from his writing."

"There's a myth that he has a birthmark on his

butt in the shape of a phallus," Ame said.

"I'd give anything to see it," Gretchel smiled dreamily.

Ame laughed, and then let out a big sigh. She had dreamed of having this sort of conversation with Gretchel—easy, fun. The discovery that her mother loved Graham Duncan as much as she did should have been awesome. Instead, Ame was stuck with the role of unwelcome messenger. She stood up and handed her mother the letter. "Zach wanted me to give this to you."

Gretchel ripped the letter open, and Ame crouched behind her to read along.

Mom,

I'm sorry for all the grief I've given you lately. Things are hard for me too. I'm not dealing with Dad's death very well. I need to be with Grandma and Grandpa Shea for a while. I need to get in touch with his side of the family. I need to know why Dad was such a prick. Please don't be mad, and don't chase me down. Just let me go for a while, and I'll be back when I'm ready. I need to be able to sleep, and I need to be able to remember Dad in a good way. I feel like every time you look at me you see him. It feels like your judging me. It feels like you hate me, because I know you hated him. Everything's going to be okay Mom. Ame will take good care of you, and I'll be back after I sort through things.

Please don't forget that I love you,
Zach

Gretchel wadded up the letter and held it between her clenched hands as she stared up at the buck. Ame was afraid to speak. She walked around the chair and sat down at her mother's feet. Ame was crying. Her mother was not.

"Mama, please say something."

Gretchel continued to stare at the buck, saying nothing.

"Mama," Ame pleaded apprehensively, touching Gretchel's hand.

"Don't touch me!" Gretchel screamed. Her whole body shook.

"I didn't mean to..."

"Go to bed!" Gretchel bellowed. Ame burst into a full-blown sob. "*Go. To. Bed*!" Gretchel screamed.

Ame grabbed her bag and ran up the stairs to her room. Her mother had never treated her this way. Her first thought was to get in touch with Eli. She considered calling him, but something held her back. She sent a text instead.

Eli. Are you there? My brother left for Chicago, and my mom is going berserk. I'm sorry I keep forgetting to check in with you. I've been busy. I hate to ask, but can you please fly out to see her soon? Please. I'm begging. I need answers. I need to know how to help her. Nobody will talk to me, and I'm stuck dealing with the lunatic on my own. I'll never ask another thing of you! Please.

Then Ame put in her earbuds, and tried not to notice that her mother was talking to people who weren't there.

Gretchel was pacing the front room of the cottage.

Keep the heid, love, or the devil's bride 'il have you for dinner.

"Let her come. I don't care anymore," Gretchel said.

Dinnae get gallus on us, love. If ye do, yer jus scunnered. Hawd on, then. Chin up! Keep the heid en hawd on!

"I'm done holding on. I dare you, bitch, to show your face!" Gretchel yelled into the empty room.

CHAPTER TWENTY-FIVE

Irvine, 2010s

Eli had been traveling all day. After arriving at Lambert Airport in St. Louis, he decided to rent a car and drive the two hours to Irvine that evening. As he checked into the Irvine Hotel, he was exhausted, mentally and physically.

He had thought about getting in touch with Ame, but he changed his mind. He needed a decent night's sleep before he made his next move. Eli switched off his phone while he was checking in. He didn't expect to hear from his mother, but he didn't want to deal with the guilt of screening her call.

Eli stepped into the elevator with another hotel guest. He got a glimpse of his face as they both turned to face the doors. It didn't take him long to realize who he was looking at. He had seen this kid on Ame's Facebook page. Gray eyes. Dark red hair. Unmistakable.

They were both headed for the seventh floor.

"Where you from?" Eli asked.

"What's it to you?" the boy answered.

Eli had no reply. None he could possibly share at the moment, anyway.

After they both exited the elevator, he watched the boy walk down the hallway with a couple of duffel bags and a suitcase. Eli walked in the opposite direction. He let himself into the room and collapsed on the bed.

After all this time, he was finally going to see Gretchel again. He had no idea what might come from this reunion, but he did know that he was about to destroy the quiet, steady life he had created for himself over the past seventeen years. He had ceased to be inertia's bitch, and he was grateful.

Eli brushed his teeth. He splashed water on his face. He got ready for bed like it was any other night, and smiled at the contrast between his mundane actions and his inner agitation. As he pulled up the covers and turned off the light on the headboard, he tried to remember the last time he had touched Gretchel. The difficulty wasn't that the memory was lost or buried; it was, rather, that it was so difficult to bear that he never let himself near it.

∞

Irvine, 1990s

Gretchel had risen early, as Eli knew she would. He didn't follow her when she went for her morning run. He showered, shaved, and dressed. Then he sat on the cold sun porch and waited. When she returned, he watched as she threw rock after rock at the old truck in the Wicked Garden. The sight was slightly terrifying, but he didn't try to stop her.

Gretchel headed straight for the bath as soon as

she got back. Eli heard water running. He entered the bathroom without knocking.

She was covered in a blanket of bubbles, but Eli could still see the soft, white skin of her arms and neck. He closed his eyes and stilled himself before he sank to the floor and leaned against the tub. "I need a drink, Eli. I need a drink, but I don't want one. Do you know what I mean?"

He did, but he didn't. Eli, his parents, and his grandparents had an easygoing relationship with mood-altering substances. Acid, mushrooms, pot—these were just a normal part of his life. But he knew enough to know that alcohol's hold on Gretchel was something entirely different than he had ever experienced or seen.

He wanted to help her. He wanted that more than anything. He thought about the baby in her belly, and he accepted that she had already made a choice that did not include him. There was only one thing left that he could do.

"Do you believe in magic Gretchel?"

She looked at him oddly. "That's a stupid question to ask a witch. You know I do."

He nodded and pulled something from his pocket. It was the amulet his mother had given him. "I want you to have this. I don't totally understand what it can do, but I know that it's very old and very special, and I think that it might protect you and the baby. I hope it will, Gretchel. I want you both to be safe."

Gretchel reached out her hand and took the necklace. "An amethyst. I've never seen one so lovely," she said as she fingered the jewel. "Where did you get it?"

"It doesn't matter," he said. "Do you know the

story of Amethystos from Greek mythology?"

"Yes, I think I remember it. Amethystos was a maiden who refused Dionysus. He pursued her, and she begged the gods to save her. Artemis answered her prayer by turning her into stone."

Eli nodded his head in agreement. "The name 'Amethystos' means 'not drunken,' Gretchel. She was able to resist the god of wine, and this stone is what she became. Even if you can't believe in me, or yourself, I'm begging you to believe in this amethyst. I want you to believe that it will keep you safe. I want it to keep the baby safe."

Eli took the necklace from Gretchel and clasped it around her neck. It rested between her breasts, just above the bubbles.

"Give me your hand, Eli." She guided his hand beneath the bubbles and under the water, and pressed it against her belly.

He felt a kick, and a huge grin spread across his face. Gretchel smiled, too. Then she seemed to remember herself, and her smile collapsed. "I want to get out now. Can you please turn around?" Eli did as she asked and turned away, but the full-length mirror hung on the bathroom door exposed him to a vision that would haunt him for the next seventeen years. It was if Aphrodite were stepping out of the sea already pregnant with life. It was the most awe-inspiring thing he had seen. The most beautiful poem ever written could not do this moment justice, though for years he tried over and over again to form the words.

He watched her pick up a brush, and he covered his head just as she hurled it at the mirror.

"Take me back to Carbondale," she commanded.

Eli waited until Gretchel had left the bathroom before he uncurled. He carefully brushed the broken glass from his sleeves, and ran his fingers through his hair. Silvered shards fell to the floor.

He stood in the hallway for a while. Gretchel had rejected him. He had given her the amulet. He didn't know what else to do. He decided to say his goodbyes.

Gretchel was emptying dresser drawers, tossing everything into a duffel bag.

She was still naked.

She stopped and turned to Eli when he stepped into the bedroom.

Eli found that he had nothing else to say.

Gretchel stepped toward him and entwined her fingers in his hair. She pressed herself against him. "Oh, Hermes," she whispered, "I am going to miss you."

And then Eli was naked, too, before he even had time to think.

They were spread across the bed in a deranged bliss. He gently rubbed her belly over and over again. Her scars were stretched to silver slivers. There was a new mark right above her ribcage—fresh, jagged, different from the older scars. Eli tried to ignore it, but it was hard.

Tears began to fall down his face. "I love your baby, Gretchel. I love your baby and I love you. I want to protect you both, and I want you both to be mine." Eli was sobbing now.

Gretchel turned to stone. "Take me back, Eli. Just take me back to Carbondale. I don't want to face my mama or Miss Poni again. I've shamed my family enough already."

∞

Carbondale, 1990s

The two-hour drive back to Carbondale was brutal. Gretchel held Eli's hand the whole way. Every time they stopped for her to use a gas-station bathroom—which was often—she clutched his hand again as soon as she got back in the passenger's seat. It was like she was on her way to the gallows, and she had to hold onto the last thing she had left in this world.

Gretchel became agitated once they got to Carbondale. "Where are you going?"

"I'm taking you to the house on Pringle Street."

She squeezed Eli's hand.

"No! He's waiting for me. If I'm late he'll punish me. If he knows I've been with you he'll kill me."

"If he wants you, he's going to have to go through me," Eli said. He'd had two hours to think of something brilliant, and this was the best he could come up with.

Gretchel began to cry.

Eli didn't want to hurt her. He didn't want anyone else to hurt her, either, and he didn't want her to hurt herself. He had no idea what he was doing. He kept driving toward the house on Pringle Street.

There was a black car sitting in the driveway. A very expensive black car. *Oh, shit,* Eli thought. *What the hell is she doing here?*

"Oh no," Gretchel moaned. Eli glanced behind him and saw Troy getting out of his red convertible. He hadn't noticed it parked on the street, waiting for them.

Eli turned back toward Gretchel. "The doors are locked. Do not get out of the car. *Stay with me, Gretchel.* I can keep you safe. I can take you away from here."

Troy beat his fist on Gretchel's window. "Get the fuck out of the car!"

She turned to Eli. "I have to go or he's going to kill me. You don't understand."

"He's going to kill you if you *do* get out," Eli yelled as he opened his own door.

He circled the car and stepped up to Troy. "Back the fuck off!" Then he shoved him several feet across the yard.

"Look, hippie, Gretchel's baby isn't your problem. Just walk away and nobody will get hurt this time." Eli looked around. All Troy's friends had probably gone home for the break, too. He was alone.

"I guess that's the difference between you and me, Shea, because I don't see Gretchel's baby as a problem."

Troy threw a punch, but Eli backed up, and then surged forward, tackling him to the ground. He couldn't help it. He had never been so furious. He was about to land a punch when two very strong pairs of hands pulled him away from Troy. Bewildered, Eli looked to his left and his right and saw a couple of extremely large men he had never seen before.

Troy stood up and brushed himself off. "Bodyguards? Who the hell are you, hippie?"

Eli struggled—adrenaline and anger had taken him over—but he wasn't budging. "It's time for you to move along," one of the men said to Troy.

Troy looked at Gretchel, who was still locked inside Eli's car, crying. "Get out!" Troy yelled, as he pounded on the window.

"Don't do it Gretchel. You're worth so much more than this," Eli shouted.

Eli watched in horror as Gretchel opened the door, stepped out of his car and let Troy lead her to his. As walked away, she said, "No, I'm not worth more than this, Eli. This is exactly what I deserve."

Eli watched her get in Troy's car, and watched as they drove away into the dismal, rainy afternoon.

Suddenly, he was hyper-aware of being restrained. "Get your fucking hands off of me." The bodyguards complied. Eli marched into the house.

His mother was sitting on the chronic couch. Eli could only assume that she had watched the scene in the driveway.

"Hello, Elliot. I flew in this morning, and I've been sitting on this sofa that reeks strongly of marijuana for a very long time. I haven't seen you in six months, Eli. I allow you to go to school here, and all I ask in return is for you to come home for a few days, and you can't even do that. Now I see why. A girl. *The* girl. I think I also understand why a bill from Carbondale Memorial came in the mail."

"There's a speeding ticket on its way, too," he said, taking off his jacket, and hurling his car keys across the room.

"You're going home. The fun is over, though it doesn't appear to have been much fun," she said.

All the fury drained out of Eli, leaving him looking very much like the devastated boy he was. "Jesus, Mother. I already knew you were obsessive and cold. I never realized that you were actually heartless."

Diana took a deep breath. "I apologize, dear. I suppose knowing that this was going to happen inured me to it somewhat. I've just been expecting this for so long."

"You *knew* that Gretchel was going to leave me? You told me to look for her! You gave me the amethyst and told me to find the girl who needed it! Why would you do that to me, Mother, if you knew that this was going to happen?" Eli's voice cracked.

"I couldn't tell you everything. It wouldn't have been fair to you, sending you out to find the girl, if you knew that your heart would be broken."

Eli just stared, incredulous.

Diana pulled a piece of paper from her handbag. She handed it to Eli. He took it from her and began to read.

Then the huntress will have a son,
and her son will have two loves.
The first will be a girl with hair as dark as blood
and scars that go deep beneath the surface.
He will give her the stone that saves her,
and she will give him despair.
When he finds the stone again,
He will find his heart,
and all may be redeemed.

Eli felt tears gathering, but he refused to cry in front of his mother. His face looked like it was carved from marble when he held out the piece of paper to her after he had finished reading it.

Diana tucked it back into her purse, snapped her bag shut, and stood up. "You're coming home with me now, Eli. You can go to whatever school you'd like, but you cannot stay here."

He shook his head, trying to come up with words to convince her otherwise. He was tired of trying to persuade the women in his life to see things his way. It was exhausting. The best he could manage was to mutter, "No, I'm staying."

"You are *not.* All of your belongings were shipped back to Oregon this morning. Your father's waiting for you with open arms. The girl isn't coming back, Eli. Forget about her."

Eli wiped at his face, and stared out the living room window. "If she had known who I am, I could have talked her into going with me. I could have helped her. I could have helped her baby." He looked back to his mother. "I would give up everything for her, and, right now, I would give up every penny of my trust to have a normal mother—a mother who actually loves her son more than a crazy fucking prophecy."

"I know you're hurting, Eli, so won't take offense at that comment."

"Well, you should."

"This is your fate, darling. I can't change it any more than you can. But another girl will come along, wearing that same necklace. *She's* your true love. The girl who just walked out of your life was just a stepping stone toward your destiny."

"The girl has a name, Mother. The girl's name is Gretchel."

"As far as we're concerned, her name *was* Gretchel," Diana retorted. "As far as we're concerned, *she* was, and now she's gone."

CHAPTER TWENTY-SIX

Irvine, 2010s

Gretchel was not surprised when the Woman in Wool appeared in her living room holding the old family shotgun. Standing there, with the gun in her hand, the Woman in Wool no longer looked pitiful and ragged. She was still filthy, her clothes were still worn, but she radiated a fearsome power. In the past, the Woman in Wool had been a terrifying shade. Now, her presence was overwhelmingly physical. The smell of mossy decomposition filled the cottage.

"Whit's fur ye'll no go by ye," she hissed. Gretchel began to weep in terror as she watched this newly corporeal presence linger in front of the old fireplace and gaze at the ancestral portraits on the mantelpiece, touching each one in turn. "Pretty lasses. All so pretty."

"Who are you?" Gretchel asked. "What do you want? Why do you torture me?"

"You don't know the meaning of torture!" the Woman in Wool screeched.

Gretchel dropped to her knees and clutched at her

head pain as the banshee wail reverberated around the room and inside her mind. When she felt still again, Gretchel raised her eyes to the stag mounted above her. She whispered a prayer to the god of the forest, and breathed in his protection. She turned back to her antagonist and tried to banish her. "Be gone, demon. Go forth from here, troubled soul. Your pain is not mine." Gretchel's words were clear and strong, but her voice shook.

"My pain isn't yours?" The Woman in Wool sneered. "Of course it is, girl. Our fate is the same, and greetin' at a dead stag's heid wilnae change that."

Gretchel collapsed. "No. This has to end."

"Nae, lass. It doesna end." The Woman in Wool assumed a placating tone. "Come now, dry your tears, lass. I understand. But we're wicked ones. Wicked ones cannae change. Wicked ones suffer, and then they drown."

Gretchel thought about her great grand mama. Miss Poni had told her that she had died by drowning. Gretchel thought about the ghost in the lake. Maybe the Woman in Wool was right.

"Yer time is still to come. Ye've work to do yet." The Woman in Wool handed Gretchel the shotgun, and Gretchel took it.

"What do you want me to do with this?"

"The guides, lass. The busybodies who move between this world and the other. The horse, the hound, that great redheaded girl—" Gretchel's shriek drowned out the rest of the litany.

The Woman in Wool cackled as she faded from the room.

∞

Eli was allowing himself to be lulled by the song of three redheaded sirens when their wordless melody became a scream. Their hands clutched at him as he struggled to wake.

∞

Peter crouched in the forest behind his house. He was experiencing the first bad trip of his life.

∞

Diana watched the Solstice Twin burn in her dreams.

∞

Miss Poni and Ella sat inside a circle made of salt, chanting prayers of protection for Gretchel and Ame. Ella wanted to intervene. Miss Poni knew that they should not.

∞

Ame heard the backdoor slam closed. She raced down the steps and pushed back the curtains to see her mother running across the yard, shotgun in hand.

CHAPTER TWENTY-SEVEN

Irvine, 2010s

The full moon illuminated the fields and outbuildings that surrounded the cottage, a divine light keeping the shadows at bay.

Gretchel would have preferred darkness.

Even though she was barefoot and bare-armed, she hardly felt the frosty April air. Her hands shook, but it wasn't from the cold. The pain in her head was a physical presence, a vast and endless pounding, like surf beating against the shore. Agitated voices were audible just beneath the waves of pain, but Gretchel couldn't tell what they were saying, and she didn't care. She knew what she had to do. She was just concerned that the din was so loud that it was seeping out of her head. If Epona heard her coming, the horse might whinny, which might wake Ame. That simply would not do. She needed to keep Ame well away from all this.

Gretchel stopped, closed her eyes, and tried to center herself. It wasn't easy, in her current state. The shotgun in her hands made her think about hunting with her father, and, as she did so, she felt his energy emanating from the Wicked Garden. This sense of his presence was a source of both comfort and wrenching sadness. She stifled tears as she whispered, "I'm sorry Daddy. For everything. For everything I've done, for what I'm about to do."

He won't listen, lassie. On with it, now!

"Daddy, what should I do?"

Gretchel tried to cling to her father's presence, but she could feel him slipping away.

The Woman in Wool, who had resumed her familiar place inside Gretchel's head, answered instead. *He would want you to move with the wind to mask the noise.*

Yes, Gretchel thought, *she's right.* And so she did. She hunted just like her father had taught her. She held her breath. She kept her eyelids low and her weight high. She moved slowly, silently, and deliberately toward her prey.

The Woman in Wool cackled quietly.

A sob caught in Ame's throat. "What should we do?" Ame was talking to Suzy-Q, who was pacing near her, whining fretfully.

Startled by the sound of her phone, she fumbled as she tried to answer the call.

"Ame, it's Eli. I'm on my way to Snyder Farms—almost there. Are you all right?"

Ame slumped against the wall in relief. She wouldn't have to handle this on her own.

"She's got the gun."

"Where is she?" Eli cried.

"Walking toward the Wicked Garden."

"Stay put. Do not move! I'm coming, Ame!"

Ame continued to watch her mother. For several minutes, she stood perfectly still, and Ame hoped that she was coming to her senses. Then Gretchel was on the move again, and a chill ran down Ame's spine when she realized what she was seeing. Gretchel was hunting. She wondered if her mother was tracking one of the spirits that tormented her. Then she heard a low growl rumble in Suzy-Q's throat, and she saw what was happening with terrible clarity.

"No!" Ame screamed.

She dropped her phone as she ran through the cottage and into the night, Suzy-Q close on her heels.

Ella stomped around the kitchen in the house on the hill. She slammed a kettle on the stove, turned on the burner, and tried to calm herself a little before she spoke to the relentless old woman sitting at the table, waiting for her cup of Darjeeling.

"I've listened to you and I've followed your advice all my life, Mama, but you cannot expect me to sit quietly and sip tea while my daughter is in danger."

"Whit's fur ye'll no go by ye, girl. Our only role here is to pray and be strong. The spirit has materialized, and it's up to Gretchel to dispatch it. This is our war, but this is not our battle. Sit, Elphame."

Startled by the sound of her given name, Ella took the chair across from her mother. Miss Poni sat up straight and tall, determined to see this long night through, a completely different creature from the confused old thing that Ella had been so worried about. But, still, neither of them was young anymore. Ella meditated on her own gnarled hands, and then she began to weep.

Miss Poni covered her daughter's hands with her own crabbed claws, and sent all the healing energy she could muster. She knew that she could never make up for everything that Ella had lost. Her daughter would have to do that work herself. But Miss Poni also did hope that the healing would begin soon, and she trusted that the battle Gretchel was waging right now was the next step in a process she had started a long time ago.

Ella's fingers tensed within Miss Poni's. "I've lost too much, Mama. I can't—I *won't* let a member of my family face this kind of danger alone. She's my child!" Ella broke her mother's hold on her hands and stood up. She turned with a start when she felt a hand on her shoulder.

It was Claire. "Sit, Elphame," she purred. "It's time for tea."

Ame had never been trained as a hunter, but she had youth and fearlessness on her side. As she raced across the yard, Suzy-Q stayed at her heel, not making a sound. Together, they stalked Gretchel as Gretchel stalked Ame's horse. When they got to the barn, the dog stopped. She seemed to be acting as sentry, as if she understood that whatever came next was up to Ame.

Gretchel was raising her weapon when she was grabbed from behind. A forearm cut off her breath, threatening to choke her, as her toes dangled just off the ground.

"Mother, put the fucking gun down." Ame's voice was low and clear, her words a command rather than a plea.

Kill her! The voice inside Gretchel's head was more

frantic, but no less forceful. Gretchel's body struggled with her daughter, while her mind tried to resist the Woman in Wool.

Then she was there with them, embodied. Ame gasped, and her grip slackened for a moment. Gretchel tried to raise the gun. Ame let her mother go and tried to wrest the gun from her hands. The Woman in Wool watched this struggle for a moment, and then she bellowed, "*Enough!*"

"I thought ye could do for yerself, girl." Her voice was calm now. "I thought ye understood. Ye cannae save them—ye cannae save yerself—no matter what those old women up on the hill may say."

Gretchel and Ame's struggle had turned into an embrace. The gun hung in their hands, forgotten. "Does that mean this is over?" Gretchel asked.

The Woman in Wool laughed. "I told ye! This is never over. But it looks like I'll have to do yer work for ye." Then she turned away, raised her arms, and mumbled a tuneless incantation.

The air above the Wicked Garden swirled, and then it seemed as if reality was pulling itself apart. The weedy earth trembled and rolled. Epona bucked and whinnied, Suzy-Q bristled and growled, and Ame and Gretchel looked on in horror as figures emerged from the soil. Five were vaguely human; one had clearly been a horse.

Gretchel seemed to be mesmerized, tears running down her face.

Ame thought about her grandmother and Miss Poni. "We've got to get to the house!"

Ame's voice seemed to rouse Gretchel, and they

both raced away from the Wicked Garden, toward the house on the hill. They didn't look back to see what might be following them.

They hadn't gotten far when they heard a booming sound, like a subterranean explosion. Gretchel and Ame turned to see a wall of water rise from the lake and expand to fill the horizon.

"Epona," Ame shrieked. "Suzy-Q." Gretchel pulled her daughter close as the water crested over them. She held Ame's head against her chest.

"I'm so sorry, baby," Gretchel breathed into her daughter's hair as she waited for them both to be drowned.

Miss Poni dropped her teacup and lurched forward, both hands clutching the table. "Mother," was all she said.

And then… Nothing. Silence.

Gretchel waited for the wave that never came.

She lifted her head and saw a full moon over a cold April night. The wraiths were gone. The Wicked Garden was quiet and empty. In the distance, she could see a breeze ruffling the surface of the lake, but that was all.

They were safe. For now, they were safe.

Ella and Miss Poni were waiting for Gretchel and Ame, and ushered them into the house on the hill without asking any questions. Ella wrapped her arms around her granddaughter, while Miss Poni gave Gretchel a penetrating stare. "Do what you must, child."

Gretchel nodded as she slipped on a pair of boots and a barn jacket, and headed out the door. She needed to finish something she had started a long, long time ago.

Gretchel couldn't remember where she had dropped the shotgun, but she knew where to find Troy's pitching wedge. It would do. In fact, it was perfect,

The Woman in Wool was sitting in the driver's seat of the rusted-out pickup in the Wicked Garden. Gretchel had been fairly sure that it would take more than a haunted deluge to destroy her.

Gretchel swung the golf club, and busted what remained of the passenger-side window.

She remembered the accident, and sent the driver-side mirror sailing.

She remembered the figure in the road, and smashed out the rest of the windshield.

The Woman in Wool just smiled.

Gretchel was about to swing once more when she heard a voice she had never hoped to hear again.

"Gretchel, it's me. It's Eli. Please stop. Come to me, Baby Girl."

Gretchel shuddered, and dropped the club. She wiped the tears and tangle of hair from her face, and tried to catch her breath. She looked at the cab of the truck and saw that the Woman in Wool wasn't there anymore. She turned toward the voice, and there he was. She dropped to her knees amidst the broken glass, and Eli was there to catch her.

Eli carried Gretchel to the cottage and into the bathroom. She let him undress her and sat patiently while he ran his fingers over her skin, checking for cuts and embedded shards of glass.

"Is it really you?" she asked.

"It's really me," he assured her,

Slowly, methodically, he picked the glass from her knees.

It took Eli awhile to figure out what was missing. It was the amethyst. It was gone. He felt a sick chill. *Fuck it,* he decided. *The prophecy is Diana's obsession, not mine.* If Gretchel ever wanted to tell him what had happened to the amulet, he would listen, but he didn't really care. He had never been interested in looking for his second great love, and he sure as hell wasn't interested now.

After he finished cleaning and bandaging Gretchel's wounds, he helped her walk to the living room.

They were not alone. Ame was there, as was Miss Poni. Ame looked apprehensive. "You remember Eli, don't you Mama?"

Gretchel laughed and cried simultaneously as she let Eli help her onto the sofa, next to her daughter. "Yes, I remember him." Then she laughed again as she enclosed Ame's hand in her own.

Eli sat down on Gretchel's other side, and she took his hand, too. She was almost afraid to look at him, afraid he might disappear. Eli seemed to sense her fear. He gave her hand a squeeze, and she ventured a quick glance through the tears. He was older, of course, but still the most beautiful man she had ever seen. And those aquamarine eyes…. Gretchel had no idea how Eli had come to be with her that night, but an explanation could wait. Right now, she just wanted to be with him, and take joy in knowing that he was with her.

Gretchel's reverie came to an end when Miss Poni thumped her cane on the floor. She looked Gretchel up and down. "You put up a good fight, Baby Girl. I wouldn't have expected any less."

Gretchel just nodded. There was no telling what her grandmother knew, but that explanation could wait, too. Or—knowing Miss Poni—that explanation might never come.

A tall, slender woman with dark hair emerged from the hallway, carrying an overnight bag. Gretchel had never seen her before, but Ame had.

"Claire… What? What are you doing here?" Ame asked.

The black-haired beauty didn't answer the question. "I've gathered some of your things, Ame."

"You're coming back to the house with us," Miss Poni added.

"What? No!"

"We brought you here because I wanted you to see that you're mother's all right. Now you've seen, and it's time for us to go."

"Mama needs me!"

"Not tonight, she doesn't child." Miss Poni's voice was gentle. "You've taken good care of your mama, Ame. No one denies that, and no one denies how hard it's been. But now it's time to let the grownups care for grownup things while children rest easy."

"I've never rested easy, Miss Poni."

"I know, girl," the old crone's voice was gentle, almost a lullaby. "But tonight you shall."

Ame eased against her mother, suddenly overcome with exhaustion. Eli helped her to a car parked in the driveway. Miss Poni sat up front, and the mysterious Claire took the driver's seat. Then they were gone.

∞

Eli retrieved his belongings from the rental, and returned to the cottage.

Now he was alone with the woman who had haunted his thoughts for more than seventeen years, the woman who broke his heart. His father had been right, of course. She could break his heart all over again, and he would still be grateful for every moment he spent with her.

Gretchel was already in bed. For the first time since he had set out for Illinois, Eli experienced a moment of indecision. Then the moment passed. He slipped out of his clothes and under the covers. He breathed in the scent of strawberries, and gently slid his arm around her soft waist. She eased into his body and sighed.

"Tell me it's all going to be okay," she whispered.

"Everything is going to be okay. I promise."

EPILOGUE

Irvine, 2010s

Gretchel set a steaming plate of biscuits and gravy in front of Eli. It smelled rich and comforting. A colossal grin spread across his face.

The last few weeks had not been easy. Gretchel had accumulated a lot of new scars in the past seventeen years—some he could see, but some ran much deeper than he could even imagine. And Eli had had the opportunity to learn—to his surprise—that a couple of decades of being on his own had made him not entirely easy to live with.

Now, though, he felt like he was home.

"Coffee?" Gretchel asked.

He nodded, his delighted smile still ten miles wide. He took the cup she offered and stared at Gretchel as she sat down across from him. This was a moment he'd never dreamt of. In the past, when he'd thought of Gretchel, he'd seen Aphrodite incarnate, an unattainable goddess of grace, beauty, and love. Now he understood that she was also an alchemist, capable of transforming his leaden existence into the gold of passion—and the base matter of flour and sausage into what might be the world's finest breakfast.

Eli studied her intently. He had worshipped her memory for so long, but there was still so much of her to learn. He was content to spend the rest of his life learning it.

"How long do you plan to stay in Irvine, Eli?" Gretchel seemed to have recovered the capacity to read his mind—or almost, anyway.

"As long as you'll have me, Gretchel."

"So, forever, then?"

"Forever," he replied.

Gretchel's smile matched Eli's. She took a sip of her coffee and turned to stare through the kitchen window. Dawn had broken, and the brilliant colors of a Midwestern sunrise blazed across the horizon. Eli heard her catch her breath.

"Are you okay?" he asked.

Gretchel waited a few moments before she answered. "Yes. I'm okay, Eli, but I'm still not well."

His smile faded "What's going on here, Gretchel?"

She sighed, and took another sip of her coffee. "I'm not entirely sure, but I would guess a little bit of karma and a lot of magic. I don't understand it all, Eli, but what I do know is that for the first time in many years—well, since my time on Pringle Street—I feel safe. I don't feel like I'm a threat to myself or anyone else, at least in this moment. I don't feel numb, either. I feel alive and safe. Your presence heals me, Eli."

"Do you still hear voices?" His tone was careful, delicate.

"Not since the night you arrived," she replied.

Eli read between the lines. She was still struggling with the schizophrenia or possession or whatever the hell it was that compelled her to marry Troy and to cut herself and to beat the shit out an old pickup truck with a golf club. She was still struggling, but better, and she was better because he was there.

"I will never leave your side again, Gretchel. Never."

Gretchel finished her cup of coffee and laughed. "I'm going to the studio now. It might be kind of hard for me to work if you never leave my side."

Eli laughed, too. "I was speaking figuratively." Then he fixed her with a stern look and added, "But don't stray too far without me." He tried to inject a little levity into his voice, but Gretchel could tell that he was serious—and more than a little afraid.

She dropped a kiss on top of his curls as she left the kitchen.

The truth was, Gretchel was more than a little afraid herself. She wasn't being coy or mysterious when she told Eli that she didn't know what had happened at Snyder Farms the night he had returned to her. She was so happy to have him back, but their new life together—and the peace it had brought her—was still fragile. Eventually, she would see what she could learn from Miss Poni, but, for now, she was mostly avoiding the old woman.

She had also been avoiding her studio. She wanted so badly to work, but she was terrified of where her imagination—her intuition—might take her. She took a deep breath, let it out slowly, and opened the door.

Ame had restocked the studio when they had

moved into the cottage, hoping that her mother might find some solace in making art. Gretchel gathered an unused sketchpad, some pencils, and a box of pastels. Soon, her hand was flying across the paper.

Eli waited as long as he could before he went to check on Gretchel. He knocked gently before he entered the studio.

Gretchel looked up from her work, her eyes glazed and empty of recognition. She gave her head a little shake, and then she was back.

Eli set down the glass of iced tea he had brought her and looked at her drawings. There were three—intensely intricate sketches touched here and there with color.

"Gretchel, these are amazing. Did you just do these?" he asked.

"Yes. This is the first time I've sketched in ages."

He sat next to her and they studied the drawings together.

The first was the old barn by the cottage, but the space he knew as the Wicked Garden was a riot of poppies. It reminded him of the painting she had shown him so long ago. Eli winced as he took in the rest of the scene. A young girl—naked, bloody, and grimacing in pain and fear—was bound to the old oak tree.

"Do you know who that is?"

"No," she whispered.

A chill ran through Eli. He turned to the next picture. It was a clearing, and another naked girl. Her clothes were strewn about her, and a wolf stood guard nearby. Eli gasped.

"Do you know who that is?" he asked.

"Maybe," she responded.

Eli had a sick feeling that he might know, too. He also knew that he didn't want to know. He looked at the last sketch, and his skin prickled.

She had drawn a body trapped within a mass of flames.

"Do you know who that is?" he asked.

"Yes. And we will never be forgiven."

COMING SOON: BOOK TWO
THE WITCHES OF SNYDER FARMS

Go deeper into The Wicked Garden...

You've met Aphrodite and Hermes, the Horned God and the Cailleach. Let Lenora introduce you to more mythic archetypes with her monthly newsletter. Meet fellow fans and discuss the themes of *The Wicked Garden* in a virtual discussion group. And look for updates on forthcoming volumes in The Wicked Garden saga.

Watch your step, and never trust the fairies...

thewickedgardenseries.com